MW01275454

Moon
&
Muldoon

Other Five Star Titles
by James David Buchanan:

Horde of Fools

Moon
&
Muldoon

James David Buchanan

Five Star • Waterville, Maine

First Edition
First Printing: December 2003

Published in 2003 in conjunction with Tekno Books and Ed Gorman.

Set in 11 pt. Plantin.

Printed in the United States on permanent paper.

Library of Congress Cataloging-in-Publication Data

Buchanan, James David.
    Moon & Muldoon / James David Buchanan.—1st ed.
      p. cm.
    "Five Star first edition titles"—T.p. verso.
    ISBN 1-59414-073-1 (hc : alk. paper)
    1. Air pilots—Fiction.   2. Aircraft theft—Fiction.
  3. Key West (Fla.)—Fiction.   I. Title: Moon and Muldoon.
II. Title.
PS3552.U325M66 2003
  813'.54—dc22   2003049534

To Elinor, Alexa and Carrie
For everything

"It's well known that death can't bear humor at his own expense."

The "conchs" of Key West

"Niner Whisky Bravo . . . Niner Whisky Bravo . . . Come in you lying, double-crossing, ungrateful sonofabitch."

Casey Moon

"I have trouble with landings."

Max Muldoon

PROLOGUE

A gray man came to Key West and stood out in a world of color. Within a few days it was common knowledge that he was hunting Max Muldoon. No surprise to the "conchs" native to this fiery small island at the end of the longest causeway in the world. They see all manner of fugitives and predators, often by looking in the mirror.

Maude Sheldon, twenty years a bartender at the Rendez-vous Room on Pethonia Street, said about him, "I never seen nobody down here wearin' a gray suit before. It give me the goddamn willies."

Several people believed they had figured out the cadaverous stranger, and began to call him "gray man" to his face—"Hey, gray man!"—until eventually it drove him away. It's well known that Death can't bear humor at his expense.

To give up Muldoon was against the code of the islands and, besides, everyone liked him. Maureen McFee, a waitress at Carlo's, told him when he came in about this latest hunter, "But don't you worry, honey. You're safe with us."

Max merely grinned (a famous grin, a beloved grin); if he had ever in his life worried about anything, no one had been there to see it. On the other hand, who the hell was Muldoon and what had he done? One thing only was apparent, he often lied but just as often told the truth, which was even more interesting than his lies.

I

"Nobody ever knows what you're thinkin'." Casey Moon, squatting in the dust studying his companion, scowled his stock-in-trade mad-monkey scowl. He was watching Max let a scorpion work its way up the leg of his jeans with a total lack of concern and it was driving him crazy.

"That's not a bad thing, that's a good thing," Max said finally, distracted, eye on the scorpion. "Everybody knows what you're thinking."

"They should if you're an honest man. It's a sign of character."

There was a long pause in what was already a desultory conversation. "Who'd you rather be in a swimming pool with, Jesse James or Saint Catherine of Sienna?"

Casey never knew what to do with questions like that. Life was a struggle to hang on to what was real and earnest. Frivolity or abstraction to any degree carried as much relevance as particle theory.

"Who's she?"

"Piss-poor Catholic you are."

"I'm not a Catholic, I'm from Oklahoma." He worried it for a moment. "Is that the trick to the question?" When Max didn't answer, which was often the case, he said, "Anyways, you're wrong. I bet you can't tell me what I'm thinkin' right now." He bit into a Baby Ruth he had brought all the way from Key West and chewed meticulously on his doctor's orders.

"Sure I can. 'If that dumb sonofabitch lets the scorpion

sting him, this whole job's a wash, and then the whole company's a wash, and my wife'll leave me and take the kids, and where in God's name will I ever find another woman who'll put up with a cheap, bad-tempered, fussy geek like me without at least I have my own company?' " Like most of Max's calumnies it sounded disarmingly pleasant. "Something like that."

He started to ease his right hand down along the pant leg for a confrontation with the insect. Its Damoclesian tail quivered, causing a momentary retreat of the fingers. Max smiled; he required spirit in an opponent.

"Mary Beth'd never leave me." Having said it, Casey wasn't sure. "At least I got a wife."

"You do. Handsome woman."

Casey looked at the sky to reprove it; the sun was well past its apex but still burned so hot it seemed to be roaring. He took off his cap, inscribed "U.S.S. Saratoga" on a bed of scrambled eggs, and scraped his forearm across his damp face and scalp. He was wearing a navy-issue T-shirt and his arms, neck and skin around the dark glasses were burned a whole spectrum of reds.

"Christ, I'll be glad to get off this goddamned desert. How long till dark?" He checked the horizon against his naval watch and answered his own question. Sweat popped back out like mushrooms after a storm.

" 'Sonora, Sun Parlor of Hell,' " Max murmured. His darker complexion and black stubble of beard protected him.

Casey looked at him with envy. "You're part Mex, aren't you. Am I right? The way you never sweat and you know so much about these people."

"I was in jail down here for five months. Still be there if we hadn't broken out." Remembering, he smiled. "That was great."

10

"Just one more lie on the heap," Casey grumbled, shaking his head. "Sorry I asked."

The scorpion, looking disgruntled, was once again immediately in front of his hand. He pulled back the bolt of his middle finger with the ballista of his thumb and snapped it against the creature's head. The insect flew off the pant leg with his nasty little stinger flailing malignly in the air. Casey started and swore under his breath, but Max looked very satisfied with himself. "It's all in the wrist. Did you know mongooses eat these things?" He indicated the scorpion, wobbling around in the dirt looking punchy.

"I suppose you seen that."

"In the Kalahari, yeah."

"You saw it in the *National Geographic*." When that failed to get a response, which was not unusual, he went on talking to himself, which was usual. "You know more goddamn useless crap. You got any Gelusils?"

Unnoticed, Max had already begun crawling up the ridge for a peek and failed to hear him. Careful to make a small silhouette on the crest and keep the sun off the lenses, he untangled the Zeiss binoculars slung around his neck and studied the valley below.

"It's the big black one, right?" Out of his pocket he drew a much-folded, sweat-stained news-clipping from a New York paper about the abduction of a premier race horse. In red ink across the bottom of a photo of the kidnappee was written a name, "Devil's Dust."

"What's he doin'?"

"Receiving communion."

"What . . . ?!" While Max was otherwise occupied, Casey took time to squash the scorpion with his boot heel—he wasn't taking any chances on it being brought along as a pet—before scurrying up the rise to join him. Cautiously,

11

he craned his neck to see over the lip.

The scene below, in its swarming activity and violent colors, was in bizarre contrast to the gray, arid limbo where they were perched. A large hacienda with a red-tiled roof dominated the center of the valley. Gardens, pastures and out-buildings spread over miles to the foothills on every side.

Horses and cattle grazed on the far periphery. To the west where the sun was already creating a far-reaching shadow, some vaqueros were herding a scattering of strays down through a narrow canyon to the valley floor. A spotted dog ran alongside, barking at them.

The only activity of interest to Moon and Muldoon was on an improvised race track well off to one side of the main house. It was marked out with painted sticks and strands of white gravel to the size of a conventional track.

Considering the remoteness of the location, it was an amazing crowd that was beginning to stretch almost all the way around the course. Deceptively carefree fragments of ranchero music came from somewhere in its mass, sailing across the valley and up the mountain like a bird on the hot dry currents of air.

Odd for this part of the world, the patron seemed to be a democrat in matters equine, because the gathering con-sisted of peons on donkeys, aristos mounted on saddles with silver trappings, dusty Mercs and Rovers, thousand-year-old Chevy pickups with sagging springs and whole families of Indians on foot.

Only two horses, however, gray and black, were being blessed by a priest while their riders paced nearby. Neither jockey wore a uniform; they were set apart by outsized red and yellow silk scarves around their necks.

"Maybe that's the last rites," Max said. Slipping down a

ways to get out of sight, he turned to put his back against a boulder, dangling his hands between his knees and tipping his cowboy hat over his eyes.

Casey came down to join him and began the process of stuffing a pipe. "You see how nervous those two jockeys were? You know everything; now just why do you think that is?"

"Shoot the loser?" came from under the hat.

"Damn straight. See what we're up against here?"

Instead of lighting the pipe, he chewed on the stem for awhile. It was already chewed half-in-two and leaked when he did smoke. "This'll never work, Max."

"Sure it will."

"You always say that, and nothin' ever works."

"Devil's Dust looked a little wasted from here, you notice?"

"Bastards who stole him probably drag him all over this godforsaken country. They don't care that's a noble beast down there. They figure they'll get caught sooner or later if they keep him, so when he loses his first match race, cat food."

He settled in himself, removing his dark glasses and pulling the peak of the cap down to meet a nose that was up to the task. The only sounds for awhile were the high-pitched buzzing of locusts, cicadas and his frequent sighs.

Max hummed "The Streets of Laredo" in harmony with the cicadas.

"I wish you'd stop that."

A roar sounded in the valley. Both men rose up momentarily but settled back again.

"Maybe you better see what's happenin'," Casey suggested.

"You want to see him race, you crawl up."

13

"You keep on forgettin' I'm the boss."

"You're the one called him a 'noble beast.' "

"All animals are. Smarter than human beings, and a hell of a lot nicer." The excitement of the crowd crescendoed. "I gotta see . . ." He scrambled back up the ridge on his hands and knees, sending dust and pebbles down Max's way.

His "employee" didn't notice, didn't even know he was gone. "If you really believe that, you never met a horse. Honest-to-Christ, they're the dumbest things on the planet. You're not careful, you end up eating baby food and pissing in a bottle the rest of your life."

The absence of any incoming invective caused him to push the hat back and look around. "Casey . . . ?"

"Gimme your binoculars."

Max hunkered like the soldier he claimed to have been and went back up the rise. "What is it?" He got down beside Casey before handing them over. "You know, maybe we oughta go down right now and try to take him in all the confusion."

"Oh, sure. There's probably a hundred pistoleros down there, but what do you care? You can afford to be macho; nobody loves you except bartenders and bimbos. I got Mary Beth and the kids to think of."

"Mary Beth hates you. Like everybody else."

"Not the kids."

"They're three and four. They'll step up to it."

Suddenly there was a different sound to the crowd eddying around the horses. A fervid tumbling swirl of humanity, shouts and screams, then shots. Finally distinct sounds of anguish. From atop the ridge it was impossible to tell who was shooting at whom, but some kind of serious trouble had erupted and people were being hurt.

"Somebody bet the rancho," Max observed.

They slept, or at least Max slept, for several hours in the bed of the old slab-sided truck they had parked a hundred yards down the slope behind them. They purchased it in Hermosillo, and Max had driven it here while Casey flew in the plane. The sides were packed with bales of hay intended to protect the horse when they got him.

Casey lay there worrying, listening to Max snore happily, the sounds of things slithering through the underbrush, coyotes, all the while being bitten repeatedly by the denizens of the bales and tormented by hay fever. He thought about putting his blanket down under the truck but settled for the mammalian company of Max with all its limitations.

The alarm on Casey's wristwatch sounded at midnight, just as he was beginning to doze off. He leaped up, frazzled, and to his irritation found a bright-eyed Max standing beside him, stretching his muscles, taking deep breaths.

"What the hell you doin' awake?"

"I set the alarm in my head." A coyote yipped close by and he yipped back at it. "Smells great, doesn't it? Like a beautiful woman all dressed up. Like in Saudi during the war, loved the nights."

Casey regarded the same night that Max was extolling and hated it. "Would be a goddamn full moon."

"Yeah, beautiful," Max said, and began singing under his breath, "Oh, we'll go no more a-roaming, deep into the night . . . Though the heart be still as loving, and the moon be still as bright," as he strapped on his shoulder holster.

"What's that?" Casey asked, climbing out of the back to dust himself off.

"Byron."

"No, I mean what you got there."

Max held up a large sheet with a red insignia on a white background . . . "Oh, this?" . . . and proudly unfurled it for Casey.

"The Red Cross?! We're supposed to be the Red Cross?"

Max jumped down with the sheet and began to tape it to the side of the cab.

"What's the idea?" Casey demanded. His voice was on a steady incline that would inevitably lead to his screaming.

"It's an international symbol of respect. Get us through the gate."

Casey threw his cap on the ground as if he was trying to break it. "That's the dumbest bullshit you ever said. It's crazy. You'll get us killed!" He began to stomp back and forth, what would have been pacing in anyone else.

"They're gonna have my huevos with their rancheros, I just know it."

Max's off-hand voice and manner turned smilingly avuncular. "We'll be fine, you'll see."

They lit off down the trackless back of the ridge. The truck had been fitted with heavy-duty desert tires, but there was still a question as to whether or not, bouncing and skidding on this kind of terrain, it would survive the trip.

It was fifteen freighted minutes getting down to a dirt track that led into the valley and eventually to the ranch. Max, who claimed he had once participated in the Baja Race, gave the raw terrain no quarter; they spent almost as much time in the air as they did on the ground.

Casey complained loud and often, invoking the welfare of Mary Beth and the kids, along with prayers to the God of the First Christian Church of Tulsa.

"How can anyone who's ever flown off the pitching deck of a carrier in the middle of a storm at night worry about a little moonlight drive in the country?"

16

"I wasn't with crazy people. Watch out!!"

The truck careened off one track and sailed for a good six feet to a parallel one below, rattling bones, teeth and eyeballs, yet somehow kept hurtling forward. Airborne, Casey howled in terror while Max shouted, "Eeeh-haaaa!!" When they landed Casey said he was fired, but not now.

Barbed wire encompassed the ranch proper but the main entrance was open, a large wooden gate that must have been there since its founding. Above it on the arch was nailed the predictable cow's skull and horns. A guard dressed as a ranch hand with a gray mustache and considerable paunch slumped in a chair nearby, tipped back against a tree with a rifle across his lap. An unlikely NATO-issue Armalite AR-15 with a clip.

Max made no effort to be surreptitious; he came roaring down the road, creating a rooster tail of Sonora dust. The guard, startled awake by the noise, almost fell off the chair. Two old hounds sprawling at his feet sprang up. Max slowed and moved forward carefully to where they could talk and the guard couldn't miss seeing the banner.

While he was still calling ahead, *"Buenas tardes, vaquero,"* Casey beside him was muttering, "They'll stake us out for the ants. We'll look like the cow up there when they're through with us."

The guard himself was so covered in dust that with every movement it rose off him in clouds like flies off carrion. He was slow and polite, but two gringos out here in an old truck in the middle of the night was bound to put a certain glint in those sleep-sodden eyes.

"Senores?"

Max jumped out to address him in near-flawless Spanish. "We're here with the International Red Cross.

17

Naturally you know who we are. First to help the poor and unfortunate. Earthquakes, floods, hurricanes . . . even sick animals."

Casey stared gloomily ahead.

"Yes, yes, naturally I know of you. You are good men."

Before he could ask their purpose, Max told him, moving close and adopting a conspiratorial air, "Right now, we're here on an errand of mercy. But the patron doesn't want anyone to know, understand?" He quickly whipped out a bottle of mescal and handed it over. "Here, a gift from your local Red Cross."

The guard thanked him profusely and Max took advantage of that by jumping back in the truck and driving on through.

He called sweetly in English, "Pleasant dreams." The guard waved.

"What's in it?" Casey managed to ask through a voice so constricted it squeaked.

"Chloral hydrate."

"Will it work?"

They had done their reconnaissance well and knew just where to find the barn. Max drove slowly so as to keep the noise down and circled wide of the hacienda where there were sounds of partying. When they pulled between two stables and saw no guards, they stopped and got out, leaving the doors open. Relief at how easily it was going was transitory—a Doberman trotted towards them with his ears back, body pointed and the beginnings of a growl.

Casey saw him first and hissed an alert. Max was ready and tossed the dog a piece of steak wrapped in wax paper. The dog looked at them, looked at the steak and decided he preferred his meat already cut-up. The wax paper was no impediment and was very soon in tiny well-fanged shreds.

"That steak's been sittin' in the back of the truck in the hot sun for two days. That beautiful animal could get salmonella."

"I hope he gets it soon," Max said, turning to look for the horse. He went into the nearest barn, Casey following on his heels, nattering.

"You really don't care, do you?"

"There he is." Max indicated the last stall on the right where the Olympian head of a large black stallion reared as if pulling Poseidon's chariot up from the sea, fell away and reared again. One huge crazed eye rolled and darted in contemplation of Max.

"Jesus, it's Moby Dick." Nevertheless, he went towards it tentatively, murmuring sweet nothings.

Casey, trailing behind, was also beginning to gage what they had taken on. "Never again. We steal back *airplanes,* that's what we do."

Max, ignoring him, reached the horse and began stroking its long quivering neck carefully. "Nice horsey . . . good boy . . . I'm your buddy, see . . ."

" 'Nice horsey?!' "

"Casey, shut up, would you?"

"Hey, just a goddamn min—"

Max actually raised his voice: "Get the truck while I got a handle on this monster, for Christ's sake! It's a very temporary thing, okay? And they will stake you out for the fucking ants."

Casey hurried, grumbling, for the truck. Max swung open the doors on the stall and began edging the horse out. He had thought to bring an apple and some sugar from a cantina in Hermosillo but almost lost a hand in the offering. The horse balked and whinnied once, causing Max's stomach to do a double flip, but it settled down again.

19

As an inveterate gambler, he understood that the Goddess of Fortune had thus far extended herself on their behalf. So, where the hell was that truck? As if in answer, Casey came roaring in backwards, fishtailing on the straw floor. He clipped one stall, splintering wood, but managed to avoid a disaster. Even before the truck squealed to a stop he leaped from the cab with a flushed face and flailing arms.

"There's people comin' from the hacienda. Staggerin' around drunk, but they're armed."

"Get the ramp down."

Max managed to get a harness over Devil's Dust's head while Casey slid a crude gang-plank to the ground from the bed of the truck. They had improvised a set of restraints with straps and of course the bales of straw to keep the horse steady in the truck itself.

"Let's go, baby," Max cooed, stroking and pulling at the same time in his effort to get the monster up the ramp. "Come on!" The horse didn't care and dug in his hooves. "Wanna end up in French hamburgers?" he snarled. To Casey, who was frantically urging him to do *something,* he hissed, "Get behind and push!!"

Unfortunately the horse caught the flanking movement out of the corner of his eye and kicked out in a preemptive strike. Casey barely got his head out of the way in time and took a glancing blow on the side of his left hand as it rose in defense.

"Ooooh, sheeiit! He broke my hand!"

"The bastard won't go up. We're tryin' to save his worthless fuckin' life and he won't get in the fuckin' truck. Fuck him!" Max was engaged in a hopeless tug-of-war and now the horse began to buck and rear, striking out with his front legs and forcing him to back away.

"Didn't you hear me? I think my hand's broke!"

"Fuck your hand, too! They're comin' to kill us." He still had hold of the reins. Suddenly the horse, having demonstrated his place in the order of things, began to settle, but too late for Max. "It's no-go. Forget it."

Casey was vehement. "Hell, we do. You ride him." He was already hurrying toward the beast with a saddle.

"Are you nuts?! You ride him!"

"I can't ride. You said you were a cowboy once—or was that just another of your lies?"

"I said we owned a ranch."

"Then you can ride."

"If it's named 'Muffy.' This is a race horse. Tie it to the truck."

Casey ignored him and placed the saddle on a suddenly docile Devil's Dust. For someone who didn't know how to ride, he was doing a thoroughly competent job of cinching it up.

"That could kill him."

"Better him than me."

"He's worth more than you. You're supposed to be this big time thief; it's put up—" He broke off at the sound of barking dogs close by, and not much further away several angry voices in Spanish.

Both men froze for an instant. "Okay," Max said quickly, "get that door open wider and get in the truck."

Relieved, Casey drew his Colt .45 automatic and ran for the entrance. Max checked the saddle, put one foot in the stirrup, and tried to mount a little too eagerly. He managed to get upright, but then the same desperate lunge that got him there propelled him further . . . and further . . . tilting . . . sinking . . . a man sliding helplessly over a cliff sideways in slow motion.

A last second grasp of the pommel above his head saved

him; sweating blood all the way, he managed to haul himself back up the side of the cliff. Now the horse was facing in the wrong direction.

"Get outta the way!" he yelled to Casey as he struggled to turn the animal. Without warning, Devil's Dust shifted under him dramatically. It was like an ocean-going ship starting its giant turbines, except that here the engines were between his thighs. Head twisting one way and then the other, the horse appeared to be looking for its own escape route.

Suddenly he spied the widened gap in the barn doors, pivoted and bolted towards it. Max found himself trying "Whooaah," but sucking wind. It was enough to hunch over, hang on desperately and pray.

They made a blur that left sound behind as they tore out of the stable. Casey had to leap out of the way at the last instant. Hoof beats were overlapped by the shouts of enraged Mexicans who were just then coming around the corner of the barn. He ran to the truck a few steps ahead of them and leaped in.

The ancient motor failed to turn over at the first try and Casey's heart developed a dangerous rhythm. He got it going just as the posse closed, but slammed down on the accelerator so hard the tires rained rocks all over the surrounding landscape while the truck remained stolidly in place. Fortunately his pursuers had to duck while a lot of them were already unsteady on their feet. The second time he sprang loose and tore away.

At the instant of his leaving, a cratered, heavily bearded face, crimson-eyed and snarling through forty years sans dentistry, made a phantom appearance in his side window. Since there was no glass there, he could feel and even smell the man's breath, the odor of unalloyed fury. It terrified him for just an instant, but sometimes in a crisis Casey re-membered what he really was, or had been.

He grabbed the .45 off the seat next to him and thrust it into the inflamed face. That close, the muzzle of the big Colt must have appeared to the floating head like a black hole that could suck up galaxies. Casey was rewarded with a look of abject horror; then the face fell away, trailing its howl of frustration after it.

There was gunfire next and a few rounds thunked into some part of the truck, but it kept going. By the time it went through the front gate Max had disappeared. At least there was no body lying along the way. A glimpse told him the guard was snoring, mouth open, in his tipped-back chair, dogs at his feet, indifferent to Armageddon.

II

A godsend for Max, the horse, who was definitely in charge of routing, miraculously chose the only possible path to where they had left the plane. All he could do himself was to pretend he was the rider and not the ridden, while having all the control of a man being swept out to sea in a tidal bore. He kept his head down and clung to anything he could get hold of.

By the time they reached the cut that led to the upland meadow where they had parked the venerable old DC3, rented from a sky divers' club, Devil's Dust was panting and foaming, having gone several times his usual trip around the track. He geared down to a loping gait all on his own.

At first Max was not inclined to be charitable; he was panting as hard as the horse when he leaned close to its ear, "You had it your way. Now you shot your wad. Those chili peppers catch us . . ."

Somehow Devil's Dust seemed to find Max's cautionary talk soothing and further diminished his pace to a trot. Max could feel him relax beneath him and gave in, sighing and reaching to pat his sweating neck in sympathy. That show of weakness brought the beast down to a stately walk, as if he had just won the Preakness.

He heard Casey coming up behind. The engine of the old truck sounded like the keening of a madhouse in an earthquake. It was a question whether it would make it to the plane.

Casey slowed and edged as close to Max as he dared on that rough trail. He shouted over, "What the hell's the matter with you? They're coming!"

Either the horse heard him or it took the truck for a rival, because it began to trot. "He's tired, give him a break," Max heard himself saying.

"Look back!" Casey bellowed this time.

Max looked. "Oh, man . . ." A half dozen vaqueros, riding all out with the moon behind them as if they were in a movie, and behind them were three more men in a Jeep. They were several hundred yards back but obviously gaining. Max tried to put the horse in overdrive.

Casey remained alongside for the moment, waving Max forward and screaming, "C'mon!" Twice he honked the horn, which made a pathetic bleating sound like a goat with something stuck in its throat. From behind, the sound of gunfire.

Max craned his head around and saw the little winks of light that accompanied the "pop-pop" of small arms. They would be in range very soon. He maneuvered closer to the truck and shouted: "Forget the goddamned horse! Lemme in." He started pulling on the reins to steer closer.

At which point Casey, pretending not to have heard, roared away into the meadow. He did wave, beckoning almost cheerfully for Muldoon to follow.

"You sonofabitch!" Max screamed. "Get back here!!"

Survival meant forgetting his inadequacies as a rider; he leaned low again over the neck and dug in his heels cruelly, yanking off his belt to use it for a whip.

A couple more minutes and he thought he could see the plane ahead in the moonlight. Casey's truck was mysteriously some distance in front of it with the lights still on and tipped at a peculiar angle. Had he overshot it in the dark? It would be like missing Mount Rushmore.

No time to worry about it; behind him the Jeep was out ahead of the vaqueros and provided a more stable shooting platform. There was a man propped up in the back, firing what looked like an AR-15 although he apparently hadn't or couldn't set it for automatic. The main hope was that they might be inhibited by a fear of hitting the horse.

Devil's Dust broke stride once and nearly hurled them into a hitherto-unseen barranco that would have been the end of them. Somehow the horse pulled back, regained purchase and kept going, but clearly he was giving out.

Max had no idea what jockeys said to their horses so kept patting its neck and shouting, "C'mon, baby!" When it became apparent the beast had nothing left to give, he threw away the "whip," forgetting it was a hundred-and-twenty-five-dollar hand-tooled western belt.

When Casey had arrived at the plane he had been so agitated he had forgotten to put on the brake, bailing from the vehicle while it was still moving. Rolling on, it missed the defenseless wing by no more than a foot, and continued until it met a boulder.

Casey never saw the near-disaster that would have meant his death. Too busy scrambling to set fire to the rows of manzanita and Russian thistle that were intended to light the runway for takeoff. When they began to blaze, he dashed up the ramp and fought open the door.

Quickly, he explored the interior of a plane that had been left alone to cook in the Sonora desert for two days and found it seemingly intact. If only the engines worked they still had a chance to save their lives. Or, to be honest, his, if Max didn't get here damned soon. As much as he needed that money, Casey had decided in the last hour that he valued life more, and Mary Beth with her expensive shoes could go fish.

That reminded him he *was* a family man, whereas his "employee" wasn't. Max loved risks; he probably had a death wish, and if you had one of those, you ought to expect it would catch up with you someday. Anyway, the burning brush wouldn't last forever.

Granted, it had been Max who had insisted on creating that runway before they went after the horse. Admittedly he had taken the lead during the several hours of stoop labor in the Mexican sun necessary to clear it of significant obstacles and mark it with chaparral, all of which had to be pulled up by the roots, brought to the line of demarcation and anchored again with stones. And that business with the Red Cross had actually worked. Those thoughts gave Casey pause for a nanosecond.

Okay, he told himself, I'll leave the ramp down—just in case he does get here in time and we could still save the horse, but only until the engines are warmed and then I'll have to cut him loose. Too bad, good employee, took on any job and hardly ever asked for his salary.

He worked his way forward to the cockpit. Settling in quickly, he raced through the instrument check and started the engines. First one turned over . . . and then the other. Casey allowed himself to breathe again as he watched the temperature indicator begin to creep slowly up the gage. A few more minutes . . .

He slid back the cockpit side window to listen, and thought he could hear horses and yells and shots echoing off the mountains. Anxiously, he checked the gages again, and when they weren't going up fast enough panicked, throttling precipitously and risking the lives of the ancient cylinders. One engine coughed and spat out acrid smoke in complaint, alarming him to the point where he again over-reacted and this time almost yanked it out of the quadrant.

Breathing hard, the throttle hand trembling, hoping he hadn't pissed in his pants, he craned his head out the window and looked back at the area of the barranco. No sign of Max.

What did he expect? You could never depend upon the man, not even for dinner. No sense of obligation. And hadn't this whole disastrous plan been his, anyway? Nobody could fault you if you had to leave that kind of reckless bastard behind.

Max hadn't been spotted because he was too close to the plane; it loomed in front of him as preeminently as a dirigible in a burning cornfield. The posse behind seemed almost as large, as they closed in.

He sensed bullets flying past him now, a tiny buzzing that should have been subsumed in pounding hoof beats but wasn't, maybe because it was something that once heard was never forgotten.

Max still had a pistol and tried to shoot back, just by way of keeping them off, but he simply wasn't a good enough horseman for movie heroics.

There! The sound of engines—he might still make it. Head low and straining to see past the horse's mane—some of which was in his mouth—through eyes reddened and streaming, he made out the open door on the side of the plane. As angry as he had been at Casey it was impossible to avoid feeling an enormous welling of gratitude at that moment. How had he so misjudged the man?

Max arrived at the ramp just ahead of his pursuers' pistol range. First he had to slow the horse, turn it and then convince it to go up that rickety homemade ramp into a rickety old airplane, all this with the engines roaring, blowing wind and dirt back at them. Devil's Dust obviously had doubts and enough energy remaining to rear up and whinny, almost throwing his rider.

Max jammed the heels of his boots into the horse's flanks as hard as he could and was never certain afterwards that Devil's Dust's hooves even touched the ramp; it was more like he leaped straight up into the airplane. Just as well, because Max, even as he soared through the air and in the door had a flash of cognition—the plane was already moving. What the hell?!

Was it possible that Casey had seen him coming and timed his taxi perfectly? Casey had never timed anything perfectly in his life. How could he even know Max was there? The unsecured ramp was jerked out by the plane's movement and fell to the ground a split second behind him.

He would have to get that door closed, but right now he had his hands full, still astride the snorting, bucking animal, inside an antiquated airplane that was bumping along over the rough surface of a too-short runway surrounded by high mountains while people shot at it. Unable to dismount correctly, he allowed himself to fall off the horse by sliding slowly down its side and ending in a heap on the metal floor, bruised but undamaged. Devil's Dust tried to stomp and then bite him, but he rolled out of the way.

He rose and managed to get the horse calmed to an extent. The real struggle was attempting to get Devil's Dust into at least a couple of the wildly inadequate leather restraints Casey had improvised for him. Always frugal, he had bought them used from an S&M establishment next to the airport in Key West and bolted them into the frame with used bolts.

Max had difficulty convincing his over-stimulated fingers to slow and take more time with the buckles, and the hysterical horse wasn't making it any easier. Bullets began slapping against the fuselage. Two holes appeared close above Max's head.

Why was the plane moving so slowly—there couldn't be a lot of runway left. It had been agreed that they would both have to be at the controls to get the craft safely airborne, and Casey was taking it up alone.

There was no more time for the horse, who would have to shift for himself. Max grabbed the door and tried to fight it shut, but it wouldn't go. They would be climbing to a considerable altitude to get over the mountains and would never make it with all that rarefied cold air rushing in. Even if they didn't end up pinned to one like a butterfly on a board, the horse would probably freeze to death.

The door wouldn't give and there was no sign of lift-off, either. Maybe Casey had been hit by a bullet, maybe . . .

Max ran forward to the cockpit and jumped into the co-pilot's seat apparently without Casey seeing him. He glanced over and found glassy eyes, a fixed gaze, a head down so far to avoid bullets it couldn't possibly see out the windshield and whitened knuckles hopelessly rigid on the controls.

The window on Max's side bore a sizable hole and spider webbing all around it. He started to pull it open in order to see out, strapping himself in with the other hand. Casey suddenly whipped his bugged-out eyes around at the ghost pilot beside him, jumped a foot in the air and let out a terrified yowl.

The ghost was obliged to shout back: "It's me, Max. Max! There's not enough runway!"

"What?"

Max immediately saw that the wind had changed; they

had miscalculated. The plane had absolutely no lift and they were nearly at the end, meaning a fall into a ravine. He reached over and knocked Casey's hands off the controls, seized his own and braked hard, bringing the throttles back to idle.

The plane emitted cries and roars, vibrated as though it would shake itself to pieces and began to fishtail. Debris flew up on both sides and the smell of burning rubber contained in a blue cloud from tortured brakes and tires gushed into the cockpit. Also, the nice clean line of glowing embers that had defined and illuminated the runway was scattered all over the meadow.

Max worked the brakes frantically; he had never flown an aircraft of this size himself. Sweat found new courses through the topsoil on his face and made his hands sticky even with the wind bulling through. Eventually one brake locked and the aircraft began a ground loop. It slammed to a jarring stop after about a hundred-and-sixty-degree turn, which meant that it was pointed more or less in the direction from which it had just come.

Casey was bounced first against the yoke and then the wall of the cockpit, banging his head. Max reached out, grabbed his arm to drag him back into his seat and threw the strap into his lap as an added hint. The expected stream of curses and complaints was not forthcoming, however. Max, unbelieving, bent forward to see his master's face.

Casey was out of the objecting business; his head wobbled, mouth slacking open, and the eyes lolled all over the place as if someone had cut the strings. Behind them no one was home.

Max realized it was going to be up to him for the moment, got the engines revving again and started back down the course. He put on one of a pair of old-fashioned goggles that had come with the plane and hung the other on Casey's ear.

Glancing out the window, he saw pistoleros all around them now, plunging and rearing about, spread all over the plateau. They seemed bewildered by the plane's bizarre movements that had led it to career around the plateau like a limping kangaroo. Weren't these things supposed to fly?

The Jeep was missing and he assumed, the way it was being driven, it had gone into the barranco. A couple of possible survivors were stumbling around on foot. Occasionally a shot was fired but even at this close range many missed the entire airplane in the confusion.

Warming to the job, Max got a firm grip on the yoke and stormed back down the runway the way they had come, kicking hell out of the old engines in recognition of the fact that this time it was get off the ground or cancel the trip.

The Mexicans livened up, yelped and whooped and drove their horses, riding alongside like Indians firing at a stagecoach. Max couldn't afford to give their shivaree more than a glance. He just hoped that none of them got in front of a propeller; he didn't want to see that.

The instruments looked right, the power felt right, but he had to have another hand on the throttles and gear to have any chance at all. He kept calling Casey's name because he couldn't afford to look at him now. Straining to see through the dark and dirty windshield it appeared to him as though the bulky shadows on the horizon, dimly moonlit, rose higher.

He tried lift-off, pulling back on the yoke with all of his strength and will, but there wasn't enough airspeed.

The plane hugged mother earth like a kid on the first day of kindergarten. He hadn't thought about the drag that would be created by the open door. Max began giving himself Supreme Unction.

". . . Wha . . . Whe . . . Max? . . ."

"Ready on the gear, dammit. We gotta get up!!"

"What are you doing?" Casey demanded, genuinely bewildered but with a note of the old peevishness.

Max leaned his head sideways, as close to Casey as he could get and still keep his eyes on the prize, and screamed louder than he had in his entire life: "NAIL THE AIRSPEED OR WE'RE GONNA DIE!" Pulling the nose up too soon this time would mean disaster.

Casey didn't quarrel, didn't say anything; he suddenly shot up straight in his seat with a firm chin and cold, steady gaze to grab hold of the controls and fight them like a man wrestling with the devil for his soul. Pure instinct. His brain wasn't working but the central nervous system and all it commanded was dancing the mazurka.

. . . Returning to the Saratoga . . . the deck pitching in a twenty-foot swell, a night black as sin all round and his aircraft shot-up while shelter-busting at Al Taqaddum . . . Iron nerves and perfect reflexes . . . against MIGs, SAMs and the weather gods . . . the tiniest error now and . . .

Checking the gage, he found it registered ninety knots and flashed Max the "V-2" sign with his fingers, meaning take off now.

Max pulled back abruptly on the yoke and felt the departure from the ground, like escaping from the clutches of a huge spider, and hope swelled. Until they dropped down again, hard, jarring. Fortunately they bounced, higher than they had been when they started to fall back.

Casey throttled the engines well past, dangerously past, the red line. The plane rose more steadily this time, groaning from one end to the other but rising. Max felt himself urging it upwards by pushing with planted feet, thrusting his pelvis and whistling through gritted teeth.

"Gear up!" Max shouted and Casey yanked the lever to raise the wheels. They wheezed and clanked but came home to the womb.

"Climb, climb . . ." Casey kept repeating to himself softly out of his dream. The look on his face was ecstatic, born again, Elysian, nothing like the man.

"Go! Go! Go!" Max urged, as if still talking to the horse! "C'mon, baby. C'mon!"

Evidently the sound of that sparked some synapse in Casey's sleeping consciousness. "Where's the horse?"

They were undeniably leaving the earth and climbing. For the first time Max dared to look at the altimeter. A thousand feet. Twelve hundred. Fifteen hundred . . . and unknown thousands to go. The moon had gone under a cloud, making the mountains in their path indistinct.

"Better start our turn," he suggested, pointing a finger. The indistinct forms were growing exponentially in his eyes.

"Turn?" Casey asked calmly. In his partial return to reality he had not yet grasped the fact that they were taking off in a direction opposite to what had been planned.

When it was explained to him he remained tranquil, until Max was beginning to think that he ought to have been hitting him on the head all along.

"The horse?" Casey repeated mildly, as he started the turn.

Max was still preoccupied with their survival in the air. He looked back down at the ground because he didn't trust the altimeter any more than he trusted the other instruments on this flying cow.

The vaqueros were invisible but he saw a couple of tiny flashes; still firing hopelessly out of fear of what awaited them back at the rancho. The lines of burning scrub were obliterated although there were glowing spots all over the plateau, knocked this way and that by the wind and charging riders.

"THE HORSE, GODDAMMIT!!!" Casey shrieked, loud enough to damage the aircraft. Reality had returned.

Max's reality was those humps and peaks that seemed to dangle above them no matter how they struggled upward. The plane was circling in its own clumsy arc, searching out a saving grace through the montana, but the bulk of the mountains themselves was swelling rapidly, narrowing them in, tightening the circle around them like a troop of advancing gorillas.

Max felt that whatever was left over of the first tiny particle which made the Big Bang must surely be taking up space in his stomach right now.

"In the back," he answered finally, without even looking at the screamer. "I don't know if we're gonna make it here." His eyes hurt from squinting into the black void around them and he tried to rub them clear.

"Is he all right, for Christ's sake??!" Casey demanded, sounding more and more like himself.

"How the hell do I know?! He's not gonna feel too good if we hit one of these fuckin' mountains," he shouted. "Look out!" There was a giant looming in front of them.

Casey banked abruptly, Max helped and they grazed treetops falling away, presenting their belly to the mountain. "If you hurt that goddamn horse, Max, my life is over, anyway."

"Bank, bank, bank!!!"

"I am. There's not enough air room to climb. We're heavier than when I came in and I just barely made it then."

"That's it, that pass at nine o'clock."

Casey couldn't look, still banking sharply in order to stay inside the menacing ring of mountains. Hopelessly squeezed, it appeared that they would have to keep circling the bottom of the bowl until perdition, because that in turn made it impossible to gain altitude, trapping them in a deadly paradox.

"Without the horse, I don't care if I live or die."

"Wonderful."

"You strapped him in?"

"Yes!"

"Why's it so windy?" Casey looked around as if discovering it for the first time when in truth it had pinned his ears back to his head and made it necessary to constantly wipe tears from his goggles.

"Watch it! Watch it!"

Casey saw the outcropping indicated just in time and yanked hard on a yoke that was already continuously at extremes. The plane bent and arched away, missing destruction by a hundred feet or so. Both men exhaled as they pulled free of the mountain and clutched at some flying room.

"I'm getting dizzy," Max complained.

"Goddamn wind in here's drivin' me nuts. What's that noise?"

"Shot out some glass here." Max pointed to his window, then added more softly, hoping he wouldn't be heard, "Also, cabin door's open."

Casey turned to him, horrified, his eyes again expanding grotesquely, filling the goggles. His lips moved frantically but no discernible sound emerged.

"He's okay, I got him in that stupid harness. You hadn't tried to take off without—"

The plane suddenly lifted, yanked upwards in the hands of some intervening deity, up, up . . . a thousand feet . . .

Casey straightened and shouted, "Great God Almighty!"

at the same time instinctively fighting against the climb simply because it was inexplicable.

"Let it go!" Max reached over to loosen his hands on the yoke. "It's climbing. Feel it!"

Casey unfroze and sat back, murmuring, "Oh, sweet Jesus in the morning. We're gonna live. We can make that pass. I'll see Mary Beth and the kids again." His eyes teared, fogging his goggles.

"Not if you don't watch it. We need another couple thousand, then hang a helluva louie."

"I can do it, I can do it." Casey eased into a steep but careful climb, handling the plane with perfect aplomb again. "Once on the Sara—go back and close that goddamned door, for Christ's sake. It's killing my eyes, I can't see." The old snarly tone had returned with the rebirth of hope.

"You need me for the pass. Anyway, it's stuck."

"You got time. It's gotta be done."

Max unbuckled and struggled out of his seat to disappear into the main cabin. Casey took the moment to line up his approach on the pass, checking all the instruments, such as they were, and trying to estimate whether he would need another circle of the valley to make his attempt.

The wind lessened and the noise stopped abruptly, so Max must have gotten the door shut somehow. He hoped, but not fervently, that Max was still in the plane. It was pleasant being by himself doing the only thing in the world he did well.

Max did return and with a peculiar look on that part of his face you could see. Casey, concentrating, failed to grasp its meaning. "That's better."

Max slipped into his seat. "How much would you say Devil's Dust weighed?"

Casey didn't pick up on the use of past tense, either.

"How would I know? You're the gambler. A thousand pounds? Probably more."

"I think I've figured out why we're finally climbing."

"Who cares? I don't," Casey said.

"Yes, you do."

"The next time around we go for it, buddy."

"Devil's Dust's gone."

"What?"

"Jumped."

After a long pause Casey asked, "The horse is . . . is 'gone'?" staring straight ahead. "He 'jumped'?" His voice began to rise but only slightly, nowhere in measure to the crisis. "How? What do you mean? Out the cabin door?"

Max nodded solemnly. "Suicide."

Casey's amazing constraint, the words jerked out of his mouth one by one as if from a very slow computer, was an attempt not simply to obviate hysteria but fend off complete madness. "Horses don't commit suicide, Max," he said softly, almost reasonably.

"This one's an exceptional person. Was."

"You didn't strap him in, did you?"

"Those straps were for a two-hundred-pound pervert; he was a thousand-pound horse, for Christ's sake. He pulled the goddamn thing right outta the wall. Then just waltzed over to the door and did a full gainer. See for yourself."

Casey's rote voice came from the land of the dead. "I borrowed money to start this business and it wasn't from a bank. Kids'll be playing soccer with my head in Calle Ocho. Even if I live I'll be sued to death by his owner. The only consolation's you and that idiot mechanic'll be out on the street with me, and you can just forget about severance or unemployment, too—'cause I haven't been putting in."

He cackled at the thought, and even though it sounded like chalk squealing on a blackboard, Max was not the sort to deny small pleasures to a drowning man, so said nothing. Besides, he was watching the mountains just in case Casey, in his despair, wasn't.

Having talked himself around to helplessness and despondency, Casey, a catch in his voice, begged for an answer. "Why in the name of God would that beautiful animal run out an open door at four thousand feet when we're trying to save his life?"

Max shook his head. "Casey," he told him in a tone of gentle reproof, "he did it for us."

III

"Where's Casey?" Max wanted to know, strolling through the always open door—hurricanes and nighttimes excepted—of the tin-roofed shack that constituted the headquarters, the only quarters, of Moon & Muldoon, Inc., Retrieval Service. It stood unsteadily on undeveloped land adjacent to one of the salt ponds that bracketed the Key West Airport, threatening to fall in.

The door was always open—rusty hinges—and Earl was always grinning. Earl had no excuse, other than being impervious to reality. He was the other employee, a slack-jawed mechanic of considerable skill and a vastly forgiving nature that made it possible to work for Casey Moon.

No one understood how Max could do it, and the issue was hardly clarified by his claim to actually like the man. That they were an odd bunch was widely held, and this, after all, was a locality where being only half-mad was considered excessively normal.

Earl was sitting, studying a *Penthouse* photograph upside down, behind the only desk, an alarmingly neat desk if somewhat worn, in a swivel chair Casey had brought from the "Sara." It too had seen better days and swiveled in only one direction.

When he heard Max's voice and his shadow fell across the doorstep, Earl shot up to attention, banging the sacred chair against the wall, and thrust the magazine behind him. The perennial grin tilted towards apprehension.

"Hey, easy, it's me," Max announced, flopping down on

an overstuffed sofa that bled something which looked like turkey dressing from several tears.

Earl relaxed and showed the magazine, but found an old cane chair in the corner for his next perch. "Casey won't stand for nobody sittin' 'hind his desk 'cept him, 'specially they're readin' dirty magazines. He says he don't want nobody leavin' jism on it. Bein' a family man an' all. But you know I wouldn't do that, Max, I ain't no prevert."

Max put up a hand and drew the remaining half of a once-long Cuban cigar from his shirt pocket and lit it with a certain ceremonial delight.

"But you know that, don't you, Max, I ain't no prevert?"

"I do. In your presence the sheep are safe."

"Thanks. It's normal for a man to be lookin' at the opposite sex nekkid upside-down, ain't it? 'Sides, ain't mine anyhow. Found it under my oldest boy's mattress and his mama wouldn't want him havin' it so I removed it."

"Where's Casey?" Max asked again, looking around the tiny office, missing him for the second time, but without sounding as if he cared, either.

"Speakin' a them kinda people, he's over at the 'Marky Dee Sod' right now tryin' to git his money back. He says them straps was no good and cost us big time."

"Marky'll run his ass out of there with an Uzi. Those are mob guys own that."

"He shouldn't a done that, should he."

"The man hates retail."

"He says he's gunna sue 'em."

"Great headline—'Local Businessman Sues S&M Den Over Horse's Suicide.' "

"Yeah? That's good, huh?"

Max consulted his watch. "I got a game on this afternoon and seeing as how I don't have the price of a Chiclet the least I can do is be on time." He stretched and yawned.

Himself came stomping through the door as if on cue, scowling and threatening, his face a moonscape of peeling, varicolored skin earned in the Sonora. "Bunch of scumsuckin' weirdos! Bastard pulled a gun on me. Can you believe it? A pissant .22. Me? Who's fired Sidewinders at people? I'll get 'em. You watch."

Moving behind his desk, he spotted Max lounging on the couch amidst clouds of pungent cigar smoke. Casey coughed. "What in sufferin' Christ are you doin' here? You're fired—I told you."

"You also told me to be here."

"I did? Well . . . goddammit, you oughta be, since it's your fault. And this's the last chance we got to save the company and our asses with it. Horse's owner's nobody to fool with. I talked to his lawyer and sure as hell he's gonna sue us. We need a plan, and you're always full of 'em."

Max wasn't looking very interested; adversity held no terrors for him. If anything by that name showed up, he thought everyone should do what he did, light up a good cigar and stroll on down the highway.

Tapping his pen on the desk top impatiently, Casey said, "Come up with somethin' Muldoon, or you're still fired."

"You can't fire me. I'm your partner."

"What are you talkin' about? You don't have nickel one in this company."

"Then how come my name's over the door?"

Earl seemed to find that delightful; he giggled and told Casey, "He got you there."

"You shut up!"

The giggle began a self-mutilation that led to its slow death.

Casey turned to deal with Max. "I only did that 'cause it

was . . . 'euphonious.' " He worried it for a moment, decided that he had leapt upon the right word and looked very proud of himself.

"You sure you don't mean 'eponymous'?"

For a moment Casey was stuck in silent fear. Was Max playing dirty, one of his tricks? Maybe there was such a word, but God only knew what it meant. Straining for an answer, he was saved by Max's abrupt coming to his feet.

"Where is this clown, anyway?"

"Who?"

"James Weydencroft. Owned the horse. I'll go talk to him."

"Just like that, you're gonna go talk to Jamie Weydencroft?" He struck a weasely tone, "Please big bad rich man don't pick on poor little us down here in the swamp. Is that it? Or you gonna kill 'em—I wouldn't put either past you."

"Where is he?" Max asked, with his usual insouciance.

"Over at the old Flagler mansion. He's got a real estate deal down here— "

Max was already strolling out the door.

"We're finished, dead," Casey moaned and went to slump behind his desk and contemplate the ruination of his life at the hands of a mere employee. Earle looked on like a bewildered setter.

As he was going down the dirt walk on his way into town, Max saw a woman watching him from the back of a taxi cab. It was only an impression, a splash of very red mouth on a white face, like a Japanese painting, a large white hat, dark glasses in a yellow cab driven by a black man. When she saw him returning her look, she settled back without hurry and the cab drove away. Had she smiled?

43

Max's whole life was impressionistic, so naturally he was in love. But what was she about?

He didn't bother to go to the hotel. He would have if he believed the man would sue—for what, bad publicity? Standing in the grocery line, he had read something about "the Jamie's" insatiable craving for attention of the right kind. Such people have no delight in the ridiculous, and what had happened with Devil's Dust was certainly that. Instead he spent the afternoon winning five hundred and thirty dollars at five-card stud, beginning with no more stake than a very good fake Rolex and his native charm. Afterwards he sat in a saloon on Front Street where everyone who came in knew him, trying to forget that exotic woman in the cab while all around him afternoon drunks and motorcycle mamas in cut-offs played video games.

Amazing, a glimpse of only a few seconds; bizarre how that vision had affected him.

That evening he tried to call Casey at home, a restored Bahamian in a good neighborhood that the Moons could in no way afford, but Mary Beth swore and hung up on him when she found out who it was. He accepted it as in the natural order of things. Casey, cornered, would denounce Muldoon as the reason she and her babies would have to get out and work the streets or starve.

He had an idea where he might find his erstwhile employer if he had been driven out of the house. On the west-facing docks, in an area called Old Mallory Square, there was a mini-festival, musicians, jugglers, every night at sunset. Boats sounded their horns and whistles, sometimes shot off fireworks, blared rock music in accompaniment to the firing of the sunset gun. A tourist thing.

For some reason Casey liked it. Max suspected it had to

do with his political ambitions. He had recently run for the City Council on a platform of reform and been overwhelmingly defeated, proving once again that people prefer conversational piety to the real thing. Worse, he had trailed a homeless person who campaigned on a promise to make the margarita the national drink.

Max let a couple of games of nine-ball take him close to sundown and then strolled over to the Square. Sure enough, Casey was wandering the crowd but minus any hint of his usual Rotarian bounce. Earl shuffled behind like a kid removed from a ball game to be taken shopping.

The sun was almost down. Casey draped himself over a piling with his arms crossed under his chin and kept up his flow of complaint to Earl. ". . . After a man's served his country like me, you'd think a wife'd have more respect. Is that too much to ask?"

Earl had been watching two girls in bikinis prepare a skyrocket on the stern of a yacht. He loved fireworks.

Minutes passed. "Well, is it?" an angry voice demanded close to his ear.

Earl had shifted his focus to the clouds where he liked to make animals and fish—his imagination didn't carry as far as castles. "What?"

"I could have a turtle for an employee and get better conversation. Let me tell you right now, I did a lot for you, Earl, and all you done was help bring me down through sidin' with Max all the time. Well, I hope it makes you just awful happy on the unemployment line."

"What did I do?" Earl looked like a plaintive turtle.

Casey made it a point of honor never to answer any question posed by Earl, so he would have returned to his woeful tale were it not for Max's appearance. He regarded him balefully over his piling and asked, "You still here?"

45

Earl brightened, feeling some element of delivery was at hand. "Max! Boy oh boy! Casey said you'd left us."

Max clapped him on the back. "Wishful thinking, Earl."

They were interrupted when some passing fishermen saluted Max's return from Mexico and wanted to know when they were going to get together for a drink. He waved them off with a grin and a promise. It drove Casey nuts when they didn't even speak to him.

"I knew you weren't going over there, just more a your horseshit—"

Max stepped close, put his arms around the men's shoulders and drew them into a huddle. "Gentlemen." He felt Casey stiffen at the touch and instinctively try to pull away. "Listen up, everything's cool. He's not gonna sue. I got his word."

Casey didn't believe it for a minute, yet he wanted to so desperately he couldn't afford not to believe it. When he demanded an accounting of the particulars Max naturally refused, but he did things like that with such éclat that he got away with it. Casey ended by being a little grateful and very resentful that he had to be.

You could hear Earl's brain grinding as he indicated Max to Casey. "He's awful smart."

"He's an irresponsible hoodlum and it'd serve you right if your whole runny-nosed clan starved on account a him."

"Jesus, you're charming tonight." Max shook his head the way aunts and uncles do at an irrepressible child, exasperation mixed with resignation.

"I feel this way about you every night."

Tiring finally of the pettiness, Max knew exactly how to bring order out of squabble—offer to buy dinner.

At the other end of the wharf a weedy man with a junkie's sniff purchased a two-dip spiced-apple, marbled-burgundy-cherry ice cream cone at a stand and paid with a twenty. The slackness was an attitude; small-man tough, and to prove it he ate the cone while chewing gum and with a cigarette burning through the fingers of his other hand. He was wearing an Hawaiian shirt that was a couple of sizes too large. There wasn't a lot of hair on top but he had let it grow long and ragged down the back of his neck to compensate. As if the bottom half of him refused to adjust to the tropics, he was wearing brown wool pants that left him shifting from one foot to another, bowing his legs in order to better pull the seam out from between his buttocks. His shoes were sand-colored hush puppies.

When the sunset gun went off he jumped, then looked around, cursing, to see if anyone had noticed. A plump middle-aged tourist in a muumuu had, and made the mistake of smiling.

"Fuck off, lady."

When Max, Casey and Earl moved on, headed for Bagatelle a couple of blocks away on Duval Street, their watcher—who went by "Doc"—very casually turned his cone over and squashed it down on the counter the way you might put out a cigarette before following. The vendor started to yell at him, but wisely changed his mind.

IV

Casey ordered lobster with a defiant gleam in his eye. Earl took his cue from Casey but his delight came from the fact that you couldn't get lobster at McDonalds. Max wasn't eating, having had a greaseburger with fries in the saloon an hour before, but ordered a bottle of 1968 Margot and a Chateau Neuf and sat back to watch.

The owner brought the bottle himself. Along with the waitresses and of course the bartender, he wanted to personally welcome Max back to Key West and looked forward to hearing about his latest adventure. That about ruined the lobster for Casey. Then Earl had to comment that it was just like being with a celebrity.

Casey tasted the Margot. "Not bad." He held it up for study, sniffed, swished, all in imitation of an observed oenophile. "I've had better."

Max merely smiled. He liked to see people enjoy themselves.

The restaurant itself was an old three-storied Creole home graced by balconies running all the way around. Casey wanted to eat in the air-conditioned bar but Max had his table out on the Duval Street side where you could pretty much count on seeing everyone in Key West if you sat there long enough, and he was buying.

Some conch would occasionally spot him up there and yell a greeting, or the other way around. Casey said it was embarrassing, "low-brow" behavior. He had attacks of resentment the way other people have gastritis, but after awhile, under the influence of unaccustomed gastronomy, the second bottle of wine and, God save the mark, Max's good nature, even he mellowed to the point where he began to speculate as to how they might save the company and everyone's employment.

". . . Now . . . if we could just hold on a few more months, I got some ideas. 'Course, it would mean neither of you could take a salary for awhile." He looked up from under his eyebrows like a stoned, road show Uriah Heep.

"We're not taking any now," Max reminded him pleasantly.

Earl interrupted his meal long enough to say, "That why I don't have no money?"

"If you need something to carry you over, Earl," Max told him, "I'm good for it."

"You don't have a pot to piss in," Casey growled, finding that idea somehow alarming.

"I can always get it."

"Steal it, you mean. Am I right?" Somehow he felt a victim in this.

Earl's uncharacteristically fervid uttering of, "Man, oh, man, oh Birmingham!" blunted the incipient rage building in Casey's craw.

His eyes darted first to Earl's, Max's followed Casey's, then both followed that star-struck view to the doorway of the balcony.

A woman was standing there, framed as if for a cover of *Vanity Fair*, one high-heeled foot slightly ahead of the other, one hand delicately touching the door jamb, tanned legs curving up, up, up to a short white skirt, yellow silk shell and white linen jacket. All that white set off a head of dense, shiny black hair cut sharply in bangs and curving in slightly to the jaw line on the sides. Her exquisite face too was slightly tanned, not pale—that had evidently been the light—but Max didn't have any trouble identifying her as the woman in the taxi.

Those large black, slightly Asian eyes were definitely on them but she didn't bother to smile. Of course not, Max thought, not the self-possessed woman he had imagined.

She stood and looked from a few feet away, yet remote, amazingly unself-conscious about her self-conscious pose, while the three of them sat at the table and gawked. Finally Max stood and smiled, hoping it wasn't just a loopy grin, because for maybe the first time in his life he found himself feeling a little awkward in the presence of a beautiful woman.

His gesture seemed to release her; she came on out to the table. Even her movements, Max thought, were special; she had either been to Miss Porter's or worked as a model. The fragrance she brought to the table, Yves Saint Laurent's Champagne, along with the way she was dressed, all said "money."

"You gentlemen Moon and Muldoon?"

The voice wasn't quite what Max had expected, pitched closer to the earth and without any of those rounded, slicked-down, high-arrogant tones that have their own strand on the double helix of the wealthy. No, this was deeper and huskier than her delicate appearance would allow, more like whisky and cigarettes but not quite that vulgar, either, too cleanly articulated. A voice that went right to your testicles and gave them a dignified little squeeze.

The other two shot up now in imitation of Max. Casey's cane chair fell over backwards but he didn't notice, proving that he was human after all. Everyone, Earl included, rushed to agree that they were indeed collectively "Moon and Muldoon."

50

"I'm sorry to interrupt your dinner but . . ."

Another chorus of crows agreeing that there was no way in the world anything they were doing was conceivably more important than what had driven her to interrupt. Max pulled out a chair. Before sitting, she gave first the chair and then him an oddly skeptical look that caused him to wonder. As if she was on to him. In what sense?

"I was in the restaurant and saw you all. If you don't mind, I won't give you my whole name. It could lead to a certain amount of embarrassment."

Max sensed Casey putting up his guard. The fact that she was beautiful would count for a little less now, just another of life's cruel tricks on Moon. It would probably be up to Max to salvage whatever part she wished to play in their lives.

"My first name's Diana."

"I'll bet you are," Max said.

"What?"

"Goddess of the hunt."

She gave him another of those looks. "You must be Moon."

"He's Moon—Casey. I'm Muldoon—Max."

Casey turned on Earl and snarled, "Close your mouth, flies'll get in."

"I'm jist ol' Earl, Ma'am."

She had saved a firm handshake and radioactive smile for the mechanic. "Glad to meet you Earl. I'll bet you keep the whole thing going." Before he could even blush she went on, "I've been told good things about you, Mr. Muldoon."

Casey couldn't help himself; his soul erupted: "Ha!!" Diana gave him a questioning glance that carried an element of censure, but it only set Casey off. The idea that this

51

beautiful woman would start right in praising the lunatic that was Max was unendurable.

He explained, "You tell me how anyone could have a good word for this dipstick here, dropped out of a fancy Ivy-League school to be a stock car racer. Like Lord Byron wanted to be Evel Kneivel. Give me the chances he had to make somethin' of his life and you'd . . ."

"I meant as a pilot."

"A pilot??! He's dropped three goddamned birds in two years. He single-handed made us practically uninsurable." His voice rose querulously. "A pilot? Ha!"

"I have trouble with landings," Max assured her cheerfully.

She looked from one to the other and frowned, the worry lines going off of the mouth and eyes only, in Max's mind adding a dimension, a detailing that made her face more than beautiful, made it interesting.

She shrugged. "Well, I don't know if this is a put-on or what, but I came here to hire you."

That caused a certain confusion. The three exchanged glances, grunted, shifted in their chairs, and Diana was content to let the silence go on.

"Actually," Max said, "those landings were under less than optimum conditions. More like . . . they were really hairy!"

Casey shook his head and frowned while he pretended to think about it. "I don't know, we got just an awful lot of work lined up right now . . ."

"Oh? My understanding was you didn't have any." She said it in the same businesslike tone, without even arching an eyebrow. It was impressive, tough—and beautiful women never were, in Max's experience. Too many people did things for them.

Casey demanded to know who had told her that outrageous lie.

"Same person told me you'd be glad to have my business. You do steal back airplanes?"

"That's another damned lie!" He turned sharply to the others. "You hear that? I told you somebody's tryin' to get us. Now you know!" Casey was always triumphant when he discovered a plot. A rising damp appeared along his hairline, a sign he was building steam in his boiler again. As much as he wanted the job, needed it desperately, this woman frightened him on several levels.

"I've obviously made a mistake . . ." She started to rise.

Before Max could intervene, Casey himself reached out for her arm. "Just a minute now. Just a minute." She settled back. "It's a sad fact a life, people always tryin' to down another man's work. The green-eyed monster, I s'pose. But see, we're not thieves, we're respectable businessmen here in Key West."

She cast a deservedly skeptical glance at a smiling Max, needing a shave, wearing scuffed athletic shoes, jeans, a T-shirt that said "Bawdy Annie's, The Place To Be" and a Detroit Tigers baseball cap bearing the name Alan Trammel.

Before Casey could go on, she told him pointedly, "You don't look it, frankly. And I wouldn't be here if you were."

Casey's ears took on an alarming pink color and when Max laughed he growled at him. If nothing else he hated all those glowing teeth. To pull himself together he wrapped himself in his chamber of commerce pose . . .

"What we are is 'retrievers.' In the United States, airplanes, forty million a year's worth of 'em, get stolen one reason or another and go south a here. And gettin' 'em back through official channels can take forever what with the crooked governments and all the red tape and bribery. Fortunately, we got the special skills and experience to get around those problems."

"We bribe different people," Max said.

"I'm trying to explain a *modus operandi* here," Casey said, so proud of his use of language he almost forgot to be irritated. Clearing his throat and emboldened, he set out to top himself. "Actually, that's to say, through our vast experience and practical application we are in a position to circumvent those obstacles on behalf of our clients. So we perform a valuable community service, the only firm that does in this whole area."

"We steal back airplanes," Max said.

"Works for me," Diana said, preempting Casey as she extracted some papers from her jacket pocket and spread them out on the table. "Registration, certificate of ownership, bill of sale on a plane I won in a divorce settlement. My ex stole it."

Casey examined the papers carefully. "From where?"

"Palm Beach. My family spends the winter there."

"You know where this aircraft is now?"

"Bahamas."

Casey went, "Hmmm," deep down, as if something might be having difficulty getting through his lower intestines.

"He's staying on a private island southwest from Andros. A friend of his owns it and there's a little landing strip not far from the house."

"How do you know that's where he is?" Max asked.

"I hired a private detective. He's down there now. He has the exact location."

Earl asked her, "What's your husband do for a livin', Ma'am?"

"I always wondered."

Casey went, "Mmmm," again.

"What's your problem? I'm willing to pay twenty-five thousand and expenses. Another twenty-five if you get it back." They looked at each other and she applied what she must have thought was the decider, "Cash." Actually it was.

Casey groaned and lowered his head, repeating, " 'Cash,' " as if it was part of a dirge.

Max, who was tilted back in his chair, came to earth with a bang.

Casey pushed the papers back across the table. "Sorry, lady."

"Just a minute, dammit! What's going on here? What are you all afraid of?"

"Death," Max said. "We don't play on big rock candy mountain, sweetheart. You want an army of Uzis, go see the DEA or some of these wacko mercenaries who haven't had an opportunity to shoot anybody lately."

"Is that it? You think my husband's involved in narcotics somehow? That's ridiculous. Oh, I don't claim we haven't been around a little blow in our circle of friends. You know, a silver tray at a dinner party. Or sometimes people will get into their children's marijuana stash as a joke and hand it around after dinner. God knows what they tell the kids in the morning." Her tone became one of injured loftiness. "But we're certainly not involved in selling it."

They had heard her out, Max disappointed but managing to look polite, Casey still with his head down in despair. Earl had gone back to his dinner.

"Why do I have the feeling you don't believe me?"

"We don't," Max admitted.

Casey's head came up and Max was relieved to see he hadn't been crying. "We know what kind of world we're livin' in, lady. You better 'round here or you're dead pretty quick. Especially doin' what we do—they come at you from all sides."

"I can't believe this. To turn down that kind of money . . ."

"That kind of money's the point," Max said. "Especially cash. And your story . . . you're obviously rich, so what the hell's an airplane more or less to you? Buy another. But you come way down here all by yourself . . . ?" He opened his hands; enough said.

"You think I'm lying." She articulated carefully: "Well, screw you! I am not a liar." She stood, eyeing them with disgust. "They told me I'd find four brass balls at M&M, instead I find the kind they clean out people's ears with." She turned and stalked into the restaurant proper, as straight-backed and stiff-necked as a marine despite the high heels and tight skirt.

"Wha'd that mean about the ears?" Earl wondered.

Max, who was in charge of explaining the world to him, tried: "Cotton. We got balls of cotton, she was saying."

"Oh? What for?"

Casey, looking ill, said, "That wasn't very lady-like there when she left."

"No," Max agreed.

"Whoooooeeee, was she ever sumpin'." Earl kept shaking his head at the wonder of it all.

"Fifty grand," Casey said, and moaned. "Fifty thousand dollars. Enough . . ." He couldn't go on.

There was a very long silence while everyone stared into his own little quadrant of space.

"Maybe . . ." Max said.

"Don't . . ." Casey said.

V

Ten minutes had gone by without anyone being able to offer anything that might generate and maintain a conversation. Earl said he wished he was bone fishing. Casey said he wished he was too. His distress at being unable to take such a marvelous fee had for the moment overshadowed all of Max's transgressions. Max himself couldn't think about anything but Diana.

"Fellas," he said, as though thinking out loud, "look, if she was working for smugglers, would she come in here and say all that stuff to us? Pseudonym, Bahamas, I don't know what he does for a living—I figured that was just post-divorce bitchiness—but then finally she offers us this huge amount of cash. Even Colombians aren't that in-your-face-stupid."

"You got a death wish," Casey said mournfully.

Earl was worried about his friend. "Why couldn't it be a runner, Max? Lookin' to jack a plane? They're always needin' 'em."

Max whispered to Casey, "I have two words for you: 'fifty thousand.' "

"And I have four words for you. 'Mary Beth, Jane and Griselda.' Five with 'me.' "

"Your little 'Bucky' is really 'Griselda'?"

"Inheritance."

Shaking his head, Max stood and put a pile of cash on the bill, tipping his usual twenty percent, a practice Casey invariably denounced as undermining the entire economic system. "Well, I gotta date. Model from New York. Can't be late." He hurried away from the table before anyone could ask questions, the other two watching him go with dismay.

"That rhymed," Earl felt the need to point out.

Casey glanced at his watch—what kind of date was that, unless maybe she was on a shoot and they were going late. But he knew better.

Even Earl knew better. "If I had a date with a model I'd dress up. 'Course he's a lot handsomer."

"Crazy sonofabitch," Casey said when Max was out of sight on the street below, reaching over to pocket what he saw as the excess ten percent. "Can't leave it alone."

"Casey, you don't not like Max, do you?"

"Of course not. I hate him."

Inexplicably, Earl was surprised. "Why?"

"Everybody in the world likes him. You know that's not right. Enough to make you barf."

"That's all, though?"

"I got more reasons than your kids got fleas, but it's as good as any."

"He's still with the company then?"

"You got to be an idiot to do what he does for what I pay him, and idiots are hard to find. Smart ones, anyway."

"I like him too."

Working conchs, gay couples, sailors from the naval bases, tourist families, the kids with backpacks you see every-where. Duval Street, the main artery, could be a lot of things: riotous and tranquil, a lovely paseo or the private game preserve of various road warriors. One thing it always was, was lively, even when it was tranquil.

On a humid night like this, Max liked the way the sidewalk

cafes seemed to fester with a tactile sense of tropical indolence and decay. What you didn't see a lot of down here was elegance, and Diana would have attracted attention on the Rue St. Honore.

He moved along several streets in a grid pattern, asking friends, waiters and bartenders mostly, if she had passed and getting some sightings without much direction. What he heard about were her legs, hips, breasts, wardrobe. Nothing about the mystique that had seized his own imagination.

These nights were not meant for hurrying, and this was hard work. He was becoming discouraged when there she was, striding briskly along the opposite side of the street in the direction of Truman Ave. As careless as if she were shopping or meeting a lover.

He knew what he ought to do: follow her, find where she was going, who she was with. He would be a fool not to. He told himself that even as he ran across the street to catch up.

She was just ahead of him now. Her purposeful gait caused her short skirt to swirl around rounded thighs where the tan never quit. The muscles of the calves worked up and down, more sensed than seen beneath the skin, leading up to Paradise and down to high-heeled yellow shoes tapping out what Max swore to himself sounded like samba. Was she walking or dancing? Dancing. The facile way her hips moved, the whole body, mercury in a glass . . . his saturated imagination overflowed, but then he was no longer entirely sane.

It was remarkable that she didn't notice him. Or did she? He watched her so intently, also the way other people watched her, that he was no longer conscious of where he was. Now he thought she walked above the sidewalk.

He shook himself out of it, moving his head like a dog

leaving the water. Where had she been since the restaurant? Fifteen or twenty minutes later and only a couple of blocks distant? And why was she alone? Women who looked like her simply did not walk urban streets at night, and Key West was not Santa Claus land. He felt the urge to protect her.

She paused by way of recognizing his presence but remained looking adamantly in front, with her shoulders squared and head up. "What do you want?"

Max, who had to stop abruptly to avoid running into her, took a moment to recover from that near farce. "Just talk to you."

"Forget it." She started ahead again without ever having looked at him.

"Man, you don't take rejection very well." When she failed to respond and kept moving, he jumped forward and grabbed her swinging arm, jerking on it to bring her to a rough stop. "Hey, hey . . ."

She yanked her arm loose angrily but stayed put and turned to face him. "Hey, yourself! Don't you dare put your hands on me. Get out of here."

"Take it easy. I'm sorry, I didn't mean to be rough. If you'll just gimme a minute. Maybe we want to reconsider."

"What makes you think I want you to." She looked him over and crinkled that lovely face. "Why don't you shave? And a bath wouldn't hurt either."

Finally, someone had found a way to wound Max. "What are you talking about, lady? I took a shower this afternoon. This is the way I look after a shower. If I'd known I was going to be doing this, I would have taken two and a steam."

"God, you're a little touchy yourself."

"Well, I'm proud of my personal hygiene."

"Now that we've settled that crucially important matter, would you get lost, please?"

Max tried looking hurt again; it had worked the first time. "That's pretty rude when I'm trying to help you here. Didn't anyone ever say 'no' to you?"

She didn't say anything for a moment. When finally she did speak it was with undisguised bitterness. "Tell you the truth, Mr. Muldoon, I'm a world class expert in rejection and I take it very well."

Worship hadn't gotten him anywhere so Max tried an aggressive empathy. "Okay, that's a start. I hear you. Me, my own family tried to put me in prison. Can you imagine that?"

"Not offhand." She was very dry now—something she did well. "Will it be a long story if I ask why?"

He would have to talk fast to keep her, "I borrowed a little money from them, is all."

"And you didn't pay it back?"

"You could look at it that way. Or you could say I should have told them. That's what seemed to irritate them. I mean, they had plenty more and it was only a hundred and fifty."

"Your own family wanted to send you to jail for a hundred and fifty dollars?"

"Uh . . . thousand, that's a hundred and fifty thousand. But they wouldn't even have missed it if it wasn't for the lousy accountant."

"Are they still looking for you?"

He grinned, warmed by the thought, "I surely hope so."

"You're trying to tell me you're from a wealthy background? You? Where'd you go to school?"

"Yale."

"But you're a thief?"

"I know, and a liar. What I'm trying to do is keep you here talking until you mellow out a little, so maybe we could start over."

"That's the first honest thing out of your mouth."

"Now that's good—total honesty with each other."

She didn't say anything and he was smart enough to wait it out, even though he was growing weary of trying to maintain a delicate, if specious, conversation on a street corner at ten o'clock at night, brushed by tourists, drunks and hustlers.

"Look," she told him, "I apologize. You're right, that was a little rude back there. It was such a disappointment, I guess."

"Hey, you know, it's only an airplane." He hoped that sounded consoling.

"Not to me." Tears appeared, rose as in a filling glass until they covered the whole eyes, yet without running off anywhere to ruin the make-up. He wondered how she did that. At the same time he was convinced that they were genuine, because he wanted them to be.

"What didn't you tell us?"

She put her head down, denying him the eyes, taking a feast from a starving man, and a tiny sob seemed more to escape than to have been uttered beneath the ebony hair. Max longed to bury his face and hands in it, unconsciously leaning forward in the hope of detecting its sweet smell.

"He took our son."

Max whispered, "Oh, man . . ." seeing for just an instant, like a "flash cut" in a movie, the depth of a great folly, yet knowing it wouldn't matter. He took her arm gently and she let him lead her away.

"I knew if I told you, you wouldn't help me."

"Not Casey, no, but let me ask you, you obviously came

to us with a lot of doubts. Was that because of that stupid horse?"

"What horse?"

"Never mind."

They were in a small sidewalk cafe on Duval, Max with a beer and a Perrier being ignored in front of her. At this hour on a week night there were only a few rowdy hedonists still abroad, but they made a sharp contrast with Diana, face cupped in her hands, and Max leaning close over their small table to speak in near-religious tones, as if their seriousness put a glass bell around them.

"Who recommended us?"

She stiffened a little. "I'd rather not say."

"Honey, we're long past the 'rather nots.' You implied this was serious business with you. How about acting like it? Why were you at our office this morning?"

"I was just looking you over, your business—frankly, it wasn't very promising. And then the way you treated me . . ."

"Okay, but that doesn't excuse you."

"Excused for what?!"

"Lying."

"I'm not going to put up with this any longer." She made a start at rising from the table.

"See, we don't get many people like you—Palm Beach and all that. We get little guys with little insurance agencies who can't afford the hit, small town dentists and farmers, hardware store owners."

She burst out, "A private detective recommended you, all right?" then burst into tears. "He's such a sweet little boy, I love him so much . . ." She began to really cry this time. "I had a court order but when I wasn't home . . . I didn't mean to hit you with all this."

"No, it's okay. I'll have another go at Casey."

She looked up, trying to wipe the flood from first one huge expressive eye and then the other. "But he obviously hates you, from what he said. Lazy, irresponsible, a bad pilot . . ."

"That's his way of showing affection. The man is putty."

"Are you always so flip?" she snapped, then just as quickly gentled. "Please, Max, don't treat me like a child. He's not going to agree and we both know it. I'm a good judge of men, and that particular man has been heard from on this subject." She waited for him to deny it.

"Not one of the world's great sentimentalists."

"My son's only four. I can't bear the idea of him being alone with that man."

"Why'd he take him?"

She hesitated and tried to shrug it off, "Why does an alligator take your arm—because it's there. No, that's not true. Just to hurt me."

Max, studying her, said, "You're still not telling me the truth."

She looked at him in her strange speculative way. "Wow, you are scary."

"What are you holding back?"

She stared down at her clasped hands again and nodded weakly. Her voice, when it came, was very small and child-like, "It's too ugly, I haven't told anyone . . . it was why I left my husband. It's not even mentioned in the divorce. I was afraid people would think I was one of those vindictive wives. And it would have been terrible for the child." At last a single tear fell, a quivering translucency on Formica, but no sound came.

"C'mon, say it. Get it out."

She hesitated. "No." She shook her head, "No . . . I . . ."

"Never mind. I understand." Max reached out to her,

64

took her hands and held them gently, but his face above her down-turned head provided a harsh contrast. "What is it you want me to do to him?"

Again Max knew exactly where to look for Casey at the various periods of the day when he was non gratis at home. Lately, he liked to go to topless clubs and deplore them. And of course Earl would be obliged to accompany him, looking sullen until the girls removed their clothes.

The "dancer" on the stage above them was "topless" from her rock-solid implants to her anklet but no one was complaining about "truth in advertising." Maybe the "vice squad" had gone tarpon fishing for the weekend; he was an old guy, after all. The girl did wear a scarf in her hair, also earrings and black open-toed shoes with six-inch heels that would have made dancing dangerous had she ever moved her feet.

". . . Look, it's decent, it's right, it's lucrative," Max shouted above the music.

"It's kidnappin'," Casey shouted back.

"You got absolutely no heart, Casey."

"I don't need one, I got a brain."

"She was trying to get away from me, for Christ's sake. She turned me down again and again."

"You ever go marlin fishin'?"

"Of course."

"You reel 'em in, then you let 'em go again, reel 'em in . . . it's called playin' the fish, in case you haven't heard. Get his guard down, let him think you don't want him, he's home free, then you yank on him and it ruins his morale. It's like psy-ops. Women been known to play that little game when they meet somebody as pitiful as you."

Max, tired of shouting, leaned over the table, forcing

Earl to rise up to see over him, and lowered his voice. "Casey, does the word 'gallant' show up anywhere in your *Ninety Days to a Better Vocabulary?*"

"Right between 'stupid' and 'prison.' How do you know she even has custody? You see the divorce papers?"

Max wanted to reach over and get him by the throat to make his point. "He's molesting the kid."

Casey shrugged it off. "That's what she says. What's he say?"

"I'll let you know when I find him."

"Oh, sure. You'll put a 9 millimeter in his mouth and ask him if he agrees with you. Only turns out he's Dudley Do-Right and she's the black widow a Palm Beach and you don't find out till you get down there and he sues us. Or shoots us."

"Sure is a good dancer, whoooooeeee," Earl said, in a review from another planet.

"We got two planes just sitting around. I'll go alone, take all the risk myself. She'll fly her own back with the boy. She's got a license. And fifty grand for the company. Fifty grand, Casey."

"Mighty pretty lady!" Earl said. "Jist real nice tits and a cute little nose, too."

"You'll take the risks, huh? How 'bout my plane? You don't think that's a risk, I guess? Hell, I can replace you—I got my life's blood in those aircraft."

"Does that mean 'no'?"

" 'No' don't even begin to say it, buddy. Let me tell you right now, it'd be worth your life to try and sneak this deal when I wasn't lookin'."

"You think I'd do that? Steal from you? Jesus, Casey, I deserve better than that." Max leaned back to think whether he would or not.

Casey sat and scowled up at the girls, who must have found it disconcerting.

"I wonder if she's married?" Earl said to no one in particular. " 'Course I am, but you never know. Darla might get sick one a these days."

At a table far enough back from the window to put her in shadow, Diana sat in a cafe across the street. She sipped a vodka and tonic and took an occasional hit on a cheroot given her by Max. Tired and no longer making any attempt to hide it. Most of the make-up was gone, not that it cost her much; it was one of those faces.

The awful sound system from the topless club leaped across the street to pound its way through wood and glass into this one, where it melded with groups such as Pearl Jam and Nine-Inch Nails to create a sort of musical mustard gas.

Diana winced when the volume rose to unacceptable heights and demanded that it be turned down. She had become accustomed to having her way in the little things. Unfortunately, it also brought her some unwanted attention.

She was not happy about being here, stale beer smells and cigarette smoke, sweat and unappeased testosterone. The few remaining men, emboldened by a whole evening's consumption and the greaseball bravado of male drinking companions, kept staring at her pointedly, giggling, making remarks. After a while the effort to ignore them became exhausting.

Eventually a florid-faced, thick-through-the-middle youngish man with a buzz cut, perhaps a service man in mufti, came over and refused to accept Diana's polite refusal to have a drink with him. Convinced of his own charm and with his friends urging him on with grins and gestures from the bar, he was finding it difficult to accept defeat.

"Hey, c'mon, sweetheart, you didn't come in here to sit and get hammered all by yourself. Don't give me that." His small eyes continued to narrow and sink into the flesh of the face until the pupils threatened to disappear altogether. "You got that look like you could use a real man tonight. My name's Jerry but everybody calls me 'Buzz.' " He ran his hand over his scalp to illustrate. "I'm a tree trimmer," he told her unnecessarily, "but that ain't all I'm good at trimmin'." He had said something clever and was so proud.

Diana asked him to leave with less politeness this time, but someone at the bar made a derisive sound about his lack of success that could only encourage him to try harder. And if that meant "meaner," so be it. He grabbed her arm and jerked her to her feet. She yelled, as much out of surprise, and then out of anger told him, "Fuck off!"

He liked that, called her "Bitch" and shook her before grabbing her hair and trying to press his mouth against hers. She struggled, twisting her head this way and that.

The bartender yelled for him to stop, but he wasn't impressed and one of the friends at the bar warned the bartender to back off.

What did make an impression was someone behind Buzz, speaking to him in a voice that sounded like something scaly moving across glass. It wasn't the usual threat but a real question demanding a real answer: "Hey, you wanna die, you little fuck?"

The man who asked that was half the size of the one addressed. Balding, long hair down the back, Hawaiian sports shirt, sniffing.

It got right through to Buzz; he stopped and let go of Diana, who backed off snarling. He turned slowly, not sure what he would find.

He had to lower his vision. "Wha'd you say?"

68

"I said, 'You wanna die,' asshole? What is it about the concept you don't understand?" He snickered.

Now he had Buzz's full attention. "Who you think you're talkin' to, you little prick? Get outta my face." As Doc didn't jump, he felt he needed to add, "I'll knock you on your ass, you pussy."

The smaller man looked at him with the equanimity of a snake. His eyes, his attitude actually conveyed what was un-imaginable in this place on this night after a few beers with your buddies—that you could die.

"Look, dickhead," Doc said, "leave the cunt alone and go back with your stupid-lookin' buddies at the bar."

The "buddies" were obviously confused and uncertain, leaning forward, trying unsuccessfully to hear what was going on.

"You come in here . . . ? I'll rip your head off!" Buzz rolled his shoulders and flexed his hands.

Diana grabbed her purse and finished her drink in a single swallow: their fight, her flight.

Doc's answer was simply to step back and pull up his sports shirt. What had looked to be a paunch was in reality a very large .44 Magnum pistol held lovingly between his pale blue belly and the belt on his wool pants. He gripped the handle but dropped the shirt back over it with his other hand.

"You're gonna fuck with me?? You think so? Ain't how it works, punk." He smiled.

"Take it easy . . . it's not . . . you know, forget it, okay?"

He was gone, back to his buddies at the bar, telling them even before he got there; in seconds they were all gone.

Diana, standing there, said, "I never thought I'd be glad to see you, and I'm still not sure."

Doc showed his junkie's sugar-rotted teeth. "Don't men-tion it, sweetheart."

"God, let's get out of this place!"

She started, but he seized her arm. "Wait a minute. You're gonna tell me how it went."

"He'll do it."

"How do you know?"

She shrugged. "This town. Everybody thinks they're Humphrey Bogart."

"Who's that?"

VI

Three days went by during which Max avoided the office. Casey was sure he was "chasing that woman" and it was driving him crazy. On the third day Max accounted for his absence by dropping off a couple of large snappers at the house, garnering Mary Beth's forgiveness for whatever he was supposed to have done, and a good-sized grouper at Earl's, where the raggedy horde already adored him.

Casey hadn't been home at the time but he told Earl that there was absolutely no doubt they were store-bought.

For once, Casey was right. The three days had actually been spent enthralled with this new Circe, wrestling with the question of whether or not he would be justified in "borrowing" one of Casey's planes in order to save a child from a perverted father. He needn't have wrestled, it was foregone. Both of them knew it.

Casey had been allowed back into the house but was spending all of his time creeping around town trying to catch Max with "that woman." Mary Beth was used to a certain amount of obsessive behavior but finally put her foot down, go or stay.

"Just because he brought you a couple of rotten old fish, you like him again."

"I love Max, except sometimes when you say something to poison my mind against him. But I should know who the liar around here is by now. Anyways, everyone loves him, especially the gals." She snickered.

71

Casey hated that snicker more than anything.

"By the way, I noticed you ate it."

"What else am I gonna do, it was the only thing on the table." Mary Beth was not famous for her cooking but she did have enormous breasts that were the source of her power.

"De quelle couleur est le crayon, Monsieur Lenoir," came from a cassette player on Casey's desk early the next morning, not clearly since player and cassette were both secondhand. Each word was clearly enunciated with just a *soupcon* of arrogance intended to discourage anyone from actually learning the language and despoiling the culture.

Casey conducted the required response with the stem of his pipe, waving it with a rare carelessness. *"Daaay . . . kel colure . . . ay lay crayon . . . Monswere Lenwar."*

He sat back, pleased with himself, with the world, having the night before received a call from an insurance man in Dayton, Ohio, employing Moon & Muldoon to recover a plane illegally taken to Antigua. Twenty thou. The papers were being forwarded. Now all Casey needed was Muldoon, but Key West was a small place and he would get him once it was advertised that there was work and twenty grand to be had.

He put his feet up on the desk and dozed off. The sound of money had had its usual effect on Mary Beth, creating what passed for a lively night in the Moon household; Casey slept with a smile on his face.

Eventually the tape clicked off, the sound absorbed by the fan, the buzzing of flies and mosquitoes. A gecko ran across his legs without waking him. He slept through a dozen takeoffs and landings outside.

Through everything except the sound of Earl's running,

since no one could have imagined it.

Earl's cries preceded him, "Casey! Casey! Listen!"

A land mine went off in Casey's subconscious; he shot out of the chair, rushed to the door, but didn't hear anything special. Listen to what? A plane taking off? Something that happened all day long.

Panting, trying to get his breath and red in the face, Earl lumbered through the door. "I run all the way from the airport. He took the distributor cap on my pickup but I didn't know it till after and I'm tryin' to get back here and I git in it and it don't work, but I didn't expect that 'cause him and me . . ."

"Shut up! Stand up straight and give your report. I can't understand a thing you're sayin'."

Earl blurted right over him: "It's ours! Yours! The Cessna . . . Max and that girl from the other night . . . ! Listen . . ."

Casey said, "Whaaaat?" but he knew "what." He knew the signature sound of those engines as well as a parent knows the sound of his child's breathing when they're asleep. Better.

He bolted past the exhausted Earl, almost knocking him down, and began scanning the sky with his hand over his eyes. He thought he had a glimpse of it just as it disappeared over some tall palms and headed out to sea.

Behind him, Earl said, "See 'em? At five o'clock."

What had the girl said? Andros Island? Off the northeastern coast? Or was it the southwestern? Hundreds of uninhabited islands in the Bahamas. Either way, they would be banking out there somewhere right now, setting a course more or less east by northeast.

His fury mortgaged to necessity, Casey managed to keep himself under control. He looked over his shoulder at Earl, who naturally expected the sky to fall on him. "Why didn't you stop him?"

"I tried, Casey, honest. But he didn't get mean or nothin', just kept smilin' and goin' on doin' what he wanted. Boy, is she a looker."

It was a struggle but Casey remained doggedly calm and cold, very cold. "I don't suppose you got mean or nothin'?"

"Casey, it was Max."

Casey looked back at the now-empty horizon. "Yeah. It was Max."

"I told him, how come you didn't steal this at night or sumpin', Max, so I don't git in no trouble? I was real surprised when he didn't answer me. He jist said he was sorry."

"That's 'cause he doesn't fly good enough to risk landin' on any of these shitty little island strips at night, that's why. Doesn't have anywhere near 'nough hours. And that's the man who after everythin' I've done for him stole my best airplane and my future and he's gonna pay. Get over to the tower. I want his course as long as he's on the screen."

"He'll come back, Casey."

Casey's voice rose slightly in spite of his best effort. "I don't care. All that playin' around with forgivin' is over and done. This is outright, and I'm gonna see him in prison for it, I swear to Christ." He lowered his voice to something more appropriate for addressing the Maker, "God forgive me, if I don't find the bastard and kill him first."

At that, Earl fled.

"Why so gloomy? It's gorgeous up here. The plane, the sky . . . and, look, you can see the line where the Gulf Stream starts. All these extreme colors, doesn't it make you feel free? We're having an adventure, Max."

It was such an ingenuous and unlikely expression of

feeling for a woman of her sophistication that normally Max would have been further beguiled. Today he wasn't having any cheering up. He rarely felt bad; when he did, he liked to take advantage of it.

In the pilot's seat of a twin-engine Cessna 402, he didn't look down even out of courtesy; he looked at her. "I don't see you as a chatterer," he said, his tone surprisingly dour.

"Well, *excuse* me. I'm trying hard here to be cheerful even though I've got my little boy to worry about. What is it with you?"

"I stole an airplane, I don't know where I'm going, somewhere not even on the charts. I gotta deal with an angry ex-husband who may be six-eight and tote an M-16 . . ."

"He's not, and you can handle him."

"How do you know?"

"I can tell when a man's hard. You are, Tony isn't. All talk. Anyway, I heard stories—that's why I chose you. You've been in combat. You've killed people."

Max grunted unhappily.

"I thought I was flattering you."

"If that's what I'm here for, kill an ex-husband, even a molester, you can forget it. I got enough demons already.

"Pasadena. If I sounded like that, sometimes I think after I talk."

"Don't worry your little head about it, no one's asking you to. As far as the location, this detective'll tell us when we get to Andros, so relax." She studied him. "You're still grumpy."

He didn't answer but did give the glories of nature at least a glance. The demarcation of the Gulf Stream was as clean as that of a playing field; on one side that startling pellucid green which is found elsewhere only on the countryside of Ireland or in the eyes of certain women. On the other the darker, more intense and roiling blue—the color of whales—of the Atlantic, with whitecaps like lace topping.

The sky was a match, occasional clouds drifted by having the substance of wind-blown Kleenex. It was a sweet day. And Max knew it should put him in a superior mood; he was very much subject to his surroundings. Which was probably one of the reasons he kept changing them.

"I feel lousy about Casey. This is an expensive plane. It was in a crash and he got it stripped-down in a DEA sale for a hundred, but it's a hundred he doesn't have. And he'll never find another deal like that, either."

"Jeez-Louise. What's your story with this guy. Mean, greedy, gutless, anal-retentive . . . treats you like dirt? You owe him money, he saved your life, he can send you to prison, you're girlfriends . . . what?"

Max said with unexpected ardor, "Not 'gutless.' I've seen real fear and nobody's immune from it. Maybe you."

"Is that a compliment?"

"Look, Casey's parents were barely up from sharecroppers, Okies. He's spent his whole life trying to be something, only he's not gonna make it. And inside of him he knows that. Where I was born with everything and don't give a shit. I doubt you could understand, but naturally he hates me."

"You sound like a radio shrink."

"He owes bad people, wife keeps leaving him, takes the kids, company's going down the tubes . . ."

"Average day in my life. C'mon, are you that saintly? Doesn't he piss you off just a little?"

"Pisses everybody off. The man's a world class pain in the ass. How can you not love that?"

"You know, you're a little peculiar yourself." She massaged her eyes gently, then the temples with her thumbs. "It's making me tired, all this stupid guilt. Let's just do the job, okay? I get my son, you get the plane, I pay fifty thousand. We all take our toys and go home."

Max accepted that tacitly, the way he did most things, and they flew in total silence for a good ten minutes. He whistled "The Battle Hymn of the Republic" between his teeth, which got him some squinty looks.

He resumed communication typically by taking his hands completely off the yoke. There was a headwind and the plane bucked slightly. "You want to take over for awhile?"

"No!" she said quickly. "I don't know this plane. We have a Piper . . . like I told you. They're so different. And, maybe you can understand, I'm a little nervous right now."

"A minute ago you were rhapsodizing about everything in sight."

"C'mon, gimme a break, will you?"

He took back the controls. "I can bring the boy back in my plane?"

She rested her head. "That might be better, after what we've both been through. He doesn't need a nervous mother piloting him."

"I haven't been in a Piper in years. It got a transponder like this one?" He pointed to a gage on the panel.

She looked. "Yes."

"Not that different. Sure you don't want to take over?"

"Just let me rest for awhile, all right?" She closed her eyes and hummed an Elton John tune. At least it wasn't Neil Diamond; you couldn't have everything in a beautiful woman.

He looked at her, trying to figure her out. It didn't say much that she was dressed practically, in short-shorts, athletic shoes over white socks, a white silk shirt nicely open from the neck to some heroic point between the breasts and a man's light-weight black windbreaker with strap epaulettes.

No jewelry except for what could have been diamond studs in her ears, and no make-up other than the eyes where it couldn't be seen behind the aviator dark glasses anyway. Except that simple elegance said she was what she advertised.

Suddenly Max was jarred by a tiny, raspy, yet undeniably white hot voice struggling to get out of the radio. Get out and kill him. Max had unfortunately left it on the company frequency with the volume turned low, and forgotten about it.

"Niner Whisky Bravo . . . Niner Whisky Bravo . . . Come in, you lying, double-crossing, ungrateful sonofabitch!"

Max turned up the volume and exchanged a glance with Diana. However he felt, it was instinctive to try to stamp the whole business with a patina of carelessness.

"Niner Whisky Bravo, copy. Uncle Casey! We're cruising at nine thousand-five right now, visibility perfect, airspeed 190 knots, but you don't want to hear all that. Smooth flight, aircraft friendly, God's in his heaven and all's right with the world. How's Mary Beth and the kids? Over."

Casey's serrated voice could have sawed through concrete, "You fucked me over one too many times, buddy." Casey rarely used "the word," he was a family man. "You're goin' down for this one. Over."

Max acted as if Casey was in the plane. He looked out at the sky and seascape, shook his head and reproved. "Fleecy white clouds, azure sky, Gulf Stream lazing below, it's a *National Geographic* day and you come on with all this negativity. Over." He glanced at Diana, hoping she didn't think he actually talked like this.

"I'm tired a your bullshit, Muldoon. You and that

78

bimbo stole my aircraft and—"

"Borrowed. Over."

"STOLE. Over."

Max winced and turned down the volume. "Man, lighten up. It's a gig—I'm working for you. Fifty grand and back in a couple days. Where's the harm? Over."

"How do you know she's even got it? Over." Casey was even more unpleasant when he turned cunning or insinuating.

Diana pulled a huge roll of bills out of her purse, brandished it in front of the radio as if making her point, then called: "Over!"

It made Max laugh. "I'd say she does. Over."

"It don—doesn't matter. You're such a smart-ass, Muldoon, but that's all right; that's the end of you that's gonna get a helluva work-out with all those fudge-packers up in Leavenworth. And I'm tellin' you this; if I don't get justice in this matter, I'm comin' after you myself. With that big pump gun you know I got. Over and out."

Max blurted in some harsher tones of his own, "Casey, you're starting to irritate the hell out of me." The radio answered with a low disgruntled whine. "Shit—he's gone."

"You still think he's so cute?" She looked at him speculatively. "You better take him seriously, is what I think."

Max ruminated. "He's not serious."

She sat back in her seat by way of dismissing him and his hopeless views. "I thought you were smarter than that."

It was roughly a two-hour flight to Andros, the largest but one of the least developed of the Bahamian islands. Some farming, fishing, scarcely a tourist Mecca. A lot of shacks and scrub. To call the airport modest would be giving it airs. But because of its location and comparative lack of activity, a lot of smugglers and stolen planes came through there, so several of the people who worked at the airport had been Moon and Muldoon corruptees.

Max tried to contact the "tower," which in actuality was a little wooden shack, but no one was home. He had hoped to find out if they were being pursued. They were scheduled to meet Diana's private detective shortly at a cafe in Nicolls Town.

Max didn't want to get the Andros "tower" in trouble, assuming anyone in authority cared, so he decided to just go ahead and bring it in. He moved the plane around a little on his approach in order to make a visual check for other aircraft in the vicinity, asking Diana to look out from her side of the cockpit.

Despite some reservations, she craned her head conscientiously in all directions. "Is this what you always do? It doesn't seem very scientific."

Max was concentrating. He went back out to sea, banked smoothly, leveled, and began his approach, throttling down, dropping the flaps . . . checking the altimeter every few seconds while triangulating the distance visually. Careful . . . how would Casey do it? . . . going okay.

It looked and felt wonderful until they touched down at just the right spot on the runway—then bounced twenty-five feet in the air and, consistent with the First Law of Over-Compensation, slammed back to earth with teeth-loosening force, which of course led to another bounce.

Diana gave a frightened cry and uttered, "Jesus Christ!" as both plea and complaint.

Max said, "Whooaah," cheerfully enough. Then, "Rough tarmac," but it was impossible to tell if he believed that; he looked cool enough. Maybe, she thought, he's just used to it. Maybe that was the way they did it in the Navy, on carriers.

Max taxied over close to a larger building, which constituted the office, canteen bar and waiting room, and managed to ease them into a ragged line of five planes. He told Diana to wait while he looked around.

As he approached the "terminal," a slim young man in coveralls came out, surprisingly bouncy for a hot day, a Bahamian with a perfectly round good-natured face that reflected the sun and made him look like a happy black pumpkin on a stick figure.

"Hey, Mox, how you doin', mon?"

"Bil-ly. Luukin' good, mon."

The Bahamian laughed; Max imitating his accent was an old joke, and they shook hands. "Got anythin' to declare?" Along with everything else, Billy was the customs officer.

"Only that wonderful thing." He jerked a thumb at Diana.

"That don't appear a whole lot like ol' Casey," Billy said, imitating the man's perennial expression of straining at stool, and cackled.

"If it did, I would have married him a long time ago."

Billy laughed harder, but then he laughed at everything. Max envied him his *Weltanschauung,* a word that, had Billy heard it pronounced, would have brought torrential giggles.

"Her old man stole her kid and her plane. We're gonna get 'em back. You seen a blue Piper around here lately?"

"No. We don't see a whole lot of 'em any more."

"This is one of the new ones. Is there another strip on Andros?"

"No, but people do lond in the cow fields." The thought of that, maybe he visualized it, sent him into giggles again.

"Okay, fill 'er up. We have to go into town, but I may need to get out of here fast. See or hear anything it's worth a couple hundred."

"Pounds or dollars?"

Max started back to the plane to get Diana. "Drachmas."

Billy had no idea what that was but it sounded so funny he laughed anyway. "Whatever, mon."

As Diana climbed out, Max told her, "Nice guy."

"And a good audience, I notice."

There were no taxis available so they rode into town on a Harley owned and driven by Billy's cousin, Cecil. Max had tried to rent or even buy the motorcycle—he claimed to have raced them at one point in his life—because it would force Diana to put her arms around him tightly in order to go on living.

The way it worked out, Diana ended up riding sidesaddle in front of Cecil, who at least was a gentleman and refused to take advantage, while Max rode behind him with his arms tightly around Cecil. A gentleman perhaps, but one hell-bent driver on roads they wouldn't have in Albania. Diana seemed to enjoy the ride, whooping and laughing; Max did not.

At their destination, an outdoor cafe in Nicolls Town, Cecil refused a tip, saying he had enjoyed Max's embrace far too much to put a price on it. He was grinning at the time so Max wasn't sure whether this was his little joke or a declaration of love.

They were exactly ten minutes early for their appointment, but forty minutes later no one had shown up. There was annoying music blaring from inside the restaurant; if it had to be anything Max would have preferred salsa, samba or calypso. A man who liked things to fit, he was listening to Snoop Doggy Dogg. The world was getting too small.

The Snoop was giving him a headache, plus he was wired from his third cup of Jamaican coffee, starting to get all-around antsy. Diana wasn't, or didn't show it, except in that Max's squirming bothered her.

"He'll be here, I promise. What's wrong with you? I rated you as so cool."

"When I know what's going on."

"You know what's going on, because I told you." Then, as if there were no issues between them, she indicated his cap. "Is that a Detroit Tigers' cap? Is that where you're from?"

"Suburb." He couldn't stop looking around.

"I'm from Detroit—actually Grosse Pointe."

"Of course. But who the hell are you?"

"*What??*"

"And what's the scam?" he said almost matter-of-factly.

He had expected her to go ballistic with denials and outrage but, as always, she was capable of surprising him.

She looked down at the table for a moment frowning, then up, taking off her glasses so he would see her eyes. " 'Scam.' You've taken all these risks and come all this way and you think I'm some kind of crook. What does that make you"—she raised her voice slightly—"a moron?"

"Probably. Since I could have turned back in time. But then Casey claims I've got a death wish and maybe he's right, or maybe it was just you, which doesn't make any sense, either."

"I don't know what the hell you're talking about. Why don't you just try to relax and look at the scenery until this private detective gets here, and then maybe you'll believe me." As if to set an example she looked off across a poor section of the town, a shantytown, at the clean green sea and scrubbed white clouds building beyond.

Suddenly she said, "When did you figure it out?"

"You know as much about flying an airplane as I do needlepoint."

"Ah."

"C'mon, whatever I am, you're no fool, you knew you were losing that game. The 'transponder' I showed you on the instrument panel was the artificial horizon."

She took a second to regroup. "You're right, I can't fly a plane. It was my husband's and I took it in the divorce just to be pissy. Not very pretty but there you are. I had to suck you in some way if I was ever going to get my son back. You don't believe I'm in trouble?"

"Oh, you're in a shitload of trouble, lady. I believe tha . . ."

"And you're not, jack-off?"

The voice came from behind. Simultaneously Doc pressed the contentious muzzle of the .44 Magnum against the back of his skull. A singular feeling, one that enabled Max to imagine fragments of that bone and all the brain behind it raining on tables in every corner of the cafe.

VII

"Shit," Max said softly, rising from the table with caution, hands in plain view, "fucking aces and eights."

"What?" Diana asked, her voice not altogether steady.

"You too, babe—get up!" Doc ordered. He jabbed Max's head forward with the gun.

"Whoa! Careful," Max urged. "Not a good idea to hit anything with a gun when your finger's on the trigger."

"I wanna know what you said."

"For Christ's sake, I was talking to myself. It's dumb. It's . . . the 'dead man's hand,' Wild Bill Hickok. Always sit with your back to the wall. Could we have a little sanity here?"

"Who's that?" Doc insisted.

"Let's go," Diana pleaded. "It's just an old cowboy."

"Hold on a minute, okay?" Max said, sounding more peeved than anything. "Look, you can't do this in a crowded restaurant right out in broad daylight in the middle of a town."

Even as he said it he glanced around and saw the last couple fleeing the cafe, now populated mostly by overturned chairs. The streets out front appeared deserted, too, as if there was a master radar for this sort of thing.

With less confidence, voice trailing off, he said, "People are bound to see . . ."

Doc sneered, "They seen it before. Shove off."

Max was finding something disturbing about Doc's total lack of concern for consequences; the gangster as nihilist.

They went out to the narrow street and waited at the curb. No pedestrians anywhere, although a couple of cars passed, the drivers looking and then looking away quickly.

Max had put his dark glasses in his shirt pocket and didn't dare reach for them, so the white-washed walls reflecting, as they did, a pitiless sun, hurt his eyes. The whiteness enveloped him, isolated him in a foreign place where there were no laws or rules and anything could happen to you.

Standing there on the sidewalk, he thought being angry at Diana would by now be redundant. You put your hand in a cage and lose it, don't blame the tiger. He knew that . . . and it still felt like betrayal.

She seemed stricken, all the sass gone out of her. He wished it back. Would rather have had her triumphant at duping him. Unless this was simply another act, act two. Whatever else, she was a hell of an actress.

"Why did you come?" she asked in a small voice.

He gave her a look but she couldn't take it and turned away.

A dusty old Chevy screeched up to the curb and stopped so abruptly the driver's head bobbed. It was a head the size and general shape of a watermelon with a body that fulfilled the promise. All of it belonged to a Cuban called Lalo, wearing a pony tail and earring with a buck knife in a leather sheath at his waist.

Doc tore into him for making them wait and the Cuban rumbled some explanation. Max was shoved into the passenger seat next to the driver so Doc could sit behind him and keep the gun on his back. Diana got in next to Doc. Rubber was burned driving away. No one saw.

They sped out to the airstrip. When they arrived Diana had to point out the Cessna to the other two, something that demonstrated to Max how he was not in the hands of master planners. Lethal, yes. Doc was prepared to leave the car, a rental, where it was and urged the others to get in the plane. Max argued that he ought to pay Billy for the fuel and landing tax and file some kind of flight plan, otherwise it might raise questions.

"Let it," Doc told him, and Lalo, who hadn't said a word on the way out, snarled something obscene in Spanish and shoved Max hard in the right direction. It took fast footwork for him to remain upright.

Diana climbed in next to him at Doc's instruction while the kidnappers took the seats behind them. As Max started to warm up the engine, he was still watching for any sign of objection to his leaving. Hoping.

Actually, Billy had witnessed their return through the louvered window of his tiny office. He was the only person on duty for the moment and had no wish to get involved in what he saw as the situation outside. It surprised him, though, because he had never thought of Max as being involved in smuggling and that's what this looked like.

But then his friend appeared to be unhappy about something. At the prospect of going with these people? Maybe it wasn't so simple.

Taking a chance, he called police headquarters in town. Knowing that a large percentage of the civil service was on the payroll of one smuggler or another, he was afraid that if he told them what he suspected they wouldn't come. Instead he simply said that it was a kidnapping of some rich Americans. The officer who answered delivered a lecture about drinking or smoking ganja on the job, and before he hung up suggested Billy go back to sleep and quit spreading false rumors while there was rugby on the tele.

Although, among his other jobs, Billy was responsible for security at the airport, he didn't have a pistol, convinced that in a world of Uzis and Kalashnikovs having one was more apt to get you killed than not having one. Nevertheless, he felt duty required him to do something. Heart in throat, he went out onto the field and called to the plane.

Lalo saw him and grunted, the form of speech with which he seemed most comfortable, indicating his presence to Doc.

"Fuck him," Doc said, his usual response.

Max opened his window, telling his captors, "Don't be stupid. I don't say anything, they'll have jets shooting us down." It was a bit of an exaggeration, but he was worried that if Billy pushed it they might hurt him, and he still had to taxi the plane out onto the runway.

Ignoring whatever they were saying behind him, he poked his head out and shouted to the effect that they were late and Billy should put the charges on the tab as usual. They didn't have a tab.

Billy seemed stuck on that for a few seconds, but then cupped his hands to call, "What about a flight plon?"

Max told him, "Just once or twice around the island. Real Estate."

Keeping it small, he swiftly slid one finger across his throat in the universal "cut" sign, open here to interpretation. With that he slammed the window shut and revved the engines.

"Let's get this thing in the air," Doc said, in his flat, disinterested voice, and Max felt relief; they hadn't spotted his signal.

As he pulled out to the runway he took one glance back and saw Billy looking lost, his eyes large with distress and hands spread helplessly. A sight that didn't fill Max with optimism.

A moment later they left the tarmac and climbed. Reasonably, Max asked, "Where the hell am I going? You got any maps, directions, anything?"

"Go west."

"Where west? Back the way we came, to the mainland? You don't just say, 'Go west,' in an airplane like it's a snowmobile. You got to give me points on the compass, coordinates, you gotta give me—"

"Okay, go southwest."

"She said it was northeast of Andros . . ."

"Jesus, you're a dumb fuck!" He slapped Max on the side of the head, hard enough to make his ears ring and his heart roar. He bit his lip, seeking the necessary self-control through pain.

Doc went on as if nothing had happened, "Do I want the people down there knowin' we're really goin' somewheres northeast? I heard you were smart, I see I got nothin' to worry about. Drive west and shut the fuck up, okay?"

Max banked and went west; he could do that.

Earl's sleep was marked by a beatific smile that turned all the lumps, ravines and knobs on his face into innocence personified. He sat on the front steps of the office with his legs outstretched and his back to the door jamb, the sun trying hard to cook him through all that grease. Among his other accomplishments, an ability to snore while vertical.

Casey kicked his leg to wake him. Kicked him again. Finally Earl straightened, stood and shook himself. Whatever happened to the Casey who used to bring donuts in the morning?

"I want you to check out Number Eight. Now."

"You mean the Beechcraft?"

"What the hell else would I mean? Max stole—I suppose you'd say 'borrowed'—Number Seven."

Earl started off, shaking his head. "I jist never understand why we only got two planes an' we call 'em Seven and Eight."

"That's why I own a business and you're a peon. Just do it!"

Earl thought of something and paused. "This for that new cust—'client,' I know, 'client'—comin' in tomorrow? That job?"

"No, Earl, it's another job." Naturally sarcasm was wasted on the mechanic, but Casey never stopped trying. "This particular job is a Cessna stolen from me. What do you think of that? By a treacherous, disloyal employee. Who, no matter what some people I know might think, is never comin' back. You mighta heard somethin' 'bout it."

"Uh-huh."

"Oh, and the cus—client comes in, you take him over to the house and tell Mary Beth to entertain him. She won't mind. I won't be long."

"She's jist gunna git mad at me."

"Where's the pump gun?"

"Right there in the ammo locker. Why?"

One Casey mask was suddenly replaced by another, smugness. "Well, now, that's the weapon of choice when you go huntin' absconders." A new word from his *Ninety Days to a New Vocabulary*, he went grinning into the office to get the keys.

These sudden shifts were very disconcerting. Earl stood in the hot sun and shivered.

Amazingly, without any apparent knowledge of navigation, Doc seemed able to find his way over these great empty deserts of water as easily as through his natural urban rot.

Lalo was the first to spot their objective and Max was

just as glad, glad to be setting down anywhere. He had been forced to take an exaggerated evasive route that had eaten up a lot of gas and kept them wandering in the air without any kind of course on which he could hang some sense of direction. And because of the random nature of their flight he had little idea what else was in the air, other than what they picked up from radio cross-talk.

Being ten thousand feet above the earth in a tiny winged capsule he barely knew how to fly, with two unpredictable armed thugs, one possibly certifiable, was not a summer day in a hammock. He wasn't surprised to find his hands cramped from gripping the yoke too tightly.

At first sight the island looked deserted. It was unusually verdant, with a lot of pine trees, vines, some palms and palmetto scrub everywhere, and of course mangrove all around the water. More like a "jungle island" in a movie than most of them in the Bahamas.

Closer, he spotted a once-grand two-story colonial teetering in a small clearing. Part of the roof had been stolen by a storm and the foliage was encroaching on the clearing that surrounded it on all sides.

"That story about the husband running away—"

"Lies," Diana said in a somewhat stronger voice than before, but without looking at him. Color had returned to her cheeks whereas back in the cafe even the tan had looked pale.

"Is there a husband?"

"No."

"Was?"

"When I was seventeen. We divorced on grounds of ache."

"His or yours?"

"No fault."

"How much you getting for me?"

"You'll see."

Doc was leaning forward, studying the ground as Max circled, descending.

"There!" Doc said, laying his arm over Max's shoulder and pointing to a tiny clearing on the ground. "That open space there in the trees to the right, see?"

"What open space?"

"The only open space there is, prick. You see another one?"

Max made a short study of it and an even shorter judgment. "Holy shit. I can't get in there. It's tiny."

"Yeah, so what?"

"You bedder land thees fucking coffin, asshole," Lalo said, surprising everyone with his eloquence. "I'm sick sitting here, you know."

"Forget it. I'm not a good enough pilot."

"Only one we got, lover," Doc said, unconcerned as ever.

Diana was in a panic. "Wait a minute. You were a crop duster. You taught stunt flying. You were on aircraft carriers."

"That was Casey."

Unbelieving, she gawked. "That wasn't you?!"

"Who said it was?"

"You looked like the one. Oh, no, not that mean geek? Oh, God!"

Max was starting to enjoy himself. "Boy have you got it wrong. Casey's an ace. I'm a hobbyist." He felt Doc's big gun on his neck again and half-turned to address him, cruelly sincere: "I told her I had trouble with landings."

Diana groaned, but made no attempt to fight back; she was too devastated.

Doc said, "Better not with this one. I hate airplanes."

"What are you gonna do—shoot me? We'd all die."

"Big deal."

Helpless in the face of such compelling evidence of an existential vacuum, Max surrendered. What were his alternatives? He took the plane out to sea while he considered them. Passing over the house you could make out people in front waving to them. One of them a woman.

"Everyone strapped in good?" He banked and started his approach, suspecting from the beginning that he was too high. But then he had no idea what was the correct height to begin a descent to that tiny white dot. From here he could barely see it.

"I don't trust your tone," Diana said, a certain wariness in her own. "It's defeatist."

"You'd be too, if you knew what I knew."

Doc, beginning at last to sound a little edgy himself, complained: "Hey, concentrate on what you're doin'."

Max was thinking how he wished he had had more than three flying lessons, and maybe Casey shouldn't have bribed that official at the FAA to get him a license. Casey had his own reasons of course, but the arguments that anyone who could race motorcycles or stock cars could probably fly a plane and on-the-job experience was the best training anyway no longer sounded quite as convincing.

Reducing his speed, he began the descent, still without being able to see the strip. The only hope was that there was more of it under the trees than could be seen from the air. As far as the surface, it looked to be impacted earth. He hoped it was that and not sand.

"You're not rich, are you?" he asked Diana, mainly to distract himself.

"Why don't you forget me. I'm not a part of this any more."

"You'd like to think so."

"I'm not rich. One of nine kids. Old man an auto worker

in Detroit when he wasn't a mean, lazy, falling-down drunk. But I'm not asking for your sympathy, so let's drop it and you concentrate."

"You're not getting any. The clothes, the look, the attitude . . ."

"I was a model and an actress. I created myself. It's just acting."

"What do you do now?"

"Student."

Max, who was keeping his eye on the terrain below while he talked, tensed and swore. There it was suddenly, directly ahead. They were way too high and too close.

Diana saw it at the same time and shouted, "No, no, go around!!"

Forget it, there was still a slim chance of bringing it in, and if he did go for another approach he might think about it too much, might not even be willing to try, and then Doc would flip out and facilitate all their deaths.

Absolutely he was not going to lose his nerve in front of these scummers. Or this woman who had sold him and, to compound the felony, got the wrong man.

He didn't warn them, instead muttered, "Hell with it!" to himself before he put the nose over into an almost perpendicular plummeting dive. The Cessna, which wasn't built for anything like this, put its ears back and complained with terrifying whines, groans and cracking sounds through its whole tormented structure.

If not the G-forces, the sheer surprise initially petrified everyone except Max, who after all had only chosen his usual way of meeting an insurmountable problem—by plunging into it. Diana was the first to scream, and loudly. Doc yelled and Lalo emitted a peculiarly high-pitched moan that sounded like an animal being eaten somewhere in a forest.

These horrendous sounds continued all the way down, for the plane kept dropping and dropping as if there was no earth below it, and eventually it would have to go off into space.

It worked for Max, because once into the dive he began to love it. He shouted with joy but the other three assumed it was out of a fear equal to their own, which only frightened them more. A few hundred feet above the ground he pulled back hard, pure instinct, on the yoke and the plane began to level. There was the airstrip directly in front.

They were going in now; there was no alternative because the end of the pull-out had put them very close to the ground. With more determination than skill, Max, still hollering, managed to hit the very edge of the strip. The plane bounced high into the trees above, the prop slashing off branches and leaves, flopped back to the ground like a seagull on acid, veered crazily, chewing up scrub all along the edge of the cleared area.

Max, very much into his role, fought it every inch of the way, alternately swearing at and encouraging the plane with loving affection, "Come on, sweet baby! . . . C'mon, you crazy son-of-a-bitch!" Dirt and sand flew up on both sides like water.

Out of necessity, he had begun to try to stop the plane the instant it touched down. The other three continued yelling and pleading as the plane took one blow or leap after another, but Max scarcely noticed. By now he was enjoying himself immensely.

At one point the landing gear caught on something and it seemed certain they would cartwheel and burn, but it broke through and the tail that had waved frantically in the air for a dangerous moment slammed back to earth. The bottom half of the Dutch-style door dropped open, becoming a ramp, while the top half flapped up and down. A puff of smoke burst from one engine and some more came off the hissing tires while the horizontal stabilizer waggled semaphore signals. And finally, barely avoiding a large palm tree, it skidded sideways up a small sand dune to settle, tilted, with a huge exhalation, an expiring leviathan.

Inside the plane a moment's eerie quiet reigned, with little bangings and tinklings, such as after an earthquake. A few seconds of that and three of the occupants exploded out of the single door, thrusting the top half up and getting banged by it each in turn. Gasping, blanched by fear and desperate for solid ground, they fled in panic across the "runway."

Diana finally felt safe enough to flop down, panting, on a sand pile in a rag doll position. Immediately she tried deep breathing exercises, but it went awry when she sucked in a sand flea. This would not be a happy island.

Lalo lumbered to the nearest tree and embraced it passionately. Doc, more cognizant of his dignity, caught himself up before he had run ten yards, kicked some dirt, coughed and spat several times but stayed on his feet. Then, confident his land legs were back, he reached for the big gun in his belt and turned slowly, very slowly with a snarl that was all the more frightening for its display of rare emotion.

Max climbed out last as a good captain should, casually—mustn't start a panic—shut the door behind him with care, and strolled away a few paces. There he paused a moment to look back at the plane, nodding with satisfaction at what he had wrought. He turned to face his passengers with a big grin. "Not bad, huh?"

VIII

Max's view was basically that any time you survived a landing, especially one of his, it should be viewed as a success. His miscalculation was immediately made manifest. Doc approached, one foot in front of the other, with his arm extended and the pointed gun shaking at the end of it. Behind that, growing larger while twisting out of shape, a face that offered no quarter.

"You think it's funny, shit-head?!" Doc screamed at him. "You a comedian? I'm gonna blow your eyes through your asshole." He continued to march straight for Max's eyes as if nothing would satisfy him but tasting the aqueous humor on his own lips when they exploded.

At that instant, however, Lalo rushed in, snorting like a maddened boar, to blindside Max, hitting out as he came. Luckily, he was so engulfed by anger and embarrassment he had forgotten to draw his knife. Max, fixed on Doc's gun, had failed to see him coming and was dead meat, on the ground in two seconds, still wondering what the hell they were so upset about?

Doc came over and was satisfied now just to hit him with the gun butt all around the head and shoulders, while Lalo tried to kick him in the ribs and break his arms and legs.

Max made an attempt at first to regain his feet and tried to get in a few shots of his own but the other two had done so much damage so quickly all he could do in the end was lie on the ground, try to cover his vital parts and groan.

When Diana recovered she came running to stop the carnage. "Cut it out!" she screamed, "let him go! Stop it! You bastards!" She got a grip on Doc's gun arm and bit it until he cuffed her off with his other hand.

Then she threw her whole body against Lalo, but he also brushed her aside easily. "You'll kill him, for God's sake." She kept coming at him until Lalo shoved her down hard enough to keep her there for a moment. Both men went back to work on Max, whose respite had been welcome but not sufficient to get him up fighting or running.

Afterwards, he had no doubt they would have beaten him to death were it not for that lovely burst of automatic weapon fire from the direction of the house which brought everything to a stop. No one was hit, no one even ducked. It wasn't the Marines, obviously.

"Hey, hey, fellas!" the gunman called in distinctly urban accents. "Don't bruise the merchandise, okay?"

A little late for that, Max thought; he was reasonably certain he had cracked some ribs. Whatever it was, the pain was severe enough to rob him of his penchant for meeting life with dark humor.

He tried to raise his head but Diana pushed it down again. "Oh, my God, are you all right? Are you hurt?" The words tumbled out one over the other, "Jesus, Muldoon, what did they do to you?" She tried to wipe away some of the blood with Kleenex but it was all over the place, including her white shorts and blouse.

On his part, Max could hardly get the words out. He was studying the fingers of one swollen hand, wiggling them to see if they were broken. "I'm okay, I guess." Even as he said it, he hated the high tenor sound of it. When he tried to suck in enough air to change the tone, his ribs forbade it. "I need a minute."

They stayed like that for awhile in a camaraderie of pain,

managing damaged smiles. At the moment she looked less like a model than someone who had been in an ugly barroom brawl, a significant bruise darkening and spreading on one side of her face, dust and sand stuck to her skin and in her hair, a tiny trickle of blood coming from inside her mouth and the white shirt torn and dirtied as well as bloodstained.

"Oh, man . . . they really hurt you," he mumbled. "Thanks."

"Just don't misunderstand, I would have done the same for a dog if somebody was beating it."

"That's what I feel like, a dog." He winced, grunted and closed his eyes, running his tongue over the cuts inside his mouth and in particular to investigate the possibility that one back tooth was loosened. Doc and Lalo were talking to someone in the background but he couldn't concentrate on living and listening at the same time.

He heard Diana's voice. "Idiot," she said, meaning it, "why would you thank me? I got you into all this." She tried to pull him up to a sitting position.

He heard footsteps and opened his eyes but blood was streaming into them from the scalp, at the same time he was trying to help her lift. The pain remained formidable but he managed to raise himself as far as his elbows where he found himself looking up at Tony Ciufini. A large, broad-shouldered, narrow-waisted man stripped to the waist in tribute to his pecs and displaying sufficient jewelry to bring on snow blindness. He also had that cupid's mouth out of Raphael that Italians call a "kissy face."

"Get me some bandages," Diana told him sharply.

"Hey, do I look like a fuckin' nurse to you?"

Diana, who fortunately was wearing a brassiere, angrily yanked off her shirt and began to tear it into strips, applying them where needed. Max was grateful; oh, so grateful. He could smell her skin when she leaned across him and felt himself reviving.

Tony was studying him with what Max felt was a wholly inappropriate grin. What was funny? They did have wonderful teeth, though, in this case enough for two men; an orthodontist would starve to death in Sicily. And all that wavy black hair; they had specialists for everything: their cars, their money, their funerals. Was there such a thing as mob hair care? He decided he was delirious. One thing wasn't delirium, a MAC-11 dangling carelessly.

"You must a scared my boys, huh?" he commented, still amused. Turning to Diana, the grin got bigger and distinctly lupine. "Hey, you're quite a little scrapper there, sweetheart. Pulled you off the guys just in time, you could a hurt one." He thought that justified a laugh, or at least a chance to parade the teeth. "Not that I care a whole lot." He indicated Max, who was shaking his head in an attempt to clear it. "Him I care about. Him I need."

Max saw the eyes that didn't bother to accompany all this grinning, but rather had that peculiar dull hostility that comes from trying to be smart and losing. Bad sign.

Behind him was a new one, Jack Biggers, cradling a tricked-up M-1 carbine with a pistol handle called on the street an "Enforcer." He didn't quite belong down here or with the others, looked more like a ridge-runner with his tubercular body, missing teeth, stubble, and hard-time tattoos running up and down his skinny-pinny arms. Their eyes met and the man spat—that was a hillbilly!

Max tried to rise further, gasped, "Aw shit!" and eased himself all the way back to prone. Diana had put her jacket under his head but this was the first time he realized it. From this particular angle he was directly in line with the lethal end of the MAC-11.

Tony seemed to regard his injuries and all that blood with some concern. "Assholes," he addressed the boys who had brought him.

"You weren't on the fuckin' thing," Doc reminded him. Fortunately, he had calmed down, back to his old blank, empty self.

Tony gave Diana another of his appraising leers. "You done good, sweetheart. You said you'd bring him and you did."

"I brought him," she said flatly, "and look at him."

"You got more balls than most a the guys I seen."

"This your ex?" Max asked her, struggling upwards again, refusing this time to show how much it hurt.

Diana, outraged, managed through effort to look ugly for a moment. "This . . . gallstone? Are you nuts?! What do you think I am? He's my ex-brother-in-law."

Tony laughed; everything was going right and it was easy to be generous.

Diana knelt in the dust next to Max, who was sitting hugging his own ribs with his head down between his legs. "You'd better get up," she said quietly, almost kindly, then whispered, "They get the idea you're no good to them, they'll kill you."

"Hey, girl," Tony mimicked. Playing to the others standing around, he asked, "Isn't that what the niggers say? I married the wrong one of the litter," he told Diana, "you know that? Should a been you, the ballsy one. Although your sister's got a better ass. A great ass," he said decisively.

Diana gave him a look of mild disgust; in her mind, major disgust would have given him too much importance.

Tony stuck out his granite chin with the cleft. "Your loss, babe. Bring him up on the porch and lay him on the couch. See if he's gonna live. Lalo!"

101

Lalo helped Diana get Max up to a more or less standing position. She kept snapping at the big Cuban to "take it easy" and swearing at him in manly fashion. Max, with their help and at great cost, managed to get one foot in front of the other until he actually could have been said to be walking. The ribs might be cracked but they weren't broken or all this careless movement would literally be killing him.

A subversive factor was the consuming sensation of Diana's body, his first. And considering his condition, its ability to distract amazed, leaving him with the feeling that he was in danger of repeating the madness that got him here in the first place.

Jack and Doc strolled on ahead along the path to the house. Tony walked a couple of feet in front of the ambulance party, batting branches and vines out of the way, his machine pistol strapped on his bare back.

"Where are we? What's the name of this place?" Max asked him, his voice a wispy thing out of a fog.

"How would we know? We stole it."

A wallet, jewels, a life even—how could you steal an island?

Ahead on the verandah that ran around the house on three sides he spotted a woman and child as they emerged. From here, a good-looking woman of near Diana's age, early thirties probably. She was wearing a bikini bottom and Dallas Cowboys' T-shirt sans bra.

As they got closer he could recognize the family's good bones but also an excess of make-up, mouth and eyes too big, lots of blond hair pulled back with a band around her forehead. The child was a four-year-old boy with black hair, handsome, Italianate, shy, hanging back behind her.

He was startled by Diana's voice so close to his ear, "My

sister Delia and her boy. I told you about my wonderful family."

"You all gorgeous?"

They approached the house. Doc and Jack were just going inside. Delia rushed down the rickety steps to greet her sister, leaving the little boy hiding behind a pillar, peeking out. "Oh, merciful God, thank you, darlin'! Ah was soooo scared."

Diana was still struggling to support one half of Max, and even though he was doing a little better, it was still jarring when her sister threw her arms around her neck and began hugging and kissing her wildly.

She tried to shake her off. "Delia, for gosh sakes, gimme a break. Can't you see—?"

Delia, who seemed oblivious to any sort of reprimand, continued to cling to her neck, crooking it in her arm while they stumbled along. "Huhnnney, you saved mah baby. And after all the trouble ah caused you over the years. How can ah not be grateful? Your capacity for forgiveness is just sooo . . . big! Thank you, sweetheart." She tried to kiss her sister again as they struggled up the steps to the porch. "Thaaaank yooooou!"

They eased him down onto an old rattan couch with well-weathered pillows.

"If you have nine kids," Diana told him, "one's gonna be Einstein and one'll be Courtney Love, trust me."

"You hoppy, asshole?" Lalo asked rhetorically, and went on into the house. Tony followed, saying he wanted to have a word with his "boys." Diana plumped the pillows behind Max.

"Why does she have a southern accent?"

Diana, disgusted, would have liked to pretend that her sister wasn't there. "I don't know. It's cute. You okay now?"

Max nodded. Delia was watching them with a pouty expression, more annoyed at being talked around than by her sister's comments.

"Come on, Ricky, sweetheart. Come to Aunt Diana."

The little boy hesitated but finally abandoned his refuge and rushed into her arms with obvious glee. She scooped him up easily and swung him a little, then kissed him on both cheeks. Max watched closely, wondering about her as he had from the beginning. If nothing else, her physical strength was surprising in someone of such delicate appearance. He certainly would never have taken her for maternal.

"He always did like you more 'an he does his own mama," Delia complained without any passion.

Diana started to say something on the order of, "Do you blame him?" but caught herself, realizing the boy would hear. "Don't be silly, Delia."

Tony swaggered out onto the porch with his hands in the pockets of his tight, black wool suit pants. He had put on a sport shirt, even if it was the silky patterned kind of thing the street corner guys back in New York would wear to an Iranian disco, widely open at the neck to exhibit a couple of gold chains and a St. Christopher medallion plus a fur chest for them to play hide and seek in.

As a concession to the heat he had pulled the shirt out to hang over his pants, and over that he wore the narrow suit coat. None of these guys, except Lalo, in shorts and T-shirt, seemed to have any idea where they were.

Tony looked at the sisters, now into a full-on quarrel and started grinning again. Max wondered what it was about Italian men that they loved to see the women fight?

". . . After ah was so glad to see you, and lovin' an' all, an' then you treat your little sister like uh . . . uh . . . I don't know what. Ah mean, ah am grateful to you, Diana, so I don't see why you're not at least uh little itty bitty grateful to me."

Diana couldn't restrain herself; she put Richie down so she could shout without terrorizing him. "What do I have to be grateful to you about? Look what I'm into here, for God's sake. Ricky, go play somewhere, sweetheart. Your mother and I want to argue a little. It's very natural for grownups to argue, honey. Go on."

"He's seen a lot worse," his mother said.

"I'll bet he has."

If a whole body could express a pout, Delia's did. She rested her weight against a pillar, all the better to thrust a naked haunch, marred only by the tie of the bikini, out into the world for viewing. Her nipples seemed to blossom through the T-shirt, and Max wondered what would cause that in the course of greeting an angry sister, a loser captive, and two psychopathic morons. Perfect legs shown off by high-heeled sandals. They were certainly sisters over the skin, if interplanetary strangers beneath it.

The boy ran around to the other side of the house but then peeked back from the corner—destined always to be the secret sharer.

"If you're gonna be grateful to anyone, you ditz, how about him?" She pointed to Max, who would just as soon have been left out of it. "He's the one we screwed over. What's this poor bastard got to do with your stupid horny love life and your—stupidity, for God's sake? He's already got the crap kicked out of him and your stupid ex-husband there's probably gonna kill him when he's through with him. Maybe kill us all, in which case at least you'll deserve it."

Max was watching them like a tennis match; it took his mind off his injuries.

Delia looked him over darkly for a minute. "Well, he's cute but he's not part of our family so ah don't care what happens to him."

"Hey, c'mon, 'nough a this sentimental shit," Tony said at last, grabbing Delia by the arm and starting to drag her towards the open door. She whined that he was too rough and put up a little resistance, digging in her heels, but that was clearly part of a game in which she was a willing participant.

Frustrated beyond endurance and helpless, Diana turned on Max as though he were the accusing God. "I had to bring you, dammit! Tony would have killed them both. It was for the boy! And I'm not sorry, and I'm not apologizing!" She was biting her lip at the end.

Max wasn't sure she was even aware of what she was saying, but he had his own building sensation of horror.

"Not his own son? YOU WOULDN'T—YOUR OWN SON?!" he yelled at Tony before he passed through the doorway.

Without turning, he shrugged and offered, "Hey, it's business," and went on.

The two passed into the house with Tony's hand vigorously squeezing Delia's buttocks, a bellows on a fire, leaving Max shocked, open-mouthed, for what was perhaps the first time in his life.

Diana gave him a look of utter hopelessness that said, "You see now?"

IX

Casey decided to go home and pick up some things, toiletries, underwear, socks, flying gear, before he took off. Also to advise his wife that he would be away a couple of days and tell her about the client coming in. Not to mention standing in for him at "Fathers' Night" at pre-school.

Mary Beth would be upset about the possibility of losing the assignment, but entertaining the client; Earl to the contrary, wouldn't bother her. She liked men and they liked her; he could count on that. Oh, he burned to tell her of Max's infamy, rub her nose in the reprobate's betrayal of his benefactor. There was joy, but the fear was that somehow it might come back on him.

It was the middle of the afternoon by the time he headed his shiny old Cadillac for the house. He drove fast because he wanted to get over to Andros before dark and start poking around.

Pulling up at the curb he noticed that the front door was closed and the windows shuttered, like somebody had gone north for the summer. Mary Beth always had the house opened up when she was there. And the kids should be home by now, too. Early for her to go shopping. No meetings of clubs or organizations that he had heard about.

Casey grumbled to himself, just when he had important info to convey and not much time. He liked women to be there when their husbands came home; not that she paid much attention to what he wanted. Too goddamned independent, all of them.

To his surprise, the screen door was locked. So someone was home. The doorbell hadn't worked for years; he pounded loudly but got no response. Stepping over to the large bay window opening onto the front porch he hit it several times, noting that it too had the curtains drawn. Nothing.

What the hell was going on here? Somebody should hear him what with three people running around like nuts in the house and oft-times, he could never keep track, Mary Beth had a cleaning woman and her daughter in to make it five. Or girlfriends to a dozen; he made it a point to stay away on those occasions, too many soprano voices were bad for his ulcer.

As for the cleaning woman, the only reason he had agreed to that was Mary Beth claimed to have been raised with servants. He knew it was a lie; her old man was a foreman in the shipyards at Norfolk, but he couldn't prove it because when Casey found her she had been running away from home and refused ever to go back.

As good as he had been to her, never mentioning the fact that she had been twenty-five at the time, the least she could do was answer the damn door. His knuckles were beginning to wear and the whole neighborhood could hear him shouting her name. Now he became alarmed, little things running around in the pit of his stomach. He owed money but it was to Cubans; unlike the Colombians or Jamaicans, they didn't hurt the family.

His precious family, insides twisting, shriveling; he could see them lying in different rooms, sick, overcome by gas, murdered. Just as he was preparing to break a window, the shutters above him were flung open.

It was necessary to back off the porch to look past its roof to the second story. Mary Beth was stretching far out of an upstairs bedroom window, trying to see below.

"Who's making all that racket down there? What do you want?"

Casey spotted her first and didn't like what he saw. Her hair was mussed; she was wearing the negligee he had given her last Valentine's Day but it was hanging open and her monumental breasts were within a millimeter of celebrating the Caribbean sun. What she was not wearing was lipstick and Mary Beth put on lipstick to go to the bathroom.

"What do I want? In my own goddamn house. What do you think I want?"

"Casey?"

"You see Elvis standin' here?"

Casey's radar was way out in front, but as yet he was unwilling to accept what it was telling him.

She seemed momentarily confused, so he took advantage. "Where's the kids?"

She thought. "Oh, over at Dolores's. Playing with little Vincent and Michele. You know."

"Yeah, well, lemme in. I don't want to carry on a conversation out here, I got stuff to tell you. And whaddaya got the house all closed up for?" He realized he was a bit loud and the neighbors might hear, so lowered his voice. "What's goin' on here, Mary Beth?"

"What's goin' on here?"

"Don't start that repeatin' everythin' I say. Just get down here and open this goddamn door."

"Uh, no, I can't."

"What?!"

"No . . . not right . . . n-now," she decided.

Casey felt the stutter deep in his wounded heart, a tentativeness that said far more than any certainty. "Cover yourself up, woman, good grief!"

109

Mary Beth made a desperate grab at the neckline of her negligee but the breasts, strong in themselves, resisted and kept bulling their way to freedom. Her fluster only increased.

"Why can't I come into my own house?! You got someone up there, Mary Beth?" he bellowed, feeling for his pistol and then remembering he didn't have it.

"Shush! You want the whole neighborhood to hear?" Her own whisper was sufficiently imperative to have been deciphered a block away. " 'Course not. I just can't come down right now."

"You don't, I'm gonna break in. How you like them pickles?"

Mary Beth was cunning but less than swift. "Well, I been thinkin' how you oughta take some time and get your priorities straight."

She seemed so satisfied with herself after that thrust Casey was afraid she would pull back in. "What are you talkin' about? My priorities are great. Nobody's got better priorities than me. Now get down here and open the door."

He had looked around while he was speaking and realized that they were drawing a lot of attention. The elderly gay couple across the street had come out onto their porch and were sitting on a glider, rocking and nodding, no doubt gratified that someone else in the neighborhood was an object of attention.

Down the street a little ways an ice cream vendor had stopped at the curb, suspending operations to get out of his truck and smile in their direction. Mrs. O'Neil next door was leaning out of a second-story window pretending to shake out her sheets, and shaking them and shaking them. Two giggling boys on the sidewalk.

Distracted by all this, it took him a moment to understand that Mary Beth was stating her case in loud and certain terms: ". . . just sick and tired of you runnin' all over the world, goin' to bad places, hangin' out with a bunch of no-good bums like Max and that pea-brain—I take that back, a pea has a bigger brain than Earl—and you stayin' out all hours day and night weeks at a time, and never even bringin' home enough money for us to live like decent folks.

"Kids ask me alluh time where's Daddy and I have to say, 'Oh, he's probably in some whorehouse in Calexico bribin' the police to help him steal somethin', but he does it for us.' Well, I'm sick and tired of sugarcoatin' you to them. So just put that in your pipe and smoke it!"

"For Heaven's sake, everybody's listenin'! I got a standin' in this community . . ."

"To hell with your dumb ol' standin'," she hurled right back at him. "You can't spend it at Burdines." She obviously felt, voice rising to an operatic peak, that she had ended her tirade on a penultimate note and was prepared to slam the shutters, reaching out for them on either side.

Casey wasn't about to let her have the last word. If those shutters slammed, he was going to rush the house and break in. Nine short simple words stopped him where he stood.

A *basso profundo* voice rumbled from somewhere deep in the house like a miasma risen from the shaking foundations, not only of the house but of Casey's life. "What the hell's takin' you so long, Mary Beth . . . ?" it said with unabashed impatience. Only boat captains had voices like that, coming as it did from a constant contending against the sound of the sea and outsized engines.

Boat captains! If there was any consolation for a betrayed husband, it was in seeing for the first time a truly horrified expression on his wife's face. She knew how he hated boat captains. Everybody did, except the writers, of course.

111

When he had heard the voice and it penetrated to the soles of his feet, Casey unhesitatingly shouted, "That's it! I gotcha!!" but he had no idea what he was really saying. He wouldn't have been Casey if he hadn't been delighted to be proven right, but then immediately his heart was sucked out of him and trampled on the ground in the full knowledge of what he was right about.

Frantically the shutters were slammed shut; his wife and marriage disappeared in a wink. How many years of glorious uxoriousness wasted? He was distraught, couldn't remember. Years and years.

"Is that Digger Hadley up there? Captain Digger 'Swordfish' Hadley?!" he screamed, naming a notorious charter boat captain whose *nom de pecher* had more to do with the sword than the fish. "Tell that fish-stink sonofabitch to come down and show himself. I'll kill him!"

Casey had cast off shame. He swung around at the neighbors, there were many more out now, and yelled, "Can you hear me? We loud enough for you? I'm gonna kill him. You hear that?"

Some turned away and pretended not to have heard anything, others smiled and waved. The young boys ran home to tell of the fun to be had. Casey gave them all a wave of dismissal and gave it up.

He didn't kill anyone, at least not then, didn't even try to break in. Despite all the noise he was making, passion had fled along with hope. What remained was a boot-high bitterness that would not wash away with the first drink. The sand had run out of him, sailors would have said; his spirit had slunk off to the shadows, head down, like a defeated beast.

Trudging to his car, he stopped a final time to call back at the house and its faithless ghosts in a breaking voice, "I love you, Mary Beth." No answer possible and none came.

"I took a first aid course in high school." Diana, who had cleaned up and was wearing one of her sister's shirts, had her work laid out around her like a doctor. The implements came from a first aid kit in the plane. Ribs were taped first, then she went over the wounds, and there were many, cleansing from a basin of soap and water, sterilizing, bandaging and in one instance, which amazed Max, sewing up the cut with an ordinary needle and thread. He had experienced a lot of cuts, abrasions and broken bones, but insisted he had never seen it done better by a professional.

"You gonna tell me why I'm so desirable? I mean, to these guys."

"I don't know." She shrugged and he believed it. "They said they needed a plane and somebody who could fly it."

He was spread all over the couch while she fussed over him. "Would you please sit still until I'm through with this?"

"These make me nervous." He held up the handcuffs that constrained him. All the same he had a beer in his hands and a small cigar in his mouth. Lalo snored in a big chair at the other end of the verandah with a shotgun across his lap.

"I'll bet you were hyperactive as a kid, right?"

"That's what they used to tell the headmaster or judge every time I got in trouble. I thought I just liked to have fun."

"You're not having it now." With a certain deliberation she poured alcohol on a wound that went almost all the way around his arm and he winced. "I hate it that I can't make you yell in pain."

"Pain's my buddy. But why would you want to?"

"Because you're such a smartass. You're so confident and macho and all that stuff. I hate that."

"You forgot 'good-looking.' "

"No I didn't," she said quickly.

They both laughed, finding it a relief.

"Would it help if I told you I'm as scared as you can get right now? I don't know what these bastards want, but I sure as hell know they're gonna punch my ticket after they get it. I hope that doesn't include you."

"Me, too."

"These boys as bad as they sound?"

"Who could be?"

"I hate this feeling of helplessness, you know. Of being trapped. I hate it for what it makes me. A little bit of a coward, to be perfectly honest."

"Oh, get real, Muldoon. This is just some kind of ploy to get in my pants. The vulnerable, sensitive male or some such crap. It doesn't suit you, you're one of the harder cases I've seen."

"Oh, yeah, that's me."

"Look, you asked, these guys are punks, okay? Doc's a snow bunny. Absolutely soulless. Or if he does have one somewhere, it slithers. Lalo's a whole other kind of animal, I haven't figured out what kind yet. A bad kind, and really dumb.

"Jack . . . he might look like just a Tennessee cow pie to you, but don't underestimate him on appearance. He's one methed-out redneck, so he's very unpredictable. And even if he wasn't, he's done enough hard time till his brain's in the same shape as his teeth. Even these guys treat him carefully, I notice. He doesn't say a word to anybody for three weeks and then goes ballistic and wants to kill the whole world 'cause a mosquito bit him. 'Course the mosquito dies after."

"I want to know about Tony."

"Tony . . . Tony's been everything from a hairdresser to an enforcer for the boys in Miami. Although he's got a big hate on for them now. All he talks about is 'revenge,' some Italian word I don't get. I don't know why, they usually don't fire people except through the head."

"So, how tough?"

"They all got the conscience of a cockroach. There isn't one wouldn't kill you while eating a meatball sandwich. Don't make the mistake because he acts like a fool sometimes he can't be very cruel or dangerous, Tony. I saw in a documentary on TV where these guys like, you know, Adolf Hitler and . . . Stalin danced around like bears and things and just generally acted like idiots in private with their friends. Yet look how many they killed. So don't make that mistake, okay?"

He looked at her with something like awe. "You really had me, you know. I'm not usually this easy, I wouldn't want you to think that."

She pulled back from Max and put down the tools of her surgery. "What do you care what I think?" She seemed genuinely annoyed.

"I'm seeing the same terrific, elegant face, body, style, but you're totally different from the woman I met. You don't talk the same, you don't begin to think the same. And, like you say, you know so much."

"Christ almighty, Muldoon, give it a rest. I liked it better when you hated me because I was a double-crossing bitch. All this trying to understand me. I 'know so much' about what?"

"The life."

"Which?"

"Only sport that counts in South Florida: drugs, smuggling, gangsters . . ."

She gave him a disgusted look. "You don't know anything."

Ricky ran out onto the porch, the way little boys run everywhere, and threw himself into Diana's lap, causing her to go "Umph!" She got him under the arms and hoisted him up. Immediately he went into a near-fetal position and sucked his callused thumb while Diana kissed and stroked his head. Max found himself envious.

"Now I can't swear at you," Diana said softly to him, having turned into a mother on the instant. The trade wind ruffled her thick hair, and her face dissolved into that featureless glow of serenity seen in Renaissance Madonnas where the figure itself seems to deny corporeality in deference to The Mystery.

It had grown silent except for the breeze rattling palms and the roll and slap of a distant surf.

You didn't need to look to know you were in the tropics; its essence was heavy in the salty air, a seductive sweetness, you felt it stroking your skin in some palpable way, wanted to lie down under it like a Buddhist and accept dissolution.

Max was watching her from his trance. Feeling almost serene when he should have been thinking hard about going on living. Time to give himself a mental shaking-up.

The boy seemed to have fallen almost instantly asleep, and who could blame him. She combed his hair with her fingertips, staring down at him, and if it were not for the fact of her moving hand there would have been no proof that she was in the world, either. She hummed softly. Max found himself wondering what it would be like to be a father—now there was danger!

"I'm really sorry I did this to you," Diana whispered to him over the child's head. It would have been impossible to have chosen a better stage setting for repentance; he was aware of that, but it worked anyway. How could it not?

116

Max need not have worried about his subsidence; contrary to popular belief no Nirvana lasts forever and this one
was shredded by the noisy reappearance of "kidnapper" and
"victim" after their obvious exchange of body fluids, stepping out onto the verandah with their arms around each
other.

Delia was truly brimming. "Diana, he's letting us go,
isn't that fab?! Right now, right this minute. I'm sooooo
psyched, honest-to-God. I can take little Ricky home now."
She gave a frisky jump in the air and brandished her fists
like a triumphant boxer. Tony sat down within reach of her
buttocks, unwilling ever to be otherwise, waiting in case the
sisters put on a show.

Max asked Diana, "Are you sure she was kidnapped?"

She paid no attention to him, but rather was looking at
her sister with murder in her eyes. "I'm glad for you. Especially for Ricky. But I want to know something."

"Of course, darling. I owe you everything. I luuuuf you
so much—you're my only sister."

"You have five sisters."

"The others don't like me. You understand me."

Diana, dealing from a barely containable rage, put her
hands over the child's ears and hissed, "Did you fuck him,
Delia? Just now? Because if you did I'll kill you."

Delia seemed genuinely outraged. "What a thing to say to
me! That's none of your business, Diana, personal questions
like that. Mama always taught us to mind our own, and I'd
advise you to try it. Butt out."

"I think I just heard the operative word," Max said,
accepting by now that he was talking to himself.

Tony slapped Delia's left rear cheek hard, making her
squeal, although it wasn't really a protest. It did raise some red
through the tan, which he commented upon with pleasure.

Diana immediately dumped Ricky from her lap, encouraging him with a pat on his own bottom and a little shove. "Go play somewhere, Ricky. Right now! Scoot!" He went reluctantly, looking back, and she kept shooing him.

"Honestly, Diana, I don't know what you're always trying to protect that boy from. He's got to see life. Real adult affection's good for him. Says so in the *Reader's Digest*, and that's not exactly a racy magazine, darlin'."

Diana looked away, head down, gritting her teeth, digging her nails into her palms, muttering to Max, "I can't deal with it. I will kill her. I'm not kidding." She was shaking.

Tony, not to be denied any pleasure for long, took another swipe at his inamorata's bum.

It seemed to Max that by now this act had taken on the coloration of a hobby.

The proud ex-husband beamed whenever he struck home and got the requisite girlish reaction. "Oooooh, Tony. You-are-so-bad! Don't in front of my big sister, she's too pure. Although God knows what she's got to be goody-good about. At least, as a model, I make my living putting my clothes on."

She laughed, though not a friendly one, instead demanding attention to the fact that she had said something terribly clever and cutting. Discussion over, I win.

Max was beginning to feel considerable sympathy for the woman who had brought him here to be killed. And, despite having been accused of being appallingly tolerant of human foibles in the past, found himself really hating this couple in front of him.

Diana seemed especially stung by her sister's last comment and he wondered: why? Perhaps he hadn't been listening.

She rounded on Delia, face scarlet and lips pale, but

Tony deflected her: "You notice how she's got my love letter? Here." He pulled his love around to show her backside as if demonstrating a refrigerator. "Show 'em, babe."

Delia responded with a coquettish grin over her shoulder and a wiggle of the parts under discussion.

"You did fuck him!" Diana yelled.

Max thought that she was a little behind on this.

"Honest-to-Christ, you're worse than a whore, you're an idiot!"

Delia wailed, "Diaaaana, I luuuuuuf him, can't you understand? The divorce was a terrible mistake, we're gonna remarry. I don't care what anyone says."

"Read it," Tony insisted, a little put-out because no one was paying attention to the letter itself. "Must prove somethin' 'bout how I love her."

Diana felt compelled to explain to Max through clenched teeth, "It's tattooed on her behind. Only then, and naturally it took her awhile, she figured out she couldn't read it in the mirror."

However had he managed not to see the immortal words tattooed on one of those small, compact, but joyously quivering hillocks marching back and forth in salute before his eyes? Max couldn't help himself; he laughed loudly, right in their faces, or in Delia's case, lower down.

She didn't seem offended, she was proud of her role as living canvas. To exhibit the fortunate cheek to full advantage with the best lighting, she turned her back all the way to him, bending over and thrusting out one hip. At the same time tugging ineffectually at the thong that constituted the back of her bikini, as if a tiny thing like that could obstruct the view of anything.

She told Max, "It didn't matter. Tony had a videotape made of it for me to see."

Max knew he had better start keeping his opinions private, but any control was fugitive. "Jesus, I'm in the hands of lunatics."

Tony, however, wasn't through with the subject. " 'Course she can't be stoppin' to find a goddamn VCR every time she wants to think a me, so we might have it done on the other cheek backwards. That way she could just slip into a lady's john anywhere."

Diana's mouth fell open and Max, in danger of convulsing, somehow fought it back. "Respect" was such a big word with these guys and "mirth" such a tiny one.

Tony's face hardened quickly. "Hey, hey, you two, this is my wife."

Diana was back on her own ground, reality. She tore into Tony for making a mockery of "wife" and "father"; he didn't have anything to do with his son, was always disappearing, ran around, knocked his wife around, was a brute, a bully and a dictator not to mention that he wasn't even a successful gangster.

That last drew blood and Diana might have paid for it, except who should jump in to defend the beleaguered husband but Delia. "Baby, it wasn't Tony's fault. I was the one who didn't have it together. It's different now. He's gonna make gazillions of money—"

"Hey!" he shouted at her, gesturing menacingly.

With a nervous spasm of the mouth matched by butterflies in the eyes that almost made one feel sorry for her, Delia stumbled through a dissemblance, "Anyway, those bad old misunderstandings wouldn't have happened if I'd just been halfway as centered as I am now . . ."

"Delia, I'd like to center your head in a vise and knock some sense into it. If not for your sake, at least for Ricky's."

Tony stood and stretched, yawning; he had had enough.

The conflict wasn't nearly as entertaining as he had hoped: words, words, words. "C'mon, babe. She's jealous. Get your stuff and I'll have Lalo take you over on the boat." He raised his head and shouted, "Hey, Ricky, get back over here. You're takin' a trip."

The boy, never far away, appeared immediately among the nearby trees and ran towards . . . Diana. Now she had to worry how much he had heard and seen.

To her credit, Delia hesitated about "gettin' her stuff." She looked from Diana to her husband. "What about my sister?"

"Yeah, Tony, what about me? I did what you asked. You going to keep your promise?"

No hesitation on Tony's part, he knew exactly what he wanted and shook his head. "Naw, you go when it's over."

"But, sweetheart, that isn't . . ."

"Enough already! I need her. She's the hostage for you now. You talk too much, which you got a way a doin', we kill her. Fair enough? Anyway, she hates you, so fuck her! C'mon." He took the boy by the arm and led him into the house.

Lalo stirred, pried himself loose from the too-small chair and lazed off down the steps to disappear on the trail towards the water. Max didn't remember seeing a dock or boat, but he had been a tiny bit distracted at the time of approach.

Delia became plaintive, contrite. "Sweetheart, I'm sorry, really. I did try. You can trust Tony, he'll let you go eventually, I'm sure."

"And him? He's the only reason you're going free."

Delia looked at Max and her shrug told it all. "I dunno. I can't fix everything." She put her thumb in her mouth, took it out again to say, "Don't be bitter. Think of little Ricky."

"I wish you would. He'd be better off with a baboon for a mother."

"Thank you very much. I'll remember that next time you need my help." She pulled herself up very straight and marched into the house.

They were quiet for awhile. Finally, Max said, "You gotta admit, there's a certain symmetry to it."

"Oh, shut up."

X

"I never get usta this heat," Martino "Hands" Vigiletti— "Vig (Vidge)" to friends, family, and people who longed to kill him—complained, wiping his wide damp forehead with an embroidered handkerchief bearing the name of the giver, youngest of his five daughters, the precious Serafina. "It's like somethin' crawlin' on you can't get off."

He stared disconsolately out the side window of the Cadillac at the frying pavement on Biscayne Boulevard. It was the late afternoon sun slanting in on his side, easily lasering right through the tint, that was the culprit. Undoing yet another button on his bulging brown sport shirt and pulling open an electric blue jacket, he used the handkerchief to dry the hair on his chest. He didn't like the feel of it—the "chest rug," he called it—when it was damp.

"I dunno, Vig . . . seems okay in here to me. Helluva great air conditioning in this car."

"Fuck you. Yeah, it's American. First thing you see these greasers do when they score is they buy some fuckin' Nazi car or somethin'. This country's good to 'em and they do that. An' hey, whose cars won the war, huh?"

Joseph "Joe Peck" Peccarino had no idea what war he was talking about—the Gallos and the Profaccis? Joe was younger, loved clothes and—here is where he carried a great burden—in his mind smarter than his bosses, which meant that every minute of his life he must be alert to the always dangerous possibility that one of them might discover this.

"Turn up the cold air," he told the ape behind the

wheel, Vig's bodyguard. The man answered with his elo-
quent shoulders; he seldom spoke. In solidarity with his
boss he was wearing a leather jacket and cap; sweat
streamed out of the cap in rivulets that flowed down the
back of his tent-pole neck. He never touched it, which
made Joe Peck wonder if there wasn't a puddle around his
feet.

Vig had turned reminiscent on his favorite subject. "This
fuckin' Miami usta to be all ours. You didn't mind the heat
then. I used to come down alla time in those days. For Big
Pauli, you know, may his soul rest in peace."

A steel-jacketed wistfulness entered Vigiletti's voice.
"What I usta come for was to put things in order. An' when
I give an order around here it was fuckin' carried out." He
shook his head. "I usta like the town then. Now . . ."

"Them must a been the good days, huh, Vig?" He knew
where this conversation had to go.

Vigiletti squirmed his bulk this way and that, pulling his
pants and shirt away from the skin wherever possible.
Peccarino made room while the squirming continued.

Punctuated by the gasps and grunts brought on by his
exertions, Vig summed up with, "Then they let in the colored and the Spanish."

He was still on the subject when they pulled into an alley
in a manufacturing/warehouse district of North Miami
where the sun seldom shone. The inhabitants and most of
the workers in the area were black and Hispanic. The big
Cadillac under the unsubtle guidance of the bodyguard
plowed as much as drove through the alley, crushing bags of
garbage, knocking over containers and sending scavengers
scurrying in all directions. If you wanted to drive for Mr.
Vigiletti, you took the shortest route to everywhere.

The boss's remembrances made Joe Peck uncharacteristically sentimental. "My old man, maybe it was his old man, my grandfather, always droolin', make you sick, the old fuck. Anyhow, somebody usta tell how in the old days in . . . that was Philly, when they'd take the broads, like the dancers, home at night after a show, maybe for the boss, you know, they'd go through the alleys and shoot at the rats and whack out the streetlights. And the cunts'd love it, you know, and get turned-on and do 'em even 'fore they got 'em home safe. Couldn't do that no more."

Vig was still sour. "Can't do a lotta shit no more."

"I allus wanted to know," Joe Peck mused, "what's with us and the old pricks run everything, huh? You get a new suit, feelin' good, you go to this party an' first thing you gotta go out in the yard, kneel next to this old man, he's wheezin' an' noddin', an' kiss his wheelchair smells a piss. Then you got grass stains. I mean, look at old Gigante over there in Brooklyn how he walked 'round the streets in his pajamas makin' ga-ga noises so they think he's *pazzo*. It's fuckin' embarrassin'. The Irish, the old man asks for a beer they give him a whack. The Spanish they kill 'em they get too old. Only Italians gotta suck up to 'em like we do."

Vigiletti, who hadn't been listening to most of it, had heard enough to warn: "You should watch your mouth sometimes, Joey. You let it run away with you."

Naturally Joe Peck agreed with him, but he wasn't concerned.

The car pulled up close to the loading dock of a meat packing plant, screeching to a stop as it fishtailed in offal. Vig cursed the driver when he got out, but as usual the other said nothing; he might as well have been mute.

Joe Peck put on his windbreaker when he emerged, because it was always freezing inside the plant. "That's how you get bronchitis, which is like junior pneumonia, you

know, goin' from one extreme kind a temperature to another extreme kind a temperature. My croaker told me
that."

"Yeah?"

They walked swiftly to the steps of the loading platform
and trotted up the stairs. Vig always gained energy when he
got closer to the money.

"What the fuck's a 'croaker'?"

"That's what my old man allus called 'em. Or maybe
that was his old man. 'Croak' is like to kill, you know."

"That's some fuckin' doctor you got."

"Yeah, I guess so," Peccarino agreed.

A huge metal door to a lighted interior was already being
rolled open by a uniformed security guard.

"Good evenin', Mr. Vigiletti. Gonna be a nice evenin',
ain't it?"

Vig, who never listened to anybody, said, "Hiya, Charlie.
You know Joe Peck." His bald head was down and his shoulders were working like pistons, propelling him forward.

"Yessir, I sure do."

The two men on a mission went into the processing
plant proper. Vig screwed up his face at the odors but Joe
Peck didn't seem to notice.

". . . The colored and the beaners," Vig said as they hurried along, answering some inner voice. "All kinds a spics,
for Christ's sake. Cubans, Ricans, Columbians . . . an' instead a havin' the business, we gotta do business."

Joe Peck, showing his worth, knew precisely where to
pick up the litany. "That fuckin' Carter."

"You got that right! That Cuban boatlift shit.
Alamogordos or whatever they called 'em. You know what
it was?"

They entered a small office at the back of the plant. An

appropriately clerkish little man sat greenly under fluorescent lights, ledgers open on the desk in front of him, computers turned on and pens lined up like guardsmen. He tried to say hello as they burst in, but Vig cut him off with a wave and went straight to a safe.

". . . I'll tell you. A goddamned conspiracy. Give Florida to the Spanish." The accountant was obviously Latino, but Vig hadn't noticed and wouldn't have cared. "You know, so they could vote for the lousy Republicans. My lawyer explained it to me."

"I thought Carter was Democrat," Joe Peck said cagily.

Vig brought some papers from the safe to the accountant's desk, and then added a couple from his inside jacket pocket. While they were going through them, he told Joe Peck, "Whadda you know? You don't even watch the TV."

He sat down next to the accountant and spoke to him for the first time, "Listen . . . we're not puttin' the, you know . . . any more a that inta the islands for awhile. You got it?"

His strange rhythm and stilted tones didn't surprise anyone else in the room. In fact, when the accountant spoke, it was with much the same intonation.

"Mr. Vi—Mr. Victor, I got a real lot of . . . 'it' . . . here. Backed up here in town, if you understand, please. I've been told to move it out, get rid of it. That's what my . . . employer wants. He told me to tell you."

"Okay, that's what we're here for. You don't got the only problem; it's backed up like a shithouse all the way from L.A. to the yodelers. Business is good, what can I tell you. It's coming in faster 'an we can stash it or ship it."

He leaned back in the chair and spread his arms, looking around at the ceiling, the usual repository of bugs. "Like the fuckin' government—if you're listenin', assholes—should have it so good. Here . . ." He grabbed one of the pens and scribbled a figure on a pad for the accountant. "We're gonna take it with us right now. We got a place where we can keep it a few months." To Joe Peck, he said, "Get started. Get that whack-off outta the car, huh."

"Mr. Victor," the accountant asked, fear making his face spotty, "This okay with . . . you know, up north?"

Vigiletti stared at him with scorn. "Do I look like someone to you calls New Jersey every time I gotta take a shit?"

"Nosir. It's . . . it's just such a big number."

"So I'm responsible. Anything happens, I'm the one. You got a problem with that?"

The accountant didn't; he even tried to smile.

In the cold storage room, Joe Peck and the bodyguard had already gone to work by the time Vigiletti got there. Vig liked to think of himself as a boss, or underboss, who would roll his sleeves and get down in the trenches if, for instance, there was killing to be done. Could pitch in and get his hands dirty, or in this case bloody, with his troops any day.

"The money's gettin' cow blood all over it," the bodyguard complained.

"So what!" Vigiletti told him. "It'll spend, won't it?"

He picked up a meat cleaver that someone had left stuck in a chopping block and went to work. Inexperienced, it took several hacking strokes to find the canvas bag, and, as he was a strong man for his age and notoriously impatient, the hanging beef carcass was afterwards in shreds.

He dropped the bag at his feet and called over to his Number One, "Hey, Joey, whaddaya think they tell the civilians work here 'bout these beefs, way they look after we get through with 'em?"

Joe Peck, who already had a pile of the bags at his feet, said, "Hey, we done 'em a favor—they're halfway to hamburger."

Vigiletti liked that; he laughed above his usual barking sounds as he went to work on another carcass. As he flailed and hacked viciously, bovine blood, bone and sinew flew everywhere. It gave him a good feeling.

"Could we get some lights on in here?" Max asked. He was straining to see photographs of a certain building in a small town, The Dexter City Bank of Commerce, they had placed on the table before him. The residue of dinner still sat around and he used his handcuffed hands to try to wipe a little marinara sauce off the glossy surface.

"You think we got Con-Ed on this pile a birdshit." Doc pushed a candelabra closer. Everyone was there except Lalo.

Diana leaned on Max's shoulder to look. They had not handcuffed her which, he had to admit, bothered him a little; why would they trust her more than him? Unless . . .

So close; he could smell her skin, feel its emanations from a couple of inches out, and all doubts, foolish or otherwise, vanished. The night was, like most at this time of the year, close, warm and humid, alive with insects. Her body seemed immune from all that, clean and fragrant in contrast to the three damp kidnappers in their varying degrees of misery.

She smacked a mosquito on Max's nose, for which he was grateful. Screens were long since rotted or absent. The bugs, real and imagined, were driving Doc up the wall; he kept waving them off and snarling, obviously longing for something he could shoot. Jack would have been bothered but was for the moment immobilized by a wicked cough.

Diana looked at the pictures. "You serious, you guys? It doesn't do much for me." She wrinkled her face, dismissing the whole idea, and wandered away.

"I'm still hungry," Max complained. He rubbed his eyes

and looked around. "I'm not here to run a shipment? I can't believe it."

Tony was contemptuous. "Don't demean us, okay? Any dumb prick, any civilian can smuggle these days. College students, old ladies . . . retards do it. Give us some credit, man. This, what we're doin', takes imagination, it's bigtime. It takes . . . 'belly.' " He obviously hadn't been able to come up with the Italian term, but to make the point he pounded his own just as if he had, delivering a little touch of Palermo.

Doc brought Max what was left of the spaghetti; it had been good an hour ago although now it was cold. He stopped to eat it anyway. Tony had fixed the dinner and was very proud of it. In truth, it wasn't half-bad, steak, peppers and pasta with some of their plentiful supply of beer laid on. They were being indulgent with their captives for the moment.

"Hey, look, these snapshots don't make it; I need like street maps of the town and aerial photographs."

"Would we go through all the shit we did to get you here we hadda pilot already?"

"Okay, but you don't have anything on where I can land."

Diana drifted, examining the badly-used elegance of the house like a potential buyer. She had accepted that things would have to go forward for now, that it was out of their hands.

Doc dragged himself over to the table, so bored and enervated Max could hardly understand him. "There's a big field out in back-a there where they grow somethin' short."

"How do you know I can land on it? You ever walked it?"

"It's the Everglades, man. Flat as a nun's ass for a hunnert miles 'round."

Max looked at Tony as the only one remotely rational. "Flat—and under four feet of water. I got news, I can't land on water without pontoons."

Tony looked at him with exaggerated tolerance and shook his head. "Well somebody's gonna land it, baby. Tomorrow. Now look 'round here and who you think that's gonna be?"

Max clung to the practical considerations because they had a calming effect on him. Losing himself in the job.

"Maybe if I knew more. What the hell's it all about, anyway? Goddamn town's so small it's not even on the Auto Club maps. Middle of the sweating, stinking, alligator and mosquito-infested 'Glades and it's got a bank?" He picked up one of the photos and stared at its modest facade uncomprehendingly. Behind him, Tony laughed, a sound like a flushed toilet.

When Max turned to look up at him, he had his head cocked to one side. "You don't know, do you? Really don't know." His view was always that anyone who wasn't in on the skinny of what went down on his street corner was hopelessly flawed.

"What's he gotta know for?" Doc asked.

"No, no, it's better he does." No one could doubt Tony's motive; he was already preening and pacing like a movie executive about to floor someone with his brilliance.

Diana, opening a beer at the other end of the room, knew him best and told Max, "You get a show with dinner."

"I used to work up in Miami on a crew for the goombata own this little shit-hole bank you're lookin' at. I did everything, broke my ass for 'em and got shit for it. 'Cept time, I did time. An' you think they took care a me inside like they promised? An' my wife I had then, you think they took care a

131

her like they said? Or the kid? Fuck 'em. They got no honor."

"You gonna tell him or you gonna make a speech how you got pissed on by a buncha guinea faggots?" Doc complained. "I wanna get outta here sometime."

"Wha . . . you goin' somewheres? Enjoy yourself? Hey, party, huh?! Watch the crabs eat each other on the beach or the seagulls shittin' all over? That where you're goin'? Fuck you."

"Who exactly did you say owned this bank?" Max asked.

"Who else? The Messinas." Tony bent his legs long enough to pull the heavy pants loose from his crotch.

"The Messinas?" Max said, without a clue.

"Jersey. Bayonne. An' they don't own it, you know, but they own it. There's a lot a these little set-ups aroun'."

"Why?" At this point the point was to keep Tony talking.

Max's ignorance never ceased to amaze him. "Madonn! How'd you get smart enough to fly an airplane? Okay, you allus got a cash problem, right? Too much, right? You're allus lookin' for places to hide it or wash it or do somethin' with it. Okay, I opened the fridge for you—see the light?

"Big corporations, like make cars an' shit, they don't have nothin' like this. They don't need it, give their execs a hunnert million in stock end a the year and nobody says nothin'."

"Are you telling me you're robbing this thing and it's mob-owned?" Max asked, not hiding his alarm.

"Well . . . like 'mob,' we never say that word, you know . . . what the meek call it, but it sounds fuckin' stupid to us, you know, it's . . ."

Max, sounding more and more less like a captive, raised his voice. "I don't give a shit what you call it. Is that what you're going to steal from?"

"Not 'you,' 'us.' "

132

Max groaned; he had understood but for some reason had been driven to hear it.

Tony addressed everybody in the room; it was his Agincourt moment. "Listen, it's the easiest score goin'. One old guard, no cops for miles out there. The nearest's like forest rangers or whatever. Smoky the Bear, right?" He laughed, encouraging the others to join in his contempt. "They got millions in there. I happen to know 'cause I been lookin' at this thing a long time, settin' it up. This ain't rippin' off no neighborhood crap game; it's planned real good.

"But anyways, tomorrow mornin' they're gettin' like a fifty million deposit." He stopped to let that have its proper effect. "And the beautiful thing, they can't even tell nobody it's gone!" He was positively triumphant at the end.

Diana had come back to the community around the table and sat. "They can tell the Messinas of Bayonne," she pointed out matter-of-factly. As if, Max thought, none of this concerned her.

Tony raised a fist and chopped the crook of that arm with his other hand in the Italian salute. "That to them. I know 'em all. Losers."

"And after this," Max pointed out, "they'll know us." He added, with a glance at Diana, "All of us."

Jack had his opinion. "I ain't 'fraida no fuckin' dagos."

Tony gave him that ancient Sicilian killing stare. "Hey, I know one you better be a little worried about. Just take it easy with my people, okay?" His gaze took in Doc as well. "The two a you."

Jack managed to look indifferent while twitching all over. Max found it a strange sight. "I ain't 'fraid of 'em," Jack repeated, showing Tony his vacuumed eyes and gap-toothed grin which indicated, apparently, that he either hadn't heard or he had, but it had not yet percolated up to his worm-ridden brain.

He went back to pulling strenuously on his left earlobe, which already drooped an inch further in the direction of those famine-case shoulders than did his right. *The Grapes of Wrath*, Max thought, that's where I've seen him. The beloved carbine was right there with ol' Jack, lying perilously on the table.

Tony let the question of ethnicity go. Very large fish to fry only a few hours away and four cooks was a minimum for the job. He tried to get back to the planning, but Diana had decided that if Tony was attackable she wanted to be one of the swarm.

Her first mistake was leaning towards him. "I can't believe you." She glanced at Max, questioning. "Is there a college that teaches stupidity?" Max started to shake his head, trying to warn her off, but she ignored him and turned back to her target. "If there is, you must of got a Ph.D., Tony, because robbing these dudes . . ."

He reached over with surprising quickness and determination to slap her hard across the face with his big-knuckled hand. It sent her spinning out of her chair with a rending cry of pain.

But Diana had been struck before and had the appropriate instincts, recognizing instantly what was about to happen, turning away and pulling back from the blow almost in time. Time enough, at least, to mitigate serious damage to her face. Some of the falling and yelping was an act, knowing from experience that when a man chose to hit you it was safer to leave him satisfied. Until such time as you could get behind him with a bat.

Jack whinnied and Doc's face gleamed with pleasure; here was entertainment of a sort they understood. Max let out a snarl of anger and tried to jump up but, with his hands restrained, had trouble getting out from under the heavy oak table. For his effort he further bruised his bruised pelvis and Doc yanked him back down with one hand.

"You got a mouth on you," Tony said quietly, almost as an afterthought to show his low regard.

Diana spent a moment on the floor recovering. She shook her head, felt her face, took some deep breaths; everyone waited, watching her.

"When I'm stickin' thousand dollar bills all over your naked body, bitch, you're gonna have a whole 'nother song to sing."

"It'll be a dead naked body." With two hands on the back of a chair she pulled herself up off the floor, seeming to force herself to stand up straight with her head high.

Now the other side of her face bore a large spreading patch of blue that threatened to engulf it, her lip and cheek were cut, some of her hair stuck in the blood. Her eyes, however, were almost triumphant in the way they shone.

Max had never seen a beautiful woman who could be indifferent to what a battering had done to her appearance. He hoped it wasn't simply masochism, that instead she ruled over an unruly and forbidding anger somewhere deep inside.

"Have it your own way, sweetheart." Tony had made his point and was feeling great about it; he went on with his account to Max as though nothing had happened. "I worked for the Messina guy in Miami, Vigiletti. An' that fuckin' Joe Peck, underboss. So I know 'Hands' real well and he ain't no rocket scientist, I'm tellin' you. Trust me, we'll be okay."

" 'Hands'?"

Tony dismissed it. "I dunno. They say 'Vig' strangled

his school teacher. Maybe he did."

"Tony," Diana said, but in an entirely different tone, one close to pleading, "don't fool with these people. It's way out of your league and you'll get us all killed. Jesus, use your head."

He raised his hand and she flinched involuntarily.

"You want more? I thought I told you to shut the fuck up."

Max implored her again with his eyes, raising his cuffed hands for emphasis. She surrendered by putting her head in her hands. Max suspected she was hiding tears. Doc asked, "We gotta listen to her?"

Tony did his usual imitation of thinking something over, then decided, "You two get out." He indicated the prisoners.

"No, no, wait a minute," Max said, anxious if nothing else to preempt any questions from Diana that could get her punished again. She didn't look as though she could take a lot more. "If I get you to that bank and back, what happens to us?" He made a point of including, with his limited body language, Diana. "When this deal is over, are we through?"

"After work," Tony said, "we come back here, hide the plane, play it cool a few days, maybe, then you take us to Mexico. Guadalajara. That's it."

"You let us go then?"

"Why not?" With his arms spread wide, palms open to the heavens, and a big beneficent smile he might have been a car salesman or Jesus Christ. Suffer the little thugs to come unto me. Unlike Jesus, no one in the room believed him, but he enjoyed his performance anyway.

Max and Diana stood. He wanted to point out: "Guadalajara's a stretch in this little plane."

"Everything's hard with you. You know why? No imagination." Tony pointed to his head, as if people had doubts.

"I read books. About the great generals, you know. Caesar, Alexander the Great. Caesar one a my people. Hannibal, some kinda nigger but he was smart. They weren't like you, they dreamed big, they took chances. Tomorrow, wiseguys all over the fuckin' country are gonna look up at me."

Max headed for the door, murmured, "More like you'll be looking up at them through a parking lot." He made a quick exit, pushing Diana ahead of him despite the handcuffs.

They got out onto the verandah without retribution and moved along the railing. At a point out of sight of the interior they leaned on it side-by-side. She fussed at his wrists, massaging them where the cuffs seemed to abrade, and he worried about the damage to her face, exploring it gently with his fingertips. Neither were aware of what they were really doing, unwilling to admit it.

After being inside, it was disarmingly soft and delicate out here with odors so varied and complex that at least some of them must have drifted on the wind from islands far away. Close around the verandah, a gift of the previous owner, were overgrown gardenia bushes, hibiscus, bougainvillea. Beyond, a three-quarter summer moon made huge moving shadows all around the house where the pines and palms closed in, weaving and ducking in the evening trades.

With his manacled hands Max stretched out over the railing to break off a hibiscus blossom, and handed it to Diana. She bowed her head to suggest he place it in her hair, smiling while her face was masked at the spectacular inappropriateness of it; very much Max. Also the smile women use when they are feeling something and pretending they don't.

Further out, mangrove, cypress and sea grape joined with scrub to form a black wall between them and the sea, although as usual you could hear it pounding to its night-time beat. There were a few insects, not as many as inside, crying for mates, some birds, and the air itself sang.

"Weird," Diana said, a darkness descending upon her abruptly, Max noticed.

"You mean deceptively peaceful?"

"I mean weirdly beautiful." She inhaled and then burst out with, "When you think how the poor bastard owned the place's buried out there somewhere."

He looked at her quizzically.

There was no doubt in her mind. "Delia told me. Lalo cut his throat. Then Doc chopped him up with a hatchet. That's 'cause he's supposed to've wanted to watch the birds eat . . . the remains. Or feed the fish with them, I don't know. Tony at least made them stick him . . . the remains, in a hole and cover him up." She paled and Max reached out to put a steadying hand on hers where it gripped the railing.

Her response was to snap at him, "You don't like hearing it? You're the hard man. Things like that happen, right?"

"I didn't say anything." He might have smiled reassuringly, but it would only have upset her more.

She had worked herself up to where she was close to tears, the look of someone who was terribly ashamed. In bitter, resentful tones she said, "Delia's great defense about knowing all this was she didn't know but threw up when she found out. Isn't that the Nazi excuse or something?"

"Nuremberg Defense."

"Yeah, 'I barfed and felt bad for five whole minutes; then I fucked his brains out because after all he was my husband, and he's really good at it, too'?"

"Sounds like the woman I met."

"God help me, I hate her!"

"Better than confusing her with yourself."

"Don't try to make me feel better. What I meant before, I'm part of what they did."

"I knew what you meant, and you're not. As for the dead guy, he won't feel any less dead if you enjoy this evening. *Carpe Diem.*"

"Huh?" She gave him a taunting, skeptical look right off the schoolyard. "Where'd you say you went to school?"

"I forget."

"You forget where you went to school?"

"I forget what I said. Harvard? One of those places."

He laughed and she joined him in spite of herself. "You're sure you weren't just released with a year's supply of Thorazine?" The laughter ran down and, sobering, she looked long and intently at the sky, as if to swallow its secrets. "I hope they don't kill us. It's crazy, but I'm starting to enjoy things, little things."

He took one of her hands where it rested on the railing with both of his and squeezed it.

She said, trying to brighten, "They're nuts; that's on our side."

"Yeah, but dumb, vicious and deluded."

"Isn't that good?"

"It's the dumb ones kill you. Not that there's any other kind. All this stuff about Moriarity and Dr. No, supercriminals, is bullshit. No point in kidding ourselves."

"Gee, thanks a lot."

The sound of quarreling, loud and obscene, came from within, rising to a crescendo that did manage to boost their hopes for a few minutes. They held their collective breath and waited . . . until eventually it slacked off.

"I was hoping we'd hear gunshots," Diana said, disappointed.

139

"Nothing's ever that easy. Look, I didn't mean to scare you. We got time yet."

"I was already scared, but that's not it. I got a person who's totally innocent—you—into it and . . . I feel terrible."

"Could we stop that? Get over it? In your place I'd do the same thing, a kid like that."

She leaned over and kissed his cheek. "Thanks anyway. I've been fighting the idea, but maybe you really are a nice guy."

Max, who hadn't blushed since his confirmation, when he lied about a potential jail sentence hanging over his young head, was actually flustered. He raised his cuffed hands and put them down, muttering, "Shouldn't take advantage of a helpless man." It was lame but that innocent peck on the cheek had rattled his brain.

"Why do you think they're letting us wander around?" she asked.

"Where we gonna go?"

"Lalo's not back. Only three of them now." She made a humming sound, then, "Any chance you could get the plane up?"

"I doubt it. But we could try." He indicated the wounds on her face. "You okay?"

She brushed it off, already moving to the steps of the verandah, motioning for him to follow. The moonlight helped them to find their way but made it difficult to stay in shadow. For some reason the handcuffs made Max feel heavy-footed, along with his ribs. At one point he had to ask her to slow down.

Still, they went rather quickly down the path to a clump of trees beside the makeshift runway where it was prudent to kneel and listen. The noisy rattle of dry palm leaves and pines forced together by the wind above their heads made it difficult, but there was nothing of an ominous nature.

"If we could get it straightened around, can you fly with those on?" Diana whispered, touching the handcuffs.

"You help me with the controls." He moved out towards the plane, alternately hunching and frog-marching over open ground. Fortunately the sand topped with seagrass was relatively quiet underfoot. Diana, more lithe, was able to simply scurry with her head down and still keep a lower profile.

Neither spoke when they got to the plane. Max reached up carefully to try the door. It was locked. He shrugged at Diana who mouthed, "stuck?" Sliding his hand up the side of the door again, he tried to finesse, then force it.

Suddenly there was a rumble like an incipient earthquake, a moment of total confusion, and Lalo loomed in the window like that of a bear in spring taking a tentative peek out of its cave, sleepy and hostile. With the same eerie slow-motion he brought up a pistol and placed it against the glass opposite Max's nose.

They didn't need any more signals, but began slowly to back away without comment . . . exactly the way you would from a bear. The gnarly, thick-lipped, dead-eyed moon of a face slowly set beneath the horizon of the window's edge.

When they got back to the trees Max stopped them, looking around with some desperation for an alternative. If Lalo was back, the boat must be back. Diana remembered the direction they had taken when they left.

They rode their hope hard all the way to a little dock at the other end of the island and on out to the end of it, running in case Lalo decided to wake up and sound an alarm. If they were caught they expected to be punished and Max dreaded any more violence inflicted on Diana. They found a small fishing boat at the end, sure enough, or rather they could see it—but it was under water.

She sagged against him and he put his linked hands on her shoulder. "We could hide somewhere maybe," she suggested without conviction.

"Nowhere to go. Might as well wait here."

He sat down on the edge of the dock, feet dangling, and urged her to join him. It smelled of tar, old wood, sea life or death and brine. The wind off the Gulf Current was full and fresh in their faces but the water itself was quiet, lapping, in this tiny inlet. A fish jumped close to them.

"Not so bad," Max said, closing his eyes, accepting the moment and the inevitable. He inhaled deeply.

She ran her fingers over the rough wood planking and smelled them, seeming to like it. "Okay . . . we're marooned on a raft in the middle of the ocean. Just the two of us. No future, no past, no hope except that for at least a little while nobody can harm us."

"What was your childhood like?"

"I don't want to talk about it. But yours couldn't have been too bad. Born rich, at least I think you were, and you had to be smart and an adorable little guy and everybody loved you until you started getting into trouble, and then they forgave you everything when you did . . . up to a point, and . . ."

"You're dreaming."

"Who knows about you? Not even you."

The fact that he laughed reassured her; in her life there had been so few men who could laugh at themselves, and in a primitive way she had always thought it was the starting point of a decent human being.

She said, "People are such bastards."

"Including you and me. And we're not so bad." He grinned, "I think maybe I just defined original sin."

"You don't know me. The mistakes I've made, wow.

You're probably the good guy I always thought I was looking for. Bad timing." She twisted to look at him with such fondness and then touched his face as if to see if it was real, if he was real. Yet it seemed to come from a vein of deep melancholy.

It was strange, Max thought, how beautiful women were always in some way unhappy; he had never figured that one out. Perhaps life could never fulfill its promise.

Usually he didn't care, but in that moment he found he did. Gently pressing his head against the hand that was caressing his cheek, he was unprepared for the white squall of emotion it unleashed in him. Like an injection of something blazing hot or ice cold directly into a vein and feeling it run all through the body unchecked, and nothing could call it back.

As much to control these feelings as anything else, he raised his locked hands over her head and brought them down, encircling. She must have felt his tremor because she reached up to each of his forearms to help guide them around her, but said nothing. Women were like that, knowing and gracious.

He brushed her lips with his, then passed on. She did the same to him, and both smiled for their own reasons. When they truly kissed, it was with a restraint born of the situation. How long that would have lasted was left unanswered by someone close behind them . . .

"Hey, that dude conquered Mexico? You know, Spanish dude?"

Max was embarrassed to have to struggle free; this time Diana helped raise his arms so that they didn't catch in her hair. She was not embarrassed.

"Cortes, Hernando," Max told him, putting a face on the awkwardness.

"Right, Hernando. This Hernando sunk all his ships so nobody in his troops could rabbit, you know. Smart. Gutsy. That's what I did." He nodded in appreciation of his own wisdom.

Helping Max to a standing position, Diana asked him, "Do they make history comics?"

Tony snapped, "Okay, get your asses back up to the house." He stepped aside to let them go by and watched as they started up the path before following.

Max waited for blows that didn't come. Tony seemed puzzled by what he had found. "You two got real cozy pretty quick. What's goin' on here?"

No one had an answer, no one tried to provide one. Max thought it was just as well.

XI

Casey had arrived over Andros earlier that evening, before dark. The "tower" didn't respond to his request to land, either. So he landed.

When he got out of the Beechcraft, he surveyed the other planes parked around the field with a practiced eye. It always paid to know who was in town. A Lear Jet was the only one that gave him pause. Expensive, fast, yet nothing here on Andros to draw the chic. Well, if he was lucky he wouldn't be here long enough to worry about it.

He found the cousin, Cecil, in the canteen-lounge, watching a replay of a cricket game on television. Billy had gone into town for dinner, he said, and he wasn't allowed to operate the radio since he had a tendency to break it. Casey inquired about Max and the girl; the cousin gave it all up without even a hint of a bribe, which thrilled Casey.

Unfortunately Cecil didn't know what had happened to them after he dropped them off in front of the cafe. They couldn't have stayed there long, though, because he had ridden past the place an hour-and-a-half later without noticing them and you wouldn't not notice a woman who looked like that. Not to mention a great guy like Max who was always a presence. And also very good-looking.

Casey heard his molars grinding. "I didn't come all the way over to this godforsaken pile of guano to hear how the smiling sonofabitch stole my airplane's the Lord Of The World. Just tell me where he's gone with that bimbo."

Cecil didn't quite catch all of that: to him Casey had a

145

funny accent. He was a little hurt by the tone, however. Suddenly he remembered to remind Casey that information was supposed to bring money into the family.

Irritated at having his good fortune reversed, Casey nevertheless came up with a twenty and Cecil recalled something else, that Billy had related how an augmented party had left in the same plane about ninety minutes after their arrival. Maybe he should go look for Billy in town and ask him for the details. Casey said that wasn't a helluva lot of information, took back the twenty and gave him a ten instead.

Cecil asked could he get the other ten back by taking him into town on his motorcycle? But Casey didn't like the idea of putting his arms around a man, especially Cecil.

He found a taxi driver at home, willing to leave his dinner and the game.

The cafe where Max and his Lorelei had been deposited was a logical first stop. A polite people, the serving staff called the night manager who was also the day manager and lived above the restaurant; he agreed to give up the game and come down.

The couple in question were remembered because there were few tourists at this time of the year. Also, they "were a very handsome couple." But not happy. Their waiter told him that the man seemed agitated, or irritated with the woman perhaps. He understood that, because he himself was often irritated by them; an infuriating race, women. Casey was not one to contradict him. Of course, the manager said, when they looked like that it was hard to feel anything but admir—

Casey brought him back on topic with something just short of a growl. It seemed that after awhile another man, a strange little fellow with an unpleasant look to him, had come in and they had gone away with him. They did not appear as though

146

they belonged together. This smaller man was very uncouth.

With a little urging Casey got him to admit that there had been some sort of a "fuss" that caused customers to leave, making him very displeased at the time. But not much of a scene, really.

"Not much of a scene," but it had emptied the restaurant. Casey understood that what Bahamians called a little "fuss" might have been a dozen gangsters shooting it out with submachine guns and rocket launchers. He pressed for more detail on the "little man" but all he got was an impression that the whole thing had been "not quite regular." Sorry, but cricket beckoned.

Casey knew better than to ask about smugglers. He was beginning to develop a tingling in his stomach that was something more than fear for his material interests.

As far as Billy went: everyone had seen him; no one knew where he was. Maybe at Miss Irma's, a most respectable whorehouse, but on the other hand he might have visited his mother. Casey walked the darkening streets for a couple of hours. He touched his pistol often as a talisman; it felt very solid and reassuring there inside the nylon flying jacket.

Eventually he gave up and got a room in a cheap little motel on the water's edge, some walk out of town but worth it for the coolness and quiet. It had a small open-air bar attached where you could hear the surf; he went in there to get a beer nightcap.

This bartender knew Billy, too; nothing unusual about that in a small town, except of course that he was talking about someone who was putatively the local "air controller." Hadn't seen him since dinner at Mama Lea's downtown.

Thinking about it, though, he did recall that Billy had appeared to be concerned about someone he apparently liked who might have been kidnapped. That happened all the time, the bartender said, but it seemed to have bothered Billy, and most of all because no one wanted to do anything about it. So he had decided to get drunk instead.

"Anyway, this is the story he tell to me, but he like that bad black rum, so I don't pay no attention to Billy when he is drinking."

Casey thanked him and actually left a tip, breaking a life-time policy with bartenders. It was an index of his concern.

He had always felt that pilots had a certain panache apparent to everybody, that he stood out in any public place, so he had to worry because smugglers were always after planes and pilots. Leaving abruptly, because of some dubious types entering the cafe, he went to his room, barricaded the door and put the .45 on the bedside table with a round in the chamber.

After which, he lay awake half the night and agonized over Mary Beth. Wondered what she was doing, who she was screwing in what position and how much was she enjoying it? And the kids, what would happen to them, especially with a mother like that for a role model?

He had always been faithful, so at least if he started going to church again he wouldn't have to worry about the sermon. Damn preachers were always coming up with something. By two o'clock he thought it might not be so bad if smugglers came and killed him.

Max and Diana spent a less comfortable but more interesting night stretched out on a large upstairs bed in their clothes, except for shoes. As a result of their attempt to escape, both were sentenced to be placed on their backs with hands cuffed above their heads, the chains hooked around adjacent posts on the headboard.

For a long time after the door closed they lay in silence, in a stupor of fatigue in Max's case, watching the shadows of palms weave bizarre patterns on a hurricane damaged high white ceiling. Not much choice; it was the only show in town considering that to look in any other direction required painful effort.

"God, what an irony, huh?"

"What?" Max asked, for once not much interested in ironies.

"It's such a beautiful, romantic place. Like a movie."

"We did that." His voice trailed away, drifting into, if not sleep, a doze.

"I'm serious. If we weren't tied up and prisoners and worrying that they were going to kill us."

Max opened his eyes for a moment, considered that, closed them again. He felt, "We are," was sufficient comment.

"Are you really going to try to sleep? You don't want to talk?"

"Diana, I got some tricky flying tomorrow. To be frank, it's probably beyond my skill level, but we don't have any other option right now. So I need sleep."

She seemed to accept that for awhile, shrugging and singing something under her breath. Max tried not to hear her, pressed his eyelids down hard enough to cause pain and called it relaxing.

Another long pause and: "I'm really scared."

He tried grunting, then felt he ought to add, "That's natural."

"When you're in a spot like this you kind of long for human contact."

"I thought I was one," he mumbled.

She twisted onto her side to look at him through one and a half eyes. "No, I mean like close. Like physical contact. Touching."

His eyes popped open this time. "What?"

"Max, kiss me." She strained to get her face closer.

"What?"

"Quit saying that. C'mon and kiss me, Max. Please. It could be my last, for God's sake."

"That's a little melodramatic. We'll be okay."

"You mean you don't want to?"

"Of course I want to. I wanted to ever since the time I saw you in that cab watching me and I couldn't even see your lips then, not really, but when you walked into . . . Yes, I want to! Kiss you."

She strained to get closer. "Well, it might just take a little more effort on your part."

"You don't think this situation is a little crazy for this? Besides, I ache all over."

"I'll lick your wounds like a mother lion, and make them well."

"A mother lion, yeah . . . I just don't know if I can, I—"

"Try, dammit. Use your ingenuity."

He wiggled and stretched. Their mouths came closer . . . closer . . . some acrobatics were in order, and there was some pain, but then miraculously their lips were touching. With a little more strain his mouth was covering hers. The effort made them both tremble, quivering against the other's permeable flesh, resonating through every cell in their twisted bodies.

He sighed, she moaned. Needing every bit of reach, the two tongues were pushed out to answer the call and touched, bulled against each other for precedence, circled for an advantage that would be an advantage to both no matter who won. Eventually, they simply held like that, moistly locked, neither willing to give it up, preferring death.

Max, in his perverse male frustration, broke it with a snarl, swearing.

She laughed. "Hard to do is kind of a turn-on, isn't it?"

Panting, he whispered, "I felt that," trying to be cool.

"I meant to tell you, looking back on it, that was a terrific landing under the circumstances." Pelvises tantalizingly only inches apart, she began to run her knee up his leg, complementing her compliment. "I'm sorry it wasn't appreciated at the time."

"Actually, it wasn't bad. Thanks." He found himself smiling in the dark.

"Max . . . let's do it."

"What? Oh . . . ah!" Her knee had made tumefacient contact.

" 'It,' for God's sake. 'It!' Everybody knows what 'it' is, especially when a woman asks them to do 'it.' Unless—"

He broke in on her, "You trying to drive me nuts? I never wanted anything more, I'd trade heaven for hell, I'd—but Jesus, woman, look where we are! The condition we're in, the future we face!" He raised his voice well beyond what was safe. Fortunately there was more noisy drinking and fighting downstairs. "I don't even know if I'm able!"

She simply smiled, that smug, all-knowing perfectly feline look that makes men desirable children and, with a soft-fur voice to match, reassured him beyond any doubt, "You are, Max. You are."

Moisture showed on his face, his breathing deepened and quickened. When he looked down in the dim light to see if she was telling the truth and found it confirmed, his eyes glazed with yearning.

He murmured, "I am, aren't I. But it's still a problem in geometry . . . clothes . . . How . . . ?"

151

She was already working on it. "I work out and I'm really agile. Also, I have talented feet."

"And beautiful, too," he whispered more or less to himself between gasps, "beautiful . . ."

She already had her socks off and was working energetically on any part of his clothing that presented itself.

He tried pulling her shorts down with his feet but met with less success, as they banged knees and shinbones against each other. "If they come in," he puffed, "We'll have to commit suicide. Okay, my belt, how you gonna get my belt? Oh, Jesus."

"Teeth!" Both were panting so hard now they could hardly speak, some of it simply exertion. "If you could . . . sort of . . . twist your body and throw it across my face . . ." she suggested. More like an order.

"I . . . never . . . worked so . . . hard . . . for 'it' before . . . in my life . . ."

"I'm worth it."

"I've always known that."

"Zipper!" she commanded.

He was losing heart, wearing down in the face of her incredible energy; she was indomitable. Like a great commander she could see that victory lay just across the ridge from total defeat. Clothes were being stripped away painstakingly, raised, pulled down, kicked aside. Some torn.

"I'm sorry . . . I can't be more romantic," he gasped. "About . . . as romantic as . . . a feeding frenzy of sharks."

"Listen," she said, and then took a second to suck in oxygen, "sharks are great lovers. They bite pieces out of the female when they . . . hump."

"I don't think I'm up to that."

Suddenly she said, "Ooh!" and they froze; realizing with a shock that they had been so involved with the mechanics and sheer drive of the struggle that they had forgotten the essentials. He had already pushed something formidable between, not deeply into but between, the top of her thighs.

"Ooh," she repeated. They held like that without moving, exploring in their minds the possibilities, not wanting to give up the hard-won anticipation. Again they stared into mutually lustrous eyes for the answer, this time as to what happened next?

"Okay," she whispered in that docent manner, "we're going to play pirate. You bring your ship up alongside mine and board me."

"I already have," he whispered back, weak from the effect.

"Oh, yeah." She gave it a confirming squeeze using only the available although obviously highly skilled muscles, causing him to moan. "That's right. Good, good . . . Ooooh . . . Now!"

"I'll never make it. I can't get close enough." He sounded as though he might be in real agony, and a lot she cared.

"Shhhhhsssshh. Don't be greedy. You've already seized my ship. How much of a prize do you need? Maybe you won't get all the way into the hold . . . but I'm going to show you how to have a hell of an interesting time on deck." While he was contemplating that, she added, "Show you what women know."

He liked the sound of that.

She began very gently to thrust against him, easing him back and forth to further suck him in, and he, a fast learner in these matters, picked up the rhythm instantly. Her voice grew even softer. "Remember, any port in a storm, 'hard to do is a turn-on' . . . and . . ."

"Aw, yeah . . . shit . . ."

"Oh, God, yes . . ."

"I'm in love . . ." he said.

"Me, too . . ."

He began to groan so loudly that she had to knee him.

Casey was, as usual, up early, but this was not a good time to go looking for a man who was obviously on a debauch. By noon Billy had still failed to return, and Cousin Cecil was beside himself. His greatest concern was to keep this fact from the civil authorities. Personally, he had nothing more to tell Casey, no matter how much he offered.

Moon was loath to start flying all over the Caribbean looking for his airplane without a little more direction. In fact, the longer Billy stayed away the more suspicious the whole affair became.

Meantime, various aircraft took off and landed blithely, as if nothing had happened. And maybe it hadn't.

Casey went back through Nicolls Town, all the bars, all the whorehouses, all the relatives he could find, and even down to Staniard Creek, the island's only other habitation of any size. Nothing . . . no one had seen Max, Billy, or the girl. Well, maybe they had seen Billy, but they weren't admitting it.

Bulling your way through didn't work here; it called for finesse. Not his strength. If only Max were here to help find Max.

A different awakening awaited Diana and Max, lying exhausted on the soaked sheets, still with beads of moisture dotting their bodies. They had managed to reestablish a little of the decorum of their dress. Both pairs of pants were loose and low about their hips, her shirt was torn open and the brassiere pulled partially off, exposing one breast.

Fatigue and the spiritual ease that emanates from successful loving had sapped their devotion to norms of survival. That much was quickly made apparent by Tony's surprised, informed gaze upon entering.

It was early for a gangster. The vulcanous red ball that begins most Caribbean mornings and strikes you like a blow if you're out in it, had barely risen against a perfectly innocent, accepting blue sky. The heat was already working up and steam rose from the vegetation outside.

The door being thrust open had jarred both prisoners awake, showing that while they might have been enjoying a certain post-coital bliss in sleep, their subconscious minds never stopped knowing where they were. To have Tony's evil, gonadal grin the first thing seen of a morning was nerve-jangling even to Max.

Really bad way to start a bad day, he told himself. In her helpless state it scared hell out of Diana, and made the bare skin feel as though it had caterpillars on it.

"Che cosa!" Tony shook his hand at the wrist. "I'd take some of that myself if we had the time."

As gruesome as that sounded, he did advance on them with the keys to the cuffs in his hands.

The Dexter City Bank of Commerce usually opened about an hour later than most and even that was flexible, as was the closing hour. None of the half-dozen rustic customers who shuffled in out of the swampy heat on a normal day seemed to mind. All of the bank's real business was conducted when it was closed, anyway. The sign in front was very small.

If Vigiletti hated the heat in Miami at this time of the year, the middle of the Everglades gave him a precursor of what to expect at Dante's Seventh Level. He had felt it would be undignified to take off his sweat-soaked shirt in front of all these WASP banking types even in a dink town like this, and toughed it out. The bank itself had air-conditioning but it was old and diseased and, since neither customer relations or employee working conditions had a high priority with the real owners, nothing was ever done about it.

The clerks were counting stacks of bills inside the vault, the coolest place in the bank, watched carefully by Joe Peck while the bodyguard stood sentinel in the front window, studying the streets, such as they were. There was so little room in the vault Vigiletti had to stand in the entrance with the bank manager, a small, innocuous bald man in a stained tan suit and light brown tie with little animals on it. Someone had told him that bank managers dressed up all the time even in the Congo, which this resembled.

Chewing at some loose skin on the side of a fingernail, he found the nerve to bring up something that had been bothering the staff. "Jimmy says a lot of the bills seem to have something on them that's . . . oh, dark and sticky? As if it could be blood," he added timidly. "Of course it isn't."

"Don't worry about it."

The manager swallowed but tried not to let it show. "Ralph, who's doing the counting in there, estimates it's almost fifty million dollars."

On this issue he made it a point to be very specific and always added the qualifying "million" or whatever was called for, whereas these people would toss around an endless number of horrendous numerical expressions like "fifty big ones," "bones," "K's," "yards," "bills," "bananas," with only the Good Lord knew what precise meaning.

He was a man who understood that the penalty for a mere momentary monetary misunderstanding could be draconian. Let them play their games and speak their abominable patois; he would be exact.

"Whichever these mooks is 'Ralph,' you tell him just make sure he don't mention that sittin' 'round the barber shop."

"Oh, no, Mr. Vigiletti. Everybody here understands." He had practiced a banker's sincerity. "We've had the same personnel for years, thanks to your people's extreme generosity. You don't have to worry."

"I don't worry."

The manager used an embroidered handkerchief to dab at his face and neck with the enthusiasm of an ante-bellum belle. "Gosh, it is warm today." He had to think for a minute as to how he might again put forward his concerns effectively. "It's just that it's such a big amount of cash to have on hand at one time." He couldn't seem to stop clearing his throat.

"If it wasn't," Vigiletti growled, "I'd take it to Chase Manhattan."

"Yes, of course."

"Don't sweat it."

"It's just that the only security we have is old Mister Orbie there." He indicated a drooping, poorly shaved, carelessly uniformed security guard minimally in his late sixties, leaning against a wall. His belly pushed out to where it made his shirt look like a sail over a jib. And with all that, his milky eyes gave the impression that he might lack a certain focus.

Vigiletti didn't bother to look. "Nobody fucks with us."

It took about an hour, which caused Tony to pace and curse and threaten, but finally Max got the Cessna straightened around to a takeoff position. In that time he made some small repairs to the aircraft while the rest of the crew, bitching all the way, managed to lengthen the makeshift runway by a few yards. Max had to point out to Doc and Jack what ought to have been obvious, that since they were going to be in the plane when it took off, it might be in their self-interest. With effort, they ultimately saw the logic of that.

By the time the props had been shown to turn the mood too had turned; Tony was exhilarated, striding around grandly, pumping his fist and encouraging the troops like a conqueror setting off for new worlds, and even the other two were checking their weapons and equipment with some alacrity. Lalo came out with his charge, Diana, to watch their departure. He was scowling because he had not been allowed to come along on the raid; Tony said it was his weight.

Diana appeared worn and the effect of the blows she had taken to the face were more pronounced today. While she was not a woman easily made to look bedraggled, too much like a cheetah for that, it still caused Max's heart to ache to see the damage and lowness of spirit.

Tony took the occasion to inform him that if they failed to return, Lalo had instructions to kill her. He said it quite cheerfully, the way a coach might say, "We're all in this together so we have to pull together." Max believed him, believed Lalo would do it with total indifference. He believed in evil; he had seen it.

Eventually they all piled into the plane, the hoodlums scrambling like eager kids now that they were getting closer to a hitherto inconceivable fifty million dollars, and settled in. Tony sat in front beside Max, who was still revving. Doc warned that the takeoff better not bear any resemblance to the landing while Jack spat quite a load out the door because he thought he might not be able to for awhile.

When they began to taxi Tony waved his MAC-11 out of

the window like a baton, leading them on to victory. Even the two in back grinned, something Diana had not seen except when Tony hit her, and hoped not to see again.

As the plane pulled away, she tried to look past the others to pick out Max, calling his name and waving frantically. Unfortunately her view of him was limited to the sight of two hands raised high above the pilot's seat in a "thumbs up" salute. She knew he wanted to ease her anxiety but all she could think of was, Oh, God, now he's doing "wheelies, no hands" during a dangerous takeoff. There was such a thing as too much reassurance.

Still, after only a couple of wobbles, a lurch and a bounce, the aircraft left the ground and climbed rapidly. As it gained the upper air, things smoothed out and it took on some of the natural grace of flight. Lalo left Diana there and slumped back up the path to the house, chewing his cud and thinking of beer.

Alone, she gave into her emotions and sat down heavily on the ground, yet managed to keep the plane in sight all the way out until finally it disappeared into the sea mist that marked the horizon. It had seemed so tiny, vulnerable, helpless and then it was swallowed in a gulp by the vastness of the sky. She stayed on and stared at the place where it had vanished.

Casey's normal temperament, along with that raised and inflamed by the nips, scratches and pinches the Furies were seemingly taking out of him on a daily basis since that stupid horse defenestrated, was not suited to waiting around for Billy to reappear. Especially was that true since Cecil had finally admitted his cousin was convinced he was witness to a dope kidnapping and terrified that they would probably come after him to prevent his testimony. He wasn't just drunk; he had gone to ground.

As for finding Billy himself, Casey had done everything except dig up the island in search of his burrow. It was the usual conspiracy of silence, but the usual bribes had no effect. He was hardly in a mood to wait much longer. Frustrated, he called his office to badger Earl; there was entertainment in that.

Bad news right off; the new client had come in and demanded immediate action. "I told him you'd be right back. An' that old lie 'bout you doin' sumpin' for the CIA? He only laughed. When are you comin' back, boss?"

Naturally the question irritated Casey, "How the hell do I know? What did you do with him? You entertainin' him?"

"I sent him to see Mary Beth to get entertained."

The outraged groan that followed would not have required a telephone to reach Key West. "You dumb shithead, why did you do a stupid, goddamn idiotic thing like that for?"

"You told me to."

Casey started to yell again, but as much as he wanted to blame Earl, to scream at him, curse him and all his ancestors and progeny, and call them by the names of unnatural things, memory brought him up short. "I did?"

"Yessir. Was that wrong?"

"No . . . no, it'll probably be good for business." In a voice that was a continuing diminuendo, he said, "And I can always shoot her afterwards."

"What's that?"

"Nothin'. Do you have to know everythin' I'm thinkin'? Listen, keep that client there if you have to put a gun in his ribs."

"Oh, I couldn't do that, boss. Anyway, you got all the guns."

"I don't care how you keep him in town—just keep him, or you're fired! I'll get back as soon as I can." He hung up before Earl could ask any more questions.

Now he felt he had no alternative to taking the plane up. He certainly wasn't enamored of the idea of flying all over Andros and its environs without a single clue as to where to look, unless of course he believed everything that evil female had told them back in the restaurant in Key West.

To talk himself into it, he posed it another way: what was the alternative? Some rotten smuggler could at that very moment be loading up his beautiful Cessna for a trip of no return. And Max might never return. He tried to convince himself that the latter was a lesser matter, served him right.

He took a cab out to the airport. Cecil, watching a body builder's contest on the TV, was too busy to attend to the refueling. A helpful Casey said not to worry one bit about that, he would be happy to do it himself. This enabled him to top off the tank and then report that he had required only a couple of gallons. Opportunities like this didn't come along every day.

Along with landings, navigation was another area in which Max knew that he could use some improvement. In this case, however, the weather had held and the Everglades was one of the more readable landscapes in the world, flat as a chessboard and even divided into the appearance of one with the dead straight highways that bisected it, often at right angles. Plus there were few areas in it with vegetation over eight feet high. Max had been over it before, flying with Casey into Tamiami Airport to meet clients.

His biggest worry was to avoid being taken out for a smuggler. The fact that it was midday would help. The plan in his head entailed flying due west towards the coast at very low altitude to avoid radar, then climb rapidly to enter Florida airspace north of Key Largo where it was relatively less populated, and slant just south of Homestead Air Force Base for the very good reason that no smuggler in his right mind would do that. Also, he would be masked by a sky full of traffic.

From there the flight was easy. Turning north to go straight up through the void of the 'Glades itself, across the Seminole Reservation, follow State 883 northwest to the Devil's Garden and there between the Slough and the Lake was Dexter. After that he would have to improvise a landing, but he wasn't as worried about that any more; the challenge was beginning to sound exciting. He had been winging it his whole life, why stop now?

The "town" wasn't hard to spot, a raisin floated on a gallon of cream. Max went down low, less than a thousand feet, and circled it for his reconnaissance. He noted a black Cadillac and a van pulling away from the bank and heading out of town, but no one else seemed to.

Tony complained about the low altitude, worried that it was a tip-off.

"I gotta find someplace to land, don't I?" Discovery was hardly a problem; he could make out two people on the street and neither looked up.

A score of buildings, one well-paved road drawn through town with a ruler east and west. The general level of ambition in architecture was such that the Bank of Commerce, a modest wooden building, represented the Dexter equivalent of the Taj Mahal. If the town had a center, that was it.

"See all that flat ground all around there," Doc pointed out, as if you couldn't see it when that was all there was. He was struggling in the jolting plane to lay out a line of coke on his dark glasses, snorting through a little silver straw he kept in the vest pocket of his shirt.

Not a good sign, Max thought, that he had to work himself up, because what his sort usually worked themselves up to had no limits. They had enormous faith in the idea of going completely crazy to get through certain things.

Tony pointed out, "Bank's the building in the middle there. Got it?"

"I got it, but there's nowhere to land down there." The bank and most buildings were white, the road through town was white, but everything else as far as the horizon was gray-green sawgrass, scrub and water.

"You gotta," Tony said, a statement of fact.

Doc tried to see through the glasses but they were covered with fine powdery residue. He made an attempt to sniff it off, then lick it off, but finally gave up and used a handkerchief.

"I know, I know, the water," Tony went on, "so we get our feet wet. We're gonna have Guccis up our ass when this's over."

Max circled again; the only thing he knew for certain was that he wasn't landing out there on the flat nothing where nothing could be seen until it killed you.

Jack had spat on the floor a couple of times on the flight over and Tony objected, so now, fooled by an unsophisticated judgment of the difference between their apparent and real speed, he stepped to the door, raised the upper half and tried to get one off into all that wind. It never traveled more than an inch from his face before returning.

Furious, he joined the debate: "Ah'm gittin' sick a all this flyin' 'round, boy." He came back to lean forward over Max's shoulder, assailing him with the effluvium of rotting insides. "You jist put this goddamn airplane down somewheres so's we can do our shit an' git it over. Ah ain't missin' out on no fuckin' score like this 'un, ah tell you that now."

"I hear you, reb. Doesn't make it any easier."

"Make it any easier if ah cut off your pecker and feed it to you on a biscuit? 'Cause that's what ah'm gonna do."

"Yeah, yeah," Max muttered dismissively. There was only so much craziness he could abide. But, since they were determined to land, he suddenly had an idea of how it might be done. No discussion, no votes, his way. He thought of Sparky Anderson, long-time Tiger manager, "My way or the highway," and laughed.

His laugh naturally raised suspicions in the paranoiac passengers, but he had flying to do and no time to care. It took less than a minute to get the plane around from where he was to three o'clock and start his descent.

"Whaddaya doin' now?" Tony demanded, with just a tiny pinprick of concern in his voice.

Max didn't answer. This was the part he had grown to love. He put the aircraft into a steep dive, straight down the road.

XII

Diana, utilizing her sister's left-behinds, was sitting on the verandah sewing up her blouse, torn in their frenzy to restore each other to a state of nature during the long night. She had her bare feet up on a chair receiving the breeze while sipping a beer. Usually she would think of her weight, but had a pretty good idea that for now fear was doing the job.

She wasn't sure where Lalo was and didn't care, so long as he wasn't near. It was a scary crew to begin with, but even worse was being left alone here with the largest, quietest and least predictable of them. True, he was phlegmatic, but so were crocodiles until they wanted to eat you.

Tony had told him to keep off her until they got back, but Lalo had the aspect of someone who obeyed orders only until such time as it suited him to ignore them flagrantly. She didn't like the way he grinned at her, as if he knew something unpleasant; those gave her the worst moments.

The shirt was finished. What to do now, except worry about Max? She had brought a book on the trip but left it on the plane; it was still there, somewhere over the Everglades right now. Maybe a swim later on . . . although it might not be a very good idea to strip the way things were.

She was even afraid to explore the island, feeling instinctively that order and structure were tied to the civilization represented by the beat-up old house, and if she got too far away from it Lalo might start thinking like Tarzan.

The day was warm, the sounds of the waves and moving palms, a cooling trade gliding along her cheeks and bare legs

. . . Diana sighed and closed her eyes, telling herself that under no circumstances would she allow herself to actually sleep. The sand fleas would hopefully take care of that. She swatted one on her forehead.

Perhaps she dozed. It was a distant, or it seemed distant, buzzing that came into her head and shook her out of it. For a moment she wondered if there were bees on these islands. She forced her eyes open.

They went automatically up to the sky, and there was a plane. Tiny, a good ways off still, but coming directly towards them and reducing altitude. Definitely not a fly-by and they had very few of those, anyway; the island had been well chosen. She stared, praying for only the brief moment of ignorance allotted that it might be the Cessna, then realized that it was coming from the wrong direction.

She stood and moved out onto the steps, shielding her eyes with her hand. Without knowing anything about planes, Diana thought it did look American, did have the appearance of a private, recreational sort of aircraft. Yet it was looking them over, surely. Customs? DEA? Maybe smugglers . . . It was a tossup whether to cheer or cry.

There was no aircraft here for the interloper to see but the "runway," even though Lalo had gone out and thrown palm branches over it, might still be discernible from the air. Criminals, in her experience, did not do a good job of work. She felt hope spurting and tried to batten it down. Max had warned her, nothing easy; they were on their own. Max was the hope.

She decided to risk it, though, looked around, failed to see the big Cuban coming from anywhere and began to wave. Almost immediately a massive forearm went round her face, blocking her mouth as if there was a danger of her alerting the plane with screams. She tried to bite it but couldn't get her mouth open wide enough. Besides, his other hand put the buck knife against her throat, pressing almost hard enough to bring blood with the terror and causing the only sound she could make, a low blunted moan.

He had evidently come from inside the house, through a door directly behind her. Come swiftly, too, for a slug, and now just as quickly dragged her back up the steps, her feet flailing in the air. When they were hidden beneath the roof he relaxed his grip enough for her to breathe adequately. She recognized that it would be foolish to struggle, so both pairs of eyes merely followed the plane.

It circled lazily at about a thousand feet and flew off. Headed back in the direction of Andros. She felt the hand that held her slide down to cup a breast, squeezing it hard. Apart from the pain the revulsion was overwhelming; she felt her legs giving out and her stomach rebel. But her struggles meant nothing; she might have been held under a pile of concrete. All she had were words.

"You rape me, you pig, and I'll kill myself. I swear to God I will. And Tony wants me. You can see it. If he comes back and I'm dead you'll never spend that money. He'll kill you. One less to share with?"

He relaxed his hold a little at a time until the grip was loose enough for her to pull herself away violently, the only gesture she could make at that point.

Lalo, to save face, shifted his gaze to the horizon and the disappearing plane, as if he might be genuinely concerned about its appearance here. After awhile his expression slipped back into its natural placidity, without malice, menace or human content apparent anywhere. Diana moved to put some distance between them.

"Who was it?" She was smart enough to grasp that she ought to reestablish an atmosphere of normality for safety's sake; questions tended to disarm.

Lalo made an indeterminate noise deep down in his throat.

"Okay, what kind of a plane was it?" She wasn't even sure why she asked that. What she had meant was, military, spy plane, smugglers, coast guard, private . . . ?

"Beechcraft," he said in his rumbling voice, and went back into the house.

Still so frightened and angry she was shaking, Diana yelled at his disappearing figure, "Why don't you take a bath now and then? It might help." She felt its ridiculousness the moment she said it.

"You crazy bastard whaddaya doin'???!" Doc screeched.

Max was concentrating. Anyway, that sort of thing from this bunch was becoming a mantra, and mantras were boring. Directly below, the road stretched out smooth and straight and empty all the way to the horizon, the best landing strip he had seen . . . ever. His heart pumped so wildly with excitement a doctor would have rushed him into intensive care, but it was joy—he was going to do it!

"You can't land there!" Doc yelled again.

The wheels touched the pavement and did not require several bounces in order to embrace it. Before anyone else really understood what he was doing, Max was taxiing down the highway towards Dexter.

For the moment Tony was frozen in place, speechless. He was supposed to be the boss with the brains and imagination, but this was too original an idea, too bizarre to absorb in a few seconds.

"Git us up offa here!" Jack said, panic elevating that toneless voice to promise a pit full of vipers.

The icy muzzle of the carbine was jammed hard against

the back of Max's skull, pushing his head forward, but he didn't care. He was getting used to that also. Anyway, it was too late to do anything else. He knew that even if they didn't, so threats and insults were nothing. Reaching back over his shoulder, he pushed the gun away. Max Muldoon was goin' downtown!

Suddenly Tony erupted, "No, no, wait a minute. This is terrific! I love it! Go on! Go on!"

Max was so tense and concentrated that this grotesque little bit of encouragement toppled his reason to where he became ecstatic about his own daring and punched the air, shouting, "Yeah!"

While there was no traffic on the highway, people in the town were coming out of buildings to gawk as the plane rolled in. One exception, the driver of an ancient pickup truck, spotting it coming towards him, swerved over onto the sidewalk, stopped by hitting a pole since he had no brakes, and leaped out to run inside a hardware store and hide. He would always claim it was aliens.

Right into the center of the town, directly in front of the bank, Max throttled down to idle and brought the plane to a stop. At the last minute Doc, fueled by coke and craving action, made a loud stink about his previously agreed-upon role of guarding the aircraft. It led to a screaming match with Tony while the bank waited a few yards away.

Max, disgusted, pointed out to them that he had a stake in this too, and any idiot could come along and put a car across that highway and then none of them would escape. The situation was tenuous and perilous, and they had better damn well get on with it.

Jack was already out of the plane; nothing the others did or said or felt ever seemed to affect him. He had, like his leader, slipped his weapon into an athletic bag, which struck Max as ludicrously yuppie for his skinny, gnarled, tattooed hands with their blackened nails. Not that anyone was looking closely.

Tony finally got out, carrying the MAC-11 in his bag with three extra clips in case he wanted to shoot up all of South Florida. They started towards the bank but then he stopped and came back to remind Max: "Keep the motor runnin'."

Muldoon found waiting as hard on his own nerves as it was on Doc's, if for different reasons. He kept the props turning slowly and had to maintain a sharp lookout lest some absent-minded citizen be turned into instant hamburger. A black man on a mule stopped close by and just stared at them. Two kids rode up on bikes and started circling. He tried shooing them away.

"Leave it alone," Doc hissed in his ear.

"These people could get hurt."

A tractor chugged by with a little boy riding on the back behind his father. He waved at Max, who returned it with a cheerfulness he didn't feel.

"Fuck 'em," Doc said. He had his large pistol down out of sight but pointed at Max through the seat.

A toothless old man in bib-tops shouted good-naturedly at them from the crowd, "Git a mule," and everybody laughed. Max waved at him too and joined in the laughter.

"I oughta shoot the old fucker," Doc said, bored.

"Take it easy. They're just small-town people; they're not hurting anything."

"What are you, some great humanitarian or somethin'? Keep your eyes on that road where we gotta take off."

Inside the bank, things were far less tranquil. Two customers, two clerks and the elderly guard lay on the floor;

three other clerks hurried about collecting the cash and loading it into bags on a dolly.

"I never know'd it'd be so goddamn big, that much," Jack said. "How we gonna—" He thought he saw movement in the corner of his eye, spun around with the carbine, set now on automatic, leveled, but couldn't find the source. He was tempted to kill someone just to set an example, but it wasn't his show. He decided it must have been Tony who moved.

The man in charge was even more hyper, pacing rapidly on the balls of his pointed Italian loafers as though about to *jete*, brandishing the gun in all directions to intimidate people who were already intimidated. "Hurry up! Hurry the fuck up!" He took an ineffectual kick at one of the clerks hurrying by.

The manager stood in the entrance to his office, hands lazily in the air, looking surprisingly unconcerned. He glanced to one side and just happened to see one of the clerks push the silent alarm in passing, but that didn't concern him, either. Unless a state police car was in the area, any sort of help was fifteen to twenty minutes away. There would be no shootout here unless, of course, the robbers were even more incompetent than they appeared. He did wish they would calm down.

"C'mon, c'mon!" Tony yelled to no one in particular. "Blow your goddamn cracker heads off . . ."

The clerks were running by now and the dolly was filled to overflowing; in fact, bundles of cash kept falling out of the sacks and were frantically scooped up again with trembling hands, because Tony damn well wasn't leaving anything. He ordered them to wheel it out and load the plane, holding the door open.

"And fast. Move it!" He kicked the only female clerk to

show he was serious. She began to cry but never slackened.

While they were distracted the guard, still stretched out on the floor, decided to be an earnest citizen and do his job. He had surreptitiously worked one hand down to his holster before recollecting that they had forced him to kick the gun away earlier.

Never mind, he had a "backup gun" for the occasion, a little .25 caliber stuck down in his belt at the small of his back. It was an idea he had derived from the movies over at Clewiston on the lake, where every noble gun-toting hero carried a backup weapon.

By now it seemed to him that time was running out and he had better hurry if he was going to do the right thing. He reached around behind him for the "backup" in one comparatively swift movement.

This too registered in the corner of one of Jack's jumping, bloodshot eyes. He spun and got off five rounds without even looking—that blur behind him could have been a rattler or cottonmouth on the ground. It was a fat old man on the floor and there was no missing from fifteen feet, three went home. One smashed through the top of his skull, a second created a fountain of blood from an artery in the back and the third clipped his side. He was brain-dead instantly and except for some gasping slid into true death without a sound. Everyone but Jack, who merely grunted, started screaming.

Tony was the most panicked of all, bellowing curses and threats and firing the entire clip from his MAC-11 into the ceiling. "Nobody move! Fuckin' assholes! I'll kill allayas."

Even Jack ducked to escape the consequences of falling debris and bullets, some of which bombarded the shooter himself, dusting him in white and edging him a little further towards madness. Luckily the ceiling was wood and plaster;

if it had been marble or any hard stone, no one would have gone unharmed; ricochets would have torn the place apart and wounded or killed everyone in it.

Jack went over and kicked the guard to make certain he wouldn't give any more trouble while Tony jammed another clip into his machine pistol as if the barbarians were coming over the walls. His breath came rapidly as he went on yelling about killing everyone in sight. By now even the manager believed him and was spread out like carpaccio on the floor, trying hard to flatten himself right down to China.

"Y'all stay jist lak that an' no body else gits kilt," Jack said quite reasonably. Like most people under tension he became more of what he was to the point where even his accent had thickened. But now that he had killed someone he was no longer jittery, instead experiencing a kind of post-sexual languor. It was sweet.

"C'mon, c'mon, that's enough. Let's go!" Tony shouted when he could get his breath, causing everyone to hurry for the door.

Appropriately, he led the way. Outside, all that shooting had put the bank clerks under the plane, cringing, and largely emptied the streets. Doc and Max were out, throwing the sacks and bundles into the back. Max stopped between every throw to holler at the few citizens remaining outside, mostly kids.

"Get away! Go home, dammit! It's dangerous!" Tony told him to shut up and work. "What the hell happened in there?" Max wanted to know.

"Jack chopped a citizen. You just drive." He dragged the clerks out from beneath and forced them with hits, kicks, curses, and jamming his gun to their respective heads when needed, to continue. Jack backed out of the bank slowly and remained watching over the scene as shotgun.

"It's too heavy. We gotta leave some of it," Max shouted, panting from the effort.

"No fuckin' way, man," Tony said, laughing at the absurdity of that.

In the distance, coming from the east, behind the plane, they heard a siren. No one had to say anything, everyone's efforts, even Max's, ratcheted up to something like a blur.

Tony began to throw the bags himself, cheerleading. "Get 'em in, get 'em in . . ."

By the time the last dollar was in the back of the plane, the streets were bare and the siren close. The assisting clerks, seeing that their job was done and afraid of being taken as hostages, broke and ran to the bank. For some reason Tony fired a burst at them, hitting one in the leg and sending him tumbling into the doorway where he lay bleeding and begging for help. Even Jack had understood that it was unnecessary.

Tony barked at Max to get in and, "Speed up the motor." The others jumped in behind him, Tony last as befitted a *commandatore*. "Let's go, let's go!"

The pursuing sound now was of at least two sirens overlapping. Everyone began to yell at Max, even Doc who was leaning over the back of his seat not to count but to fondle the stacks of cash in the back of the cabin, stroking, rubbing them against his skin, running bundles like a deck of cards.

The engines, Max pointed out, were not responsive to intimidation and would turn over only so fast, unless they wanted him to risk blowing a cylinder through a cowling, which would see all of them running for their lives through four feet of weeds and water rife with snakes and 'gators.

Finally the plane began to edge along the highway, headed out of town, and the critics were briefly silenced. It began to pick up speed but the boys were accustomed to make their getaways in cars that went from zero to sixty in seconds and in a much shorter distance.

"We're haulin' a helluva lotta freight here," Max said, shaking his head. "I don't know . . ."

Tony suspected defeatism. "Great people use their 'wills.' You know what that is? If there's a will, you can do it. Just take off and fuck it."

Max was getting a little irritated. "You don't say 'fuck it' to the law of gravity, you dumb shit."

No one listened, they continued to scream for him to take off, all the while nervously trying to look behind, which was almost impossible given the configuration of the airplane.

"Get this plane up, man, they're gettin' close," Tony ordered.

"I gotta get up to airspeed. I need room and I need—aw, Christ."

Everyone turned to see what he saw; an ancient flatbed truck chugging out onto the highway ahead of them. The driver, a tiny, very old white man, seemed absolutely oblivious of what was coming up rapidly behind him. Not so the half-dozen black farm workers in bib-tops riding on the truck bed. They rightly viewed the approaching propellers with great alarm; everyone shouted and gesticulated, and a couple began to pound frantically on the back window of the cab.

The little old driver, apparently deaf as well as blind, ignored them.

Inside the plane Tony pounded the palms of both hands against the console in front of him, shouting into Max's ear, "HONK!"

Behind them, Doc had the whole upper half of his body out of the top half of the door and was screaming insults, demands and obscenities at the driver of the truck straight into the propeller noise. Next to him, Jack was trying to push his way into the same crowded opening with his carbine, trying to find a way to fire at the pursuing police cars if they got close enough.

"Kill the old fart," Tony screamed, "Kill him!" Doc leaned back in and told them, "They're catchin' up!" with the rotating lights burned into his stoned eyes. The sirens crescendoed to a raging dementia.

Tony poked his MAC-11 hard against Max's ribs where they had already been injured. "You don't get us up, I'll kill you."

As the whirring props grew ever closer to the flatbed, the farmhands began bailing out, leaping off the truck into water-filled ditches on either side of the road.

His captor's relentless stupidity on certain issues was starting to wear on Max. "Get that thing outta my ribs, you fuckin' guinea moron." And with that, and everyone crying out in abject fear as the farm truck swelled up larger than a glacier, ballooning to be bigger than anything any of them had ever seen, Max, against every instinct, headed the plane up the gravel driveway of one of the town's outlying homes.

Past the modest clapboard house and around it through the backyard, scattering chickens and a housewife with wash in her hands. Still, he managed to avoid any obstacles, only missing a Scotch terrier that was barking at them because a patch of mud slid the plane sideways. Finally he got it turned back towards the highway on the other side of the house.

Here there was a long flat shoulder that allowed Max to actually taxi alongside and then pass the slow-moving flatbed. He gunned the engines and put the plane into a full takeoff mode. The police cars had tried to follow him around the farmhouse with less success, one getting stuck momentarily and the other clipping the barn and revealing a lot of bewildered cows. When Max looked back down the road the truck still chugged straight ahead, showing no sign that its driver had ever been aware.

One police car appeared back on the highway with a crumpled fender but was hopelessly behind now that Max was increasing speed.

Turning to look ahead, Max was horrified to find that they now had a huge semi coming down on them at sixty plus. His passengers let him know at almost the same time and loudly. There was nowhere to get off this time, nowhere. You had to assume that the truck driver had seen them but his mind refused to process it as anything except a swampland mirage.

"Throw out some money, goddammit!"

The answer came in cacophonous concert: "No! No money!"

There was no alternative but to shove the throttles through the console and try to get at least twenty feet off the ground. If they stalled or the cylinders blew, that was it. He surprised himself by thinking how he had Diana's life in his hands as well.

The engines stuttered, wheezed their complaint but finally began to gulp salubriously in fits and starts. Max pulled back radically on the yoke with both hands, closed his eyes since there was nothing positive to see, and indulged in prayers normally uttered only on an occasional Christmas or Easter and then with considerably less fervency.

No one cared enough to note his religious conversion. If they were praying too, it was to Baal. The truck's horn seemed to come howling from all across the 'Glades, pounding on the plane's thin metal as if it wanted to get in. The airbrakes were also being applied, making a rending sound like the skin-puckering screech of fingernails on blackboards, that increasingly emanated from somewhere directly under the plane.

Would they get clear? He heard a snap and felt the tug as a wheel struck off the truck's aerial, and then the aircraft seemed to leap upwards. Max cracked open his eyes, daring to look down. They were free, climbing rapidly. He, they, would live another day. And Diana.

The crew took longer to come out of their paralysis, but when they realized that they were safely in the air broke into riotous celebration. Frank actually became animated, tearing open a package of money and throwing it around the cabin with down-home yips. Tony kept shouting out unreal sums and even more unreal expectations of what his life would be like from here on. Doc laid his head back and grinned, making a phlegmy humming sound.

Max the only quiet one, concentrated on flying the airplane and feeling his body reawaken to life in the freedom of flight.

"How much we give that faggot manager, Tony?" Doc asked.

Max had wondered how it had been set up, not that it mattered.

Tony's response was predictable. "You kiddin'? What's he gonna do? Who's he gonna tell? An' I don't think he'll come after us, do you?" The idea of that struck them as very funny.

Tony went on, "Hey, you seen that fuckin' truck driver, man? You seen the mook's face?" Tony wasn't addressing anyone in particular and roared joyously in answer to his own question. "He thought he was gonna join Jimmy Hoffa."

That got a big laugh from everyone except Max.

XIII

The Cessna had disappeared over the glaucous wasteland of the horizon, over the eight-foot trees and mysterious lines of ragged shrubs planted by the WPA in the thirties that occasionally gave a specious appearance of order to what was in reality a vast spread of emptiness. It was long gone by the time the police got any kind of an investigation going. The feds would take a while longer.

Tony had demanded that they leave the scene in a deceptive direction but Max refused; there wasn't enough gas for that, not with the weight they were carrying. Again a quarrel broke out over Max's insistence that they dump some money. He gave in, the issue having already been decided, but wanted the satisfaction of warning that it was going to be a close thing, so if they all died at least he would be proven right.

They flew southeast at an altitude of just over a thousand feet. It was suspicious-looking but a choice made, and smugglers came into the country, not the other way around. He would go up to a respectable altitude when they crossed the coast, then drop below radar range again for the crossing to the islands. All of this would cost fuel.

Jack fell asleep with his mouth open, looking like a very old man or a corpse. Tony sang under his breath, something Max didn't recognize but might have been do-wop. Doc was coming down from the coke but was too afraid of flying to relax. He muttered to himself all the way back.

Max hadn't paid any attention to the time but now,

when he looked down for a bearing, the occasional palm was casting a shadow. Still, they would make it back with plenty of light left for a landing. If the gas lasted and he didn't miss the island; Max was too smart to put a lot of faith in his own estimates.

There were other risks. Should the feds get on it in time it was not impossible that someone would authorize scrambling military aircraft from Homestead. Certainly customs planes would be on the lookout. Their best hope, he thought, was scarcely a hope at all, that the real owners of the bank could somehow maneuver to impede the investigation, keeping the whole question of crime and punishment unto themselves.

The bank manager fidgeted behind his desk, listening to one of his clerks, Jimmy Dunlap, talk about the robbery. Through the glass partition he could see the authorities bustling in and out. He had closed the door to his office on the excuse that he needed to recover from the excitement. The real reason was Dunlap.

Jimmy seemed to be glowing, maintaining a very unclerk-like insouciance, while everyone else was in varying degrees of trauma. Here was one man dead and poor Mr. Beaufort taken away with a ghastly wound in his thigh and right now, right outside his door, one of the male clerks had fainted and the female clerk was throwing water on him.

The manager himself was terrified; things hadn't gone at all the way he imagined, and it was all he could do to keep from shaking the teeth out of his head.

Now here was the lean and hungry looking Dunlap acting cock-of-the-walk. Buck teeth, a cheap suit and tortoise shell glasses did nothing to ameliorate his suddenly acquired look of unholy ambition. Or had those rheumy eyes always burned too brightly? Ambition wasn't something you looked out for in a swamp.

". . . I said, did you call Mr. Vigiletti yet?"

"Uh . . . no, of course not." He nodded sternly at all the investigators bustling around outside of the confines of this cool little executive cave. "It's hardly the time, and certainly not with this phone."

"What'd be a better time?" Jimmy asked, almost a demand, brazen, slouching in his chair while knowing full well that bankers didn't slouch. "He always says to let him know right away if anything happens."

"When it's appropriate and . . . safe."

Jimmy smirked. "I'd sure hate to be there when he hears it on the TV."

The manager's voice rose a little, "That's my responsibility."

"Okaaay." The one word managed to convey both a verbal and physical dismissal.

"If you haven't given your statement, Jimmy, maybe you should go out there and not keep them waiting."

The clerk rose slowly, very slowly, like something that had been in the sun too long. "Oh, I think they wouldn't mind waitin' if they knew what I knew."

The manager came a little up from his seat, the sweat-dampened pants making a sucking sound when they came away from the plastic-leather seat cushion that was intended to make him taller. "What? What are you talking about, Jimmy?"

"I got the number on that plane."

"Number? Planes don't have license plates, do they?"

"They got numbers on the sides that identify 'em. I'm surprised you didn't see it."

"Oh . . . well, I don't know how dependable our judgment

would be, any of us, under such terrible stress . . . I don't, well . . ."

"I know what I seen, 'cause I was thinkin' it was the last thing I was ever gonna to see on this earth." He went to the door. "Mr. Vigiletti'd like to have that number, I betcha. Pay more 'an the government, too." He paused in the doorway and turned back to say, "Oh, an' I quit this damn job." He left the door open and went down the hall, his malign chuckle drifting back.

Undone by Bugs Bunny! What now? The manager considered trying to stay around long enough to collect his sizeable cut for having set up the robbery, but he had an idea that if Vigiletti caught up with any of the robbers they might tell on him. You saw that about criminals on television—not dependable people. And then . . . he shuddered, and in that shudder was a decision.

Fortunately, he had already pocketed about fifty thousand when nobody was paying attention. That was comfy in a briefcase locked in his safe. He got it out, took it to an exterior window, opened it and made a deposit on the ground. Next, he went to tell the authorities that he was going home for awhile to reassure his family, which enabled him to leave through the front door. Picking up the briefcase from where he had left it, he was soon in his car and on his way to Miami International, having just recollected that he had an aunt in Alberta, Canada.

Long before his former boss had reached Miami, Jimmy Dunlap had called Mr. Vigiletti in that city and given him the number of the plane. Unfortunately Mr. Vigiletti was far too upset to express his gratitude. Actually, he threatened to kill Jimmy.

Vig rushed to his favorite pay phone at a gas station on

Bickel in Miami Beach. ". . . There's heat all over the fuckin' place. Yeah . . . Yeah . . . On a news down here it said like they got fifty K's . . . Only off by like thirty-five mill . . .

"I know, I know—they got enough . . . 'Course there's gotta be somebody inside . . . I got an idea on that, little prick looks like a rabbit, Dunlap, allus got some kinda game goin'. We'll take care of it.

". . . Jesus Christ, Tommy, don't talk that way . . . You know me . . . You ever had reason, no! . . . Yeah, but shit, this is Vig you're talkin' to, you know, your *compadre* . . ."

He wiped his head with the monogrammed handkerchief, then flapped his arms like chicken wings in order to allow air into the armpits. He wiped his nose and blew into it to disguise a quaver that only he could hear. ". . . Yeah, well, tell the man I'm . . . tell him I hope I still have his respect, you know . . . I'm on this thing . . . okay . . . ?"

The party on the other end hung up abruptly. Vigiletti hung up regretfully, snarling at all bosses under his breath to show that he was not afraid. He paused to give his shoes a little polish with the same handkerchief, and felt better after that.

Joe Peck and the bodyguard were waiting for him in the pink vinyl booth of a coffee shop attached to a small hotel on Collins Ave. He arrived while a dumpy, worn, middle-aged waitress whose uniform and hair matched the vinyl was pouring the fourth coffee refill without comment other than a dour expression that implied everyone should have a job and go to it every day. She was not afraid of these guys; she was more afraid her feet would die before the shift was over.

There was a bottle of scotch on the table. The manager looked over occasionally and worried about it but mainly he just hoped it, and they, would go away without trouble. Peccarino poured some into the cup of coffee and pushed it over in front of the boss who accepted it as his due.

"It's cool for now," Vigiletti said.

"How long?"

"Just listen. We tracked the number on the plane. It comes from down in Key West, the airport there. So we need a plane ourselves. And some people."

"I'll get on it," Joe Peck said.

"You get on it," the boss agreed, throwing down half of the cup of coffee-laced scotch. "Jesus, I needed some a this. You know who they think it is? Tony C. Remember him? Tony Ciufini? Big good-lookin' kid allus chasin' cooze. They used to call him 'Dumb-Dumb.' He thought it was 'cause he notched his ammo."

"Yeah . . . yeah, hey, he used to work Nino's crew."

"From Brooklyn," the bodyguard put in, making a rare contribution.

"The hairdresser, right?!" Joe Peck said, and laughed. "Who you want me to get for this?"

Vigiletti had to think it over. "Call the Rasta Man and hire out some people. If it's ever tied to the bank, it's better the colored should be seen." He reinforced the whisky in the cup and took a long swallow. "I want these cocksuckers up on a hook in a basement with a torch, all the fuckin' trouble they caused me."

"You know, Vig," Joe Peck said, "we start usin' these jamochs, they don't take no prisoners, man."

"Whichever." He shot the cuffs on his sweat-stained sport shirt.

Max felt pretty good when he hit the island dead-on and without incident. Fuel was low so it was just as well, but in

184

his pride at his newly-crafted skills he wasn't thinking about that. By now his companions were spent, highs of all sorts had sunk into somnolence so if he had missed they wouldn't have known until they hit the water, losing out on the joy of shooting him on the way down.

Since the earlier plane Diana had been kept in the house while Lalo prowled around outside, scanning the horizon for any alien presence. Now, alerted by the distant purr of the Cessna and uncertain of its identity, he ran back to the house and hid beneath the roof of the verandah.

Diana came to the door and asked, "Who is it?"

"You stay."

She stepped out onto the verandah to stand next to him anyway. "I won't go out there. Is it them, do you think?"

She clutched one of the roof supports tightly, straining towards the oncoming plane, her thumbnail in her mouth and tears already making her bleary-eyed and snuffling. It amazed her, this much emotion. And Muldoon, a lunatic like Muldoon?

A luminous, largely windless sky, perfect conditions, yet she found herself praying that Max could bring the plane in safely. That he would survive—not simply for her own sake. She decided right there that she might conceivably really be in love with this guy. A whole new concept.

"It's them! It's the Cessna." Like a child galloping for a playground, Diana ran out into the clearing in front of the house to jump and wave and shout. Lalo must have agreed; he made no attempt to stop her and eventually shuffled down the path to clear off the runway. The plane slipped lower as it closed.

Max, making his pass over the house, waggled his wings and gunned the engine in salute. Diana loved it and cheered. Irrepressible Max. He was back and they had a chance now.

This time he made a near perfect approach, Casey couldn't have done it better. Straight down the improvised runway at just the right rate of descent, allowing perfectly for the added weight and drift. Plenty of light yet, sun cruising the horizon. His captors maintaining a rare silence, as if sensing the smoothly professional nature of his approach. He dipped a little too low, bringing some tension into the cabin, but corrected quickly, keeping the nose up in compensation for the weight. And finally . . . touchdown.

The "runway" was still too short, so it was necessary to fight for purchase and drag while keeping the plane on course despite the rough terrain. It bounced a couple of times and yawed but far less than before. Everything was near perfect until they were almost at a stop, and then they hit a limb that had fallen since their departure. It was dead, hence no leaves to mark it, and the trunk was white, plus the sand had drifted across some of it. Somehow Lalo had missed it, or perhaps in his dim mind it hadn't seemed important.

There was an ominous crack and the aircraft lurched sideways with its tail going into the air for an instant, but then Max straightened it and brought things to a halt without further mishap. He immediately jumped out and ducked beneath the plane to inspect the landing gear. No major damage. All things considered, not a bad job, he thought.

Lalo came down from the house to help unload the money. Diana ran past him to embrace Max, but she never got there. Tony was livid; he had seen the Promised Land and here was this fuck-up pilot endangering everything. He jumped between them, blocking her off with his bulk and yelling into Max's face. Doc and Jack crowded in also, demanding answers interposed with screaming insults and obscenities that drowned out any response he might make.

Max started out calmly, keeping his voice low, encouraging them to do the same while he tried to explain the situation. The accident was no big deal and the damage could be fixed in a day or less. If they heard him, they didn't believe it and he was soon screaming back at them. That drove everyone to a greater frenzy and Diana got into it, trying to be the peacemaker.

Tony started to slap her again but she pulled back adroitly, and before he could follow through he had reason to regret it. In a blur that no one registered, Max hit him in the stomach; or at least he aimed for it with a hard right hand. Luckily, in missing by inches, he caught the solar plexus just above, paralyzing his target. Tony's mouth shot open, wide enough to put a fist through, his eyes popped and he wheezed dramatically in a desperate search for air.

The left hook, intended to set his victim up for another right, caught the cheek and was so powerful that it instantly knocked Tony down, gashing the side of his face and loosening a couple of those marvelous teeth. Max was angrier than he knew.

Tony's weapon went flying across the ground, which was probably the thing that prevented Max's death on the spot. That and the fact that the punches had been so fast it took a couple of seconds before the others even realized what had happened. Those seconds would provide thinking time.

Max rounded on the other two who were standing close, hoping to take them out before Lalo got into it, but Doc, grinning, whipped the Magnum up, thrusting the muzzle to within inches of his face, and the fight was over. Lalo grabbed Diana, something he enjoyed, and held her fast even though she fought him, something he liked even more.

From the ground, when he could manage just enough breath, Tony attempted to scream orders for them to kill Max. The words squeaked and cracked trying to get out, bloody spittle flying, inhibited as much by his insupportable rage as lack of oxygen.

But things had changed. "Huh-uh," Doc said, "not now." Aside to Jack, he told him to put down his carbine, because the latter was on the point of carrying out Tony's demand. Doc, the new man of reason, looked around at the other two. "We're rich now. We got a lotta livin' to do, men."

Tony continued to screech in a tiny voice, "Kill him!!" Under other circumstances it would have been comical.

Doc went on as if he hadn't heard. "Tony, all a us, it's like a fuckin' miracle, you know? Okay, I don't blame you bein' pissed, you're not exactly pretty right now, but we shoot this dude just 'cause he popped you, we don't ever get to spend it. You're not thinkin' right now. You wanna work out on him a little later on . . . but you're not gonna kill him and you better be careful not to get him too mad, neither."

There's logic, Max thought.

Doc looked to the others for confirmation.

Jack changed sides with remarkable facility, "Ah ain't never heard a this much money. I ain't never even smelled it an' now I has. Ain't nobody takin' it from me now. So all ah thank is, you better be real cool, you dago piece a shit."

Here was open rebellion. Max's heart did a little dance of hope, although the moment passed quickly and apparently without consequences.

Lalo broke the tension by grinning at Tony; another first. "I don' think so, mano. I got big plans."

Doc lowered his gun in a long slow arc and it was over.

Max sagged a little in relief; he had expected to die this time. Lalo let go of Diana, who spun and hit him hard as soon as she was free. He showed no sign of having felt it. Jack helped Tony to his feet, where he tried to glare at Max through the blood and sand that covered his face, and they all dragged up to the house in silence; it had been a strenuous day.

"I don't care, I entertained him all I'm goin' to. Let Earl entertain him for awhile," Casey's wife complained when he called her on the phone.

"What would Earl do, show him dirt? He doesn't have any imagination."

"You like my imagination, do you? Maybe you should a took advantage of it now and then."

Casey, misunderstanding, felt heart and phallus leap in tandem. "Mary Beth, does this mean . . . you're willin' . . .'"

"Doesn't mean nothin'. And don't you go gettin' horny on the telephone. You know what happened last time, people can hear."

"No they can't. I just wanna know—"

"Nothin' is what you're gonna know. Now stop callin' me ever five minutes the way you been doin'. Just 'cause you're bored. I told you not to go over there."

"What about Digger Hadley?"

"I'm gonna hang up on you."

"Okay, okay, we'll wait till I get home. Just do me this one favor, it's for both of us, for the kids, Mary Beth, if you think about it. Just keep this customer there. I swear I'll be home in a day or two."

"He's ugly as a possum and he's got a wart on his chin and all he wants to do is stay home. I'm tired of tryin' to show him a good time."

Her choice of words grated on Casey. He was acerbic when he said, "I didn't ask you to 'show him a good time,' I just said entertain him."

"Casey Moon, you're the only person in the world that wouldn't think entertainment oughta lead to a good time."

She wanted a report on Casey's progress but he didn't want to give it to her; waiting around for Billy to show up didn't quite have a dynamic feel to it even though it was the only alternative he could see at the moment.

The local police had given his concerns the same reception they had given Billy's earlier. The senior officer, the ablest and most often financially encouraged in the past, was off until tomorrow.

Casey had called the Miami Police, the Customs and the Coast Guard but they saw it as a quarrel between partners and refused even to take a report. Of course there was always flying around the Caribbean, as he had earlier, expending expensive fuel, landing in dangerous places and being mistaken by smugglers for the DEA.

Mary Beth didn't understand any of that. She wanted the money from the client, she wanted him to come home. They would get the Cessna back in good time—it was her day to trust Max because he was cute and fun. When Casey swore she hung up on him.

He had to do something to keep from going crazy, so he called the office. For once Earl had something to report. A detective had called from Miami and said they were on the way down to talk to him about the plane.

That worried Casey; he didn't trust Earl and he couldn't understand why this sudden interest on the part of the authorities when only a couple of hours before he had met with indifference and buck-passing?

He instructed Earl at length as to how to talk to them,

giving neither too much, because Casey didn't trust the police on principle, or too little, because then they might not help. Earl promised.

"And don't you worry 'bout the client, boss; he seems to be havin' a good ol' time."

"You entertainin' him all right?"

"Huh-uh, Mary Beth, remember? But they seem to be havin' themselves a lotta fun. I seen 'em last night comin' out a Club Mambo. Laughin' and, you know, carryin' on."

"No, I don't know."

Earl thought he detected a certain grimness. "Jist havin' a real good time." One could have witnessed the shrug over the phone.

"Yeah? What's he like?"

Earl tried to be encouraging.

"Real nice fella. Good lookin', allus smilin' and showin' his teeth. Funny, too, I guess, way she was laughin' at him."

"What about that big wart on his chin?"

"Wart?"

Billy came back to work at dinner time. Casey found him at his tiny desk in the control shack, head in hands, moaning occasionally, crying occasionally, effusing alcohol fumes continually.

"Nobody help me, mon. I was scared the po-lice would be tellin' the smugglers and they would come to kill me. I be nothin' but a terrible coward, and I let my friend down bod. Poor Mox. It's my fault, all my bloody fault . . . I couldn't help him and he look so distressed . . ."

Casey would put up with that only so long; questions of conscience were why churches got a tax exemption. "Don't worry about that, I got a lotta influence with the police around here, bein' a businessman."

Billy stopped his lament on a dime and flashed his big Bahamian smile. If there was one thing Casey hated about the Bahamas it was all that indiscriminate smiling. "Oh, I hope so, Ca-sey. That Mox, he is the finest mon I ever . . ."

"I don't want to hear about Mo—Max. Just tell me what direction they took."

Billy thought for a moment. "Southwest."

"You better be damned sure. Not south-by-south, west-by-west?"

Billy shook his head vigorously and then held it because it hurt. "I watch real good 'cause I believe then po-lice would help me." He moved his open, upright hand away from his nose in a southwesterly direction.

"So the island's to the northeast," Casey said.

Billy looked confused.

"That's what Jap carrier pilots did in 'The War.' " He always referred to the one he had missed by virtue of being unborn, as "The War." "Everybody does that, if they're stupid. Try to throw you off doin' the exact opposite, never ninety degrees, always a hundred and eighty. If they got the fuel. Did they have fuel?"

"Filled up, yes."

"That's where that island was," Casey said aloud to himself.

Billy asked him which island he was talking about.

Casey looking out the window at the darkening sky, didn't hear him. It was too late; another day was lost.

Earl figured that as long as he had to wait for the detectives he might as well enjoy himself, so he went out and brought a six-pack of Bud back to the office along with a pile of magazines: *Penthouse, Screw, Beavers and Buttheads, Bazooms, Jugs and Jokes, Foxy Femmes* . . . He had it in his mind that the "company" might pay for this revel since Casey had left him in charge. He intended to look at them *all* upside down.

The detectives came after dark. As usual, the door was open and they simply walked in. They were imposing men, one Anglo, or at least his name was, Denton, although his skin color was more like olive, with heavy, thick features, eyebrows like bottlebrushes, a broken nose, eyes black as space. He was not tall but had a tree trunk thorax and shoulders, conveying an immovable force.

The other, who called himself Avila, was paradoxically lighter in tone, a little shorter, with an aquiline face marred by scars and with constantly moving hands and eyes. Both wore somewhat garish sport jackets, Avila a patterned tie that clashed with the pattern of the jacket.

Earl was dozing over his *Penthouse*, head down and feet up on the desk, toothpick dangling off the lower lip. The two detectives took one look at him and exchanged a glance. The larger one, Denton, slammed the flat of his hand on the wall and shouted, "Hey!"

Earl experienced a cruel awakening; he tried to bolt out of the chair in several directions at once and almost ended on the floor, which brought a laugh from Avila. Earl had bitten through his toothpick.

They introduced themselves and flashed something in their wallets while he tried to pull himself together. Eventually, he was able to stand at attention. "Yessirs."

The detectives exchanged another look. They told him gruffly to sit down, relax.

Earl sat but he didn't relax, sitting up straight on the edge of his seat, which was Casey's chair, and moving his hands nervously around the desk top as if looking for something to hang on to.

"Thank you. Y'all wanna sit down, too. How 'bout some coffee? Fresh made."

"We want some information, is what we want," Denton said dourly, taking out a notebook, "which you're gonna give to us. What's your name?"

"Earl Delroy B. Fortin."

"What's the 'B' for?"

"I dunno."

"Whaddaya do here?"

Avila sat down on the old couch with his back partially to Earl and studied the room, content to let his partner ask the questions.

"I'm the Chief Mechanic and Office Manager."

"Who's in the company, how many?"

"Me and Casey and Max. Though it's hard to know sometimes when Max's workin' here 'cause he's always fired. Like right now."

"Who?"

"Max. Muldoon. Is that what this here's 'bout, Max stealin' the Cessna? I didn't help him none, I swear to the Lord above. I don't know whatever Casey told you, but I didn't. Max jist does things and nothin' an' no one can turn him 'round. He's like a storm, you know, it jist happens— only nicer." He looked from one to the other, hoping they had understood what seemed very complicated to him.

Denton held himself back for the moment. "Fella, you're tellin' us a lotta shit we don't wanna know, okay? The plane, that's what this is about. You got that straight?"

Earl nodded enthusiastically and went right on. "I never thought Casey'd do that, turn Max in, to the law, I mean, but I guess he's really gone and done it. When he called here, 'bout seven or so, an' I told him you was comin', he wasn't least bit surprised."

"Who?" The detective's voice was taking on a certain ragged edge of impatience.

"Casey. Moon. He's the boss. He's one always firin' Max."

"Why?"

" 'Cause ever'body likes Max and nobody does Casey, if you want the honest truth. And then Max steals his airplane and stuff like that."

Avila twisted around to join the conversation, laughing. "I can see where he might wanna kill the fucker."

Denton wasn't laughing, he was a short-tempered man putting up with a lot, as he saw it. "This Cessna numbered N4694P?" he barked.

Earl, startled, had to think. "Yessir."

"So where is it?"

The man was leaning nearer and nearer and Earl could smell onions and garlic and maybe even oregano; it was making him increasingly nervous.

"Well, see, we don't know. Casey's gone over to the . . ." He caught himself up, looking constipated. What had Casey told him to say?

" 'Gone over to' where?"

"I don't know if I should tell." He wiped his face. "I sure wish he was here now to tell me what to say. Casey, the boss, he's got jist an awful temper."

"You ain't seen mine yet," Denton said, starting to rise and working his fists.

Avila, too, changed pace; he was easily bored. "Listen, shit-for-brains," he said, as if ready to go over the couch and desk, "you wanna take a little trip up to Miami tonight? We got a cell up there with nothin' in it but transvestites and rough trade. If that don't work we'll just kick the shit outta you ourselves."

Earl shuddered, appealing with his hands. "No, no, please. I'm an Amurican, I don't go for that stuff at all."

Denton pushed him against the wall. "Where's the fuckin' Cessna, man?"

Earl was beginning to quiver all over, which gave some credence to his confession. "Casey's—my boss, you know—he's over on Andros. Island. In the Bahamas. I talked to him jist a couple hours ago on the phone. He's lookin', he is honest-to-God lookin' real hard, but I don't think he's found 'im yet. Max. That's the whole truth, that's all I know about it. I swear—on the Holy Bible!"

"Hey, the Bible," Avila laughed. "Bigtime."

Denton decided for them. "Okay, asshole. You don't mention this to nobody, you understand?"

"I do, I surely do, officer. I'm a real good citizen. I served my country."

The detectives were already leaving. He heard Avila comment, "Stupido," to the other one, but he didn't care. Falling back into the chair, exhausted, he had enough to worry about in Casey's inevitable reaction.

The two men walked not to their car, a rented five-year-old Plymouth with dents, but past it to another, a Cadillac parked at some little distance.

In the back seat Vigiletti leaned across Joe Peck and ran down the window to receive their report.

Denton said, "One a the pilots, name a Max Muldoon, ripped-off a plane, a Cessna. Musta took it for the job. His boss, Casey Moon—yeah, that's their names—he's chasin' him. Moon's over in the Bahamas now. Andros Island, this prick says. He's the mechanic."

"That all?" Peccarino asked.

"He's dumber an' shit, but yeah, I think that's it."

"He bought us as dicks," Avila said, "he's in there

cleanin' out his pants right now."

Vigiletti told Joe Peck, "Get the troops down here."

"When you want 'em?"

"When the fuck you think I want 'em?"

"Okay, okay . . . gimme the phone . . ."

"What about jerk-off in there?" Denton asked.

"Vig?" Joe Peck said.

Vigiletti took another few seconds; he liked the idea of other people waiting for him. "Put him down. Too much at stake." He raised the window and the bodyguard started the car.

Denton went back to the office by himself, walking quickly on the balls of his feet now that he had a job to do, screwing a silencer on a .22 automatic. Avila got the car and moved it closer.

When Denton reentered the office Earl was standing with his back to the door, straightening up in order to go home. He heard the sound of someone entering and turned. He grinned, partially out of fear but mostly as a fact of his native good humor.

"Yessir, officer. Is there somethin'—"

Denton shot him twice dead-square in the chest, stood for a second regarding his handiwork, turned and went as methodically as he had come, removing the silencer and holstering the pistol.

Earl didn't understood what had happened. He reached out for something to hold onto and keep himself upright, examining his own blood as an alien substance . . . clutched the phone, dragging it noisily off the desk and on top of him as he fell. Wondering, why would they do that to me?

XIV

Dinner that night came out of cans, the drinks out of bottles; there were far more bottles than cans. Vodka, whisky and wine, Tony mixing all three. Most of the evening was devoted to an alcoholic counting of the money in the dining room.

Max and Diana, hands bound in front of them, were forced to watch, but then, as Diana said, they didn't have anything else to do. The hoodlums, buried in money, were on the whole in a jolly mood, although Tony couldn't really forget or forego his humiliation and was simply papering it over with thousand-dollar bills.

Certainly the old cocky, smartass Tony-in-charge was missing; between drunken outbursts of false laughter he would glare at Max, his eyes and occasionally moving lips promising revenge in whatever the human body could bear.

Max shrugged it off to Diana as part of the entertainment, and there was something almost funny about its relentlessness. Not that the man wasn't dead serious. As the counting grew to a close and the drink took hold, quarreling broke out again. There had been complaints all along that many of the bills had something dark and sticky on them.

Doc said it was blood. Tony replied that only a fool would think a bank would tolerate money with blood on it. Where would it come from? Doc said he'd seen a lot of blood in his career and there was something hinky about its presence; maybe it was a new way of marking money, a suggestion Tony scoffed at.

Jack said, "It's a sign somebody put on it. I don't lak it, I tell you that. You shoulda known 'bout this," he accused Tony.

"Bullshit. How'm I supposed to know somethin' sticky got on the fuckin' money? Maybe some asswipe accountant spilled the catsup off his baloney. You're bein' a couple a pussies, you wanna know."

Lalo said he didn't care; himself, he would wash it in champagne and spend it with joy. Maybe he'd have his own country, like Castro.

With more liquor it went downhill from there. Tired of listening to it, Max asked if Diana and he couldn't go to bed. Naturally this inflamed Tony. "You just wanna fuck her is what you want. Well, we'll fix that."

"What I want," Max said, "is to know what happens to us, Diana and me? Considering, you want me to fly you out of here."

The mere idea of Max asking questions further angered Tony, who leaned over and slapped him in the face. He was too drunk to score an unqualified hit, although it did leave a large spot that seemed to glow on one cheekbone. Diana gave a little cry but Max was indifferent, showing nothing, which naturally pumped Tony's temper another notch.

He swung again with his backhand but Max avoided it easily by jerking away in his chair and twisting his head, making his assailant look inept. For a moment Tony didn't know what to do, but half-sat, half-stood, puffing, eyes bleary and blood-shot, trying to kill Max with them since all else had failed. He was conscious of laughter, some of it feminine.

He turned to strike out at Diana but Doc's voice stopped him, "Hey, Tony, we wanna know what happens when we get there."

Tony's gaze wobbled from one to the other; they were agreeing, ganging up on him. "All right. I told you . . ." His speech was slurred but comprehensible. ". . . We stay quiet for awhile. Here . . . right here. Safe and sound. Then we go to . . ." He looked at Max. "I'm not tellin' him yet."

"You already did," Max reminded him. "Mexico. Guadalajara. What you didn't tell me was the course I'm supposed to take to get there. If you know."

"A course I know. But I'm not tellin' you, shithead."

" 'Cause if it's around Florida and then up the Gulf you're gonna have to land in the States. The tank on this plane maxes out at about fourteen hundred pounds of fuel, that's it. At over two hundred knots it uses a couple hundred an hour. If it's the Yucatan, we can make Cancun in good weather, then hop up the coast. But mostly how do we go anywhere without aviation fuel? There's enough in the tank now to just barely reach Nassau."

Tony looked drunkenly cockeyed-wise, waggling his finger and smirking. "We got gas here. Lotta gas. We brought it over before. You won't get outta it that way."

"I don't want to get out of it; I want to get it over with. There's something you may not know. The numbers on the plane? If somebody remembered them they could be all over us real soon."

He had their attention. "What numbers?" Doc demanded.

"You didn't notice either? On the side of the plane, every plane, big enough to be seen from a distance."

The boys looked at each other, and even Diana was wide-eyed at the idea. Tony was obviously on the verge of another of his rages, but at the same time he felt overwhelmed; he was the boss who was supposed to know these things.

"Why didn't you tell us, you fuck!!??" he screamed at Max. "It's your robbery?"

200

"Anybody comes, you go down first."

"Why do you think I told you?"

Jack said, "Sounds to me lak we oughta git goin' out a here."

"You listenin'?" Doc asked Tony, and got only a distracted nod.

"Kin you fix it fast?" Jack asked and Max reassured him. "Lak tonight?"

That, Max said, was not going to happen; he would rather be shot than crash and burn. And they would surely burn with fourteen hundred pounds of fuel aboard.

Doc winced. "You take us the best way, the safest," he told Max, looking at Tony defiantly. "Only you get us outta here, right?"

"Then you let us go after that?"

"Yeah," Doc said, quickly preempting Tony, who might say anything. "You do your job."

Tony belched and snorted. Not expecting agreement, he addressed himself. "I'm gonna kill 'im . . . both of 'em."

Max simply looked at him as though he were irrelevant.

The others, however, at least Doc and Jack, barked at Tony to shut up and quickly ushered Max and Diana out, up to the same bedroom where they were again handcuffed to the bed, this time a few feet apart.

They could hear the typically violent talk going on downstairs a good part of the night. The two of them were subdued and speaking very little. Max tried to say something encouraging but fell asleep in the middle of it. Unable to sleep, Diana found it somehow comforting just to watch him.

Downstairs, the others quickly let Tony know that everything had changed. It was not debatable that they were going to sit around on so much money you could wipe your ass with it and just wait to be hit. Eventually they passed out one by one on the table, on chairs, on the floor amidst empty bottles, smoking ashtrays and huge messy piles of fifty-, hundred-, and thousand-dollar bills.

Casey awoke with hope. If not clarified, his life seemed somehow simplified. His wife and family gone, company gone and with it anything resembling friends, status gone, best airplane gone, all he had to do now was find and kill or perhaps save Muldoon, and that particular skein showed promise of unraveling. He longed to be up in the clear, clean high air following it.

The motel's attached bar was a cafe during the day. He pounded on the door until they agreed to open for him, although it was six in the morning and only working fishermen were up at this abominable hour.

The waiter, who was also the cook, bartender and manager, asked him, "How 'bout a little rum in the coffee this morning, sir? Quicken the step."

"Nope. Gotta fly today. I'm a pilot, case you didn't spot it."

The waiter assured him that he had indeed recognized it the moment he had pounded on their door so loudly, and handed him the Nassau paper to keep him busy. Reading a newspaper thoroughly every day was one of Casey's self-improvement duties. Whereas most men will start with the financial or sports section, most women with the home, life-style or theatrical sections, he took pride in beginning with the first column on the first page and moving through it geometrically.

Not on this morning; a headline on the first page announced: DARING BANK ROBBERY IN FLORIDA . . . CRIMINALS USE AIRPLANE . . .

Casey slammed the paper shut and put it down as though it was infected. He dumped enough money on the table to pay twice over for the breakfast he hadn't had. He realized it as he hurried towards town and police headquarters, but decided, what the hell, such things no longer mattered. Life was short and Mary Beth would just get it anyway; live for the day. God and Oklahoma help him, he was becoming like Max—this was what the man had done to him!

The aforementioned and Diana awakened during the first pinkish-gray intimations of an island morning. Diana said this was practically a first for her, but then so was going to sleep at ten o'clock at night.

Max stretched to the extent his fetters would allow.

"What'll happen, Max? Now?"

"I don't know yet."

"Today the day?"

"Yep."

"Live or die, huh?"

"Could be."

"Max, would you ever consider marrying someone like me? Just an idle thought. Stupid question, I must be cracking under the strain. By the way, I need to pee."

"It's very quiet downstairs. Maybe they killed each other. Want me to shout?"

"No," she said sharply. "I'd rather wet my pants. If I still have any on, panties—I can't remember. It's nice to be alone."

"What was that 'someone like me' stuff? You're gorgeous. Any male in his right mind would want to marry you."

"Max, there are other things besides a cute face or body.

203

You're saying men only get married to have a trophy?"

"I don't think this is the time to discuss—" He broke off at the sound of someone coming slowly up the creaky stairs, whistling scraps of the Temptations' "Just My Imagination."

Diana groaned. "Max, did they kill those people at the bank?"

"Probably the guard. They thought so."

"They won't ever let us go, will they?"

"No."

The door was thrown open and Tony stood there in his bare feet, rocking slightly. He could have been an accident victim with his scrambled hair, face leached to the point where it resembled tinfoil, dirty shirt partially hanging out, a two-day growth of beard, and of course the cut cheek. All of which made his self-satisfied grin the more horrible. An attempt had been made to overlay the night's excess with a vile Crown Heights street corner cologne.

He was dangling a half-empty bottle of champagne in his left hand and a huge wad of bills in his right. That his eyes glittered was not taken as a good sign by the two on the bed. Neither spoke.

"Hey," Tony hailed, "to the victor belongs the spoils, ain't that right? Way it is in wars and conquests, huh?" He swigged champagne out of the bottle and then let it drop with a thud to roll away, clanking.

They watched him in silence from the bed as he approached slowly, slouching, seeming to enjoy the effect of the anticipation on them.

"What are you doing, Tony?" Diana asked, trying to sound in charge.

"You think Caesar and Hannibal and Genghis Khan didn't have their choice a the best pussy when they knocked over a town and did . . . whatever that was they called it? 'Bagged it'?"

That he was still drunk was becoming clearer as he stood over them at the foot of the bed, tilting forward a little and then alternately balancing back on his heels, the fumes emanating from his mouth and clothes thick enough to be photographed. Diana swore, made a gagging sound and told him he smelled like a sewer.

Max said nothing.

"Didn't I promise you, honey," Tony said, "didn't I say?" He threw the wad of bills high in the air over Diana, to float down over her outstretched form. "I think I said naked body, though, didn't I?"

"Oh, Jesus. Tony, get out of here."

He shook his head slowly and grinned some more. Then reached down and began to undress her, in no particular hurry, pulling off her shorts. Diana struggled against him and kicked but he was a large strong man and with her hands manacled it had no effect. She looked at Max and started to speak—knowing full well that he was as helpless as herself. But couldn't he at least say something, swear, scream insults, threaten?

She had never felt this helpless in her life, and there had been bad times. It was a feeling like being scalded slowly, her face burned with the shame; as much as she hated the idea of crying, she knew she would, was starting already.

She also hated to hear herself pleading, but she did that, too. He ripped open the blouse she had sewn, not bothering to remove it, and pulled up the brassiere to expose the breasts, giving one a squeeze, and finally yanked off her panties. By now she was crying openly, exigent tears. Tony stepped back to undress.

205

"What're you cryin' about, babe? Just think a me as another customer only you don't get paid, okay?"

Diana tried to make a denial, but emotion made it sound as though she had something as thick as blood in her throat and she couldn't get the words out.

Tony wasn't listening to anyone but himself anyway. "Others'll be up when I'm through. We'll keep you busy. It'll be like old times for you."

Tony was naked by now, his phallus cantilevering over the foot of the bed. He remained there, looking down at himself, showing a smug delight in his own grand tumescence. "Look how lucky you are, honey. Lotta cooze been happy to see that comin' at 'em." Caught-up in self-adulation, he seemed in no hurry to commit the rape.

Diana had recovered some control through an incandescent anger; this cretin with his ugly mouth had already destroyed everything she hoped for. "It isn't gonna happen, Tony."

"You'll like it, relax." He climbed up on the bed on all fours, hovering over her. "If you don't, I will, so at least one a us is gonna be happy."

All the time Max watched, inanimate beside her while she longed for him to say something to get her through.

"I'll throw up, I swear to God."

"No, you won't. You do and I'll rub your face in it. No, we're gonna have a nice little party here, you and me." He started to force her legs apart using both hands and his knees to hold them in place.

Diana began to sob again. "Max?" she called, helpless, driven to beg for his comfort against every impulse, then turned back to Tony's flushed face above her. "Goddamn you, you fucking pig!" She tried to spit. "I'll kill you, you bastard!"

Tony made kissing sounds and moved up her body as if

to put the tip of his erection against her mouth.

"You'll lose it."

"Would I?" He pretended to take her seriously. "I'd kill you, but maybe you're right, it isn't worth the gamble."

He laughed as if the whole thing had been a joke but Diana felt that she had won a tiny victory no matter what.

Max, too, noted the retreat. "I hope it's worth it," he said almost matter-of-factly.

"Yooooh!" Tony reared back to rest on his calves. "The hero talks. This's what I been waitin' for. What'sa matter, you don't gotta good view? You gettin' a little hard yourself? I don't mind. In fact, I want you to watch. You might learn somethin', asshole." He dropped the phony geniality. "I'm gonna do it right in your face. Your girlfriend, man, alla us. Look good, though, afterwards I might chop yours off so it's only a memory."

"Max," Diana said, "shut up. You can't do any good."

"Okay, go ahead," he told Tony, "pay later."

Tony was prepared to ignore him, but somehow couldn't go ahead, either. "Worth what? What are you gonna do 'bout it?"

"Nothing right now. Later." He stared at the ceiling, eerily calm, and continued to speak softly, dispassionately, as if he were the one on top, as if he commanded lives.

"You outta your fuckin' mind or somethin'? You don't do dick later without we tell you."

"I fly the plane, remember. Way out over the Gulf."

"So?" He moved back from Diana to sit on the edge of the bed, a ludicrous but unaware figure for a serious conversation about life and death. "You'll be in it, asshole. So will she."

Diana lay quietly listening to Max's sibylline voice, staring with her huge dark eyes, wondering and sensing that something was happening, indifferent now to her nakedness or what it might mean for her.

"So, what are you gonna do, you faggot?" Tony pointed a finger, threatening, unable to hide his rising distraction. "Nothin'!"

"Oh, I can do something. I can push the nose over and take us all down, down, down into the water. And there won't be a goddamned thing you can do about that."

"You'd kill yourself. You bananas? What for? Over a cunt like this? A high-priced whore?" His voice began to rise with a kind of hysterical petulance. "For any cunt? Jesus fucking Christ!"

Max refused to be dragged into the give and take, keeping the delicate reins himself, forcing Tony to carry the burden of the tension. "Honor," was all he said. That single word, and yet it seemed to echo in the room, carrying an inexplicable power for Diana, listening above her own frail breath.

And perhaps for Tony too. "What's that got to do with it? You're in no position. You're weak, you're nothin'. Honor . . . ?"

"Not mine, hers."

Tony was starting to turn in circles and shake his head. "Yeah? 'Hers'? What's 'at mean? Shit, she'd die with us. How about that, honey, rather die than get humped by me?" He seemed to have forgotten the earlier boasts and threats of gang rape and mastery.

As his nerve had slipped, Diana's retrenched. "Given a choice between your sperm and death, Tony, any woman'd choose death."

Tony had finally got off the bed, still stark naked. He looked down at Max, who could see his face clearly for the first time and saw it pocked with the spore of doubt.

"You're bluffin'," Tony said. He tried hard to put a lot of muscle in it, but it lacked the menace he had spent a lifetime cultivating. He felt it himself—without the promise that he was the one willing to kill, willing to do the unthinkable, he was not a whole man.

Max went on in his monotone, a professor sent from hell. "If I'm not, you'll find out too late. And, like Doc says, you'll never spend all those millions. If you're wrong, tomorrow you'll see those whitecaps rushing up at you couple hundred miles an hour, and you'll know it wasn't worth it. But by then it'll be too late, won't it. And I'll laugh my ass off all the way down, listening to you scream."

Tony's voice was two keys higher when he asked, "Why, for Christ's sake?" It was a demand that begged. "She's a fuckin' whore!"

" 'Revenge a dish best served cold.' You think you're the only people with a sense of honor? I'll tell you, I have to watch the four of you climbing on and off of a woman I love all day—"

He was interrupted from two quarters. Diana gasped with a noticeable awe, and Tony swore, falling back on Italian, at least the Italian of the *"nabe,"* to express his incredulity, but it lacked force.

Max went on, speaking over them, "—tomorrow, my heart's gonna be a very cold place."

Tony seem paralyzed, unable to decide. Max smiled at him; Tony had seen that smile before on old men who decreed your death with a kiss or a fluttering of arthritic fingers. Exactly that smile.

Diana had come all the way back. "Lose something, Tony?" she asked defiantly.

Instinctively he looked down to find something more than his will had gone flaccid. "Fuck you, you bitch."

"Not today, sweetheart." She hated the sound of that the moment the words escaped her lips; so hard, callused, the defiance of a whore.

Tony grabbed up the few clothes he had brought to the party and went out, predictably with words directed at Max to the effect that his day would come.

Diana muttered, "Bastard." That was better, more acceptable. She struggled to get some of her clothes back over, if not on, her.

Max, meanwhile, sighed, relaxed his body, closed his eyes. His breathing deepened.

Diana raised up a little to study him, worried. After a beat she decided to chance it, "Thanks."

He moved his head slightly up and down.

"Now you know," she said.

"What?" He sounded as though he might actually have gone to sleep and was only halfway back.

"I was a call girl, actually, if that makes a difference."

Max remained where he was, exhausted. "Hygienically."

"That's not true! That's—goddamn you! You know better than that, you bastard."

"I just meant rich guys are probably cleaner and nicer to you. That with Tony was tiring—could I get a little more sleep here for a second?"

"Cleaner, not necessarily nicer," she corrected, fumbling. Outraged, grateful, hurt, ashamed, she had no idea where to take this. Expecting the worst yet obligated by her own distinct sense of honor to make some kind of expiation. Something!

"Three months, Max, that's the God's truth. That's how long. And I wasn't even there, just the lower half of me being an actress. Although I don't guess there's any reason you should believe me, is there?"

"No. But then I don't believe anybody. That's how I stay alive and cheerful."

"Would you stop being so goddamned flip and condescending?" She felt her anger growing, knew it as a fact and not a right, and fought to tamp it down. "This is important and I owe you and you're being a real sonofabitch."

"I'm being real tired."

She was back down flat on the bed herself, wearied, like Max, by what had just passed, but she thought she saw him nod. If that was the best she could get, she would have to work with it. What she would have preferred was to cry hysterically and not care about anyone. One thing about the old life, no explanations, never the strain of caring.

"I whored three months up in Palm Beach—this isn't an apology or excuse. I have worked as a model and an actress and a few million other things; that's the truth. I made my own way my whole life; I've never lived off anyone else, any man, if that's what you're thinking. And I'm a student, although I'm over thirty.

"Maybe I lacked the guts to go to Hollywood or New York or wherever things happen. And then I got kind of desperate a year ago and a guy I'd modeled for said I could make a grand a night . . . which I did. For exactly three months."

Her voice trailed. ". . . It wasn't worth it. Believe me, nothing is."

Max seemed to gain energy. "Do I look like Saint Ignatius of Loyola to you? You're ashamed of it, right?"

"What's it sound like?"

"Good. So am I of a lotta the stuff I've done, deeply ashamed. That's what separates us from the jerks of the world. So give it a rest." He settled back again.

"I wanted you to forgive me."

"I just did. And me, and all of us sinners, okay?"

"Max?"

"Yeah?"

"You wouldn't have really done it?"

"What?"

"Crash the plane. Kill us all."

He thought before he answered. "You have to believe it or don't say it."

At that point she realized that she didn't know Max at all, and wondered if anyone did. But she was awed by him and whispered, "Wow . . ." as she closed her eyes.

Max appeared to be already asleep, or was visiting whatever strange place he went to when his eyes were closed.

"Love's a bitch," she whispered.

XV

The newspaper story had said the plane was probably a Cessna, but Casey didn't have to know that to know who was involved. He had his instincts. Over fifty thousand dollars had been taken, it said. Unfortunately no one had thought to get the plane's I.D. number.

Casey could have told them—N4694P—but he wouldn't; any plane used in a robbery would likely be confiscated or at the very least held in evidence for a period of months or years.

On his way into town to look for help, he more or less ran into it, or at least the potential in an East Indian police lieutenant with the assimilatory name—chosen when his mother gave birth to him in the London railway station—of Neville Paddington. Neville was riding his bicycle furiously along the coast road when Casey spotted him.

The policeman was resistant to the idea of stopping but Casey held up a twenty-dollar bill and that bought at least a few minutes of a busy law enforcement officer's time. He remained on the bike to reinforce the point that he needed to be somewhere else, but listened as Casey spun out the whole sordid account of Max's perfidy and the part this Jezebel had played in it. The bank robbery went unmentioned for the moment.

Unfortunately, Lieutenant Paddington had read the same newspaper.

"Mr. Moon. I have expressed myself on these things in the past. However unfortunate their methods, these terrible gentlemen were merely exercising their personal freedom while practicing a form of free enterprise. My view of this is well grounded upon the teachings of the great international moral philosopher, Ayn Rand." He indicated the small dollar sign on the lapel of his uniform.

"Who's he?" Casey asked pugnaciously, feeling that he was going to lose. International philosophers? If only Max were here.

"She. It is a woman when it was alive. A sublime and brilliant woman philosopher. Believe this or not."

"So, wha'd h—she say?"

"Her philosophy, extraordinary don't you think in its simplicity, is such that everyone should do as they wish and the strong will triumph, which is for the good for everybody."

"You'd be out of a job, wouldn't you?"

"You don't comprehend. It is very deep. Besides, these gentlemen are extremely dangerous and we don't have jurisdiction."

"You don't even know where they are."

"That is why I know we don't have jurisdiction."

"What if I told you I do know where they are and you do have jurisdiction?"

Paddington shook his head in disbelief. "You are obviously a man without a philosophy. I have to go now, please excuse me." He began to pedal off furiously.

Casey, frustrated, shouted at his back, "Where the hell you going?"

"I have a robbery in progress."

Casey was on his own.

Tony, Doc and Jack sat on the verandah of the house, nursing hangovers with a breakfast of stale donuts, coffee, and vodka. The heat was already oppressive and lassitude lay about like smog on an otherwise clear bright day. In this atmosphere the previous night's high spirits had atrophied.

Jack spoke for all. "Drunk too much last night. Gotta git sumpin' to raise me up."

Convinced that leaders didn't have hangovers, Tony pretended to be light-hearted. "Wait till you get to Mexico, man," he told him. "Got meth farms down there, pick the berries right off the bush. Fill a whole basket in a few minutes, lifetime supply." No one else laughed so he did, winking at Doc, who scowled in return.

"Mexico's the shithole out back," Jack said. "Worse'an this place."

Doc had run out of coke and was depressed. "I don't care where I am." He got up and leaned against a pillar, looking out in the general direction of where Max was working on the plane. "Life's nothin' but doin' time on the outside anyways."

He threw the rest of his donut out onto the clearing for the birds and lured a curious vulture. Nobody liked that omen; they all jumped up and yelled for him to go away. Doc threw an empty vodka bottle and that did it.

Jack listened to the distant hammering from the direction of the plane. "What'll we do with them two?"

"There's a ranch there near Guadalajara where we can land. Owner's a friend. We get a car, drive to Mexico City, we don't need 'em no more—that's it for them."

"We leave 'em at this here ranch?" Jack asked.

"Under it."

"Big waste a her," Doc said over his shoulder.

"Him right away, her maybe a little later."

Tony stood, left the porch and strolled along the path towards the plane, just far enough to make sure something was being accomplished and Lalo hadn't fallen asleep.

215

The plane itself lay under an almost professional job of camouflage. Lalo had learned about such things training with anti-Castro para-military groups during the early days of the movement. Before they threw him out.

Max was working hard beneath a canopy of interlaced branches and palm leaves. He was not a mechanic but he knew something about engines, so one of the cowlings gaped open in the search for an anomalous sound he had detected while coming in. A long flight over water dictated that he try to locate the source. The landing gear had already been dealt with to the best of his ability, although it worried Diana that he kept drawing analogies to stock cars and motorcycles.

"Hand me the spanner."

She held it up. "This thing?"

He took it and worked silently for awhile. Lalo leaned against a nearby palm, playing with his knife, occasionally leaning against the trunk and closing his eyes, letting the sun beat down on him.

"Max, when do we do something?" Diana whispered.

"I don't know."

"When do you think you will know?"

"Don't know that either."

"You're a real fountain of hope here."

"You're raising your voice."

She was, and lowered it. "Are you sure we want to fix this?"

"We don't, they'll kill us now."

"Instead of later?"

He replied, "Later's usually better," but then he looked at her and saw the measure of her distress, laid down his tools and slid off the wing.

"What's the matter?" she asked, unable to see herself.

He came and put his arms around her. Lalo opened his eyes sleepily but didn't seem concerned. "Don't lose it yet," Max told her. "Hang in, honey, lotsa time."

She buried her face between his shoulder and neck. "I finally find somebody I care about, and I get them killed."

He stroked and soothed her, whispering in her ear, until Tony's voice broke in on them. "Whaddaya you doin'?! Get to work, get us outta here."

Still, he hadn't come all the way down to them. Max thought about how often it was that when you had really hurt someone, and gotten away with it, they were always a little leery of you afterwards.

"Ready in an hour or so," he yelled back. "You can start your loading."

Casey called home, meaning the office, and got no response. He tried Earl's residence and got no answer there, which seemed odd as it was such a large tribe. For awhile he tried to think of a friend he might call, but ended by phoning Mary Beth again.

The first couple of minutes were taken up with her screaming at him, demanding to know how could he be away "at a time like this," what was he doing running around the Bahamas having fun "at a time like this," and did he have a "little colored girlfriend" he was visiting over there at "a time like this?"

After he got her halfway calmed, he heard how Earl had been shot twice the previous night by two men who had come into the office pretending to be Miami detectives. No doubt at the exact time that he, Casey, was consuming a tall drink with a little umbrella in it or one of those things that they set fire to . . .

"Did they take anything?" Immediately, he sensed that

this might be construed as insensitive, and attempted to rectify it over her protests by inquiring as to his employee's chances for survival.

Mary Beth said that only the Lord's intervention had given them any reason for hope at all. One shot had struck his metal Moon & Muldoon, Inc., employee badge, which he had always worn so proudly, and been deflected away from the heart. The other round, however, had driven through a lung, creating internal bleeding and giving the doctors considerable cause for concern.

"I trust you are goin' to take care of his medical bills. Poor man has a real big family."

His first impulse was make an argument for birth control, but for once he thought before he spoke. "This might just surprise you, Mary Beth, but our firm has insurance for our employees coverin' every medical eventuality. 'Less he dies, and then all those kids can just go out and dig a big hole in the beach and plunk their daddy in it, 'cause we're not prepared for mortality." And with that, he hung up, proud of having gotten in the last word.

Still, it wasn't just the plane any more, as much as he might deny that to himself. There wasn't going to be any police assistance, either, from here or anywhere else; it was up to him. He hailed a cab for the airport.

Upon arrival Casey went straight to the plane. He wanted to make sure the pump gun was still under the seat where he had hidden it, disassembled. He was busy putting it back together when Billy called to him from in front of the control shack. "Ca-sey!"

"No time now, Billy. I gotta get up."

"I need to see you, mon. 'Bout the account."

"I'll be back."

"No, it must be settled now."

Casey gave in and went over to see Billy. "What the hell you talkin' about?"

"I'm sorry, we can't let you go without you settle this account, Mr. Moon." He went back into the building, assuming Casey would follow.

"We don't have an account," Casey shouted after he had disappeared.

When he thought about it, Billy was behaving very oddly. Was this about bribes? Some official squeeze, keep him at the airport until a price could be arranged?

He went inside to have it out. The door was slammed behind him.

He stopped and stood still. Vigiletti's bodyguard was behind the door. Now he stepped close, reached around an unresisting Casey and removed his pistol from its holster.

The man himself was lolling behind Billy's desk with Joe Peck sitting alongside. The back door opened and three of the surliest-looking garishly-dressed Jamaicans Casey had ever seen, dreadlocks on their heads and automatic weapons in their hands, lounged in from the adjoining shed to sneer at him.

"I'm really sorry, mon," Billy said. "I couldn't do nothing else."

"Hope you know where he is, pal?" Vigiletti said.

"Who?"

That was obviously the wrong answer, because the bodyguard punched Casey hard in the kidneys. He gasped in surpassing pain, slumped to his knees and groaned against every instinct, afraid he would be sick.

"You be pissin' blood for a week," a satisfied Joe Peck told him. "But, see, time's a problem so don't fuck with us."

"I don't even know what you're talkin' about," Casey

maintained, still on his knees, trying to reach one hand around to where it could comfort the damaged kidney.

"Oh, mon, I be so sorry," Billy kept saying off to one side, wringing his hands. Everyone ignored him.

"Yeah, you do," Vigiletti told Casey. Then, to the bodyguard: "Cut off an ear."

The hulk stepped forward and pulled out a switchblade. When it was clicked open, it looked to Casey to be about the size of a saber. The sun coming in a window reflected off the blade, making little suns dart around the room. The bodyguard grabbed his hair with one hand and came at him with the knife. Casey held up a hand just in time. "Wait! Wait a minute."

"Not that long," Joe Peck said.

"This the bank I read about with the plane?"

"Cut it off," Vigiletti said matter-of-factly to the bodyguard.

"Hold it! Hold it! Damn . . . gimme time to think, willya. I just want to say, how it happened, my pilot, worked for me, Max, he was kidnapped by these people. None of us had anythin' to do with it, I swear on the head of my children. Tricked and kidnapped, that's how they got the plane. It was some female. Like always."

If he hoped to establish some sort of male-culture link with that last, it failed. "We don't give a fuck," Joe Peck said scornfully, and then looked at his compatriots. "Why would we give a fuck?"

Vigiletti leaned one elbow on the desk and took off his shades so Casey could see all the killings-past in his adamantine eyes. He pointed a plump finger straight at a point between Casey's. "Only one thing from you. Where's that plane?"

Casey stood, throwing up his hands. "I don't know!

That's the truth of it. You can kill me, torture me, but I still won't know." He could only hope he looked as helpless as he felt. "I had a place where I was goin' out to look when you got me in here. Somewhere I saw the other day and wondered about. Listen, I got a stake in this, too, you know. It was my aircraft they stole. If that was your fifty thousand—"

"Thirty-five million," Joe Peck corrected.

His boss turned on him with a look that could wither cement. "Shut the fuck up, Joey!"

For once, Peccarino looked chagrined.

The effect of his indiscretion was to stop Casey breathing; he had never even thought in terms of that much money. The stakes! These people would kill God for thirty-five million.

Vigiletti had made a decision. "We'll go in your plane. Our pilot says ours's too big to land on these dink islands they got around here."

"How many in the plane?" Casey asked, anxious now to sound cooperative.

Vigiletti looked at Billy, then the bodyguard. "You stay here with the smoke. Keep things quiet, 'cause we gotta come back here we don't wanna go inta Nassau." He instructed Billy, "You wanna live, be an okay guy. Keep it all normal-lookin', that way you and your buddies go on."

"I can take only so many, I'm tellin' you," Casey persisted.

Joe Peck stood and slapped him hard across the face. "Nobody's talkin' to you. You'll take how many we tell you."

Being a stickler for the rules, Casey tried again to impart the realities of flight, and got hit again, this time with a fist that knocked him back down to one knee, giving him a black eye. He grabbed a chair for support.

When in the course of screaming at him Joe Peck incidentally mentioned that there would be seven, Casey decided
that he, and the plane, could live with that since it was de-
signed to seat six. It didn't occur to him until later, and it
wouldn't while he was having his brains pounded like old
meat, that they would also be bringing back the thirty-five
million. But then, they might be counting on fewer people
for the return trip.

Vigiletti told him that time was short and he had better
have the right island, but Casey had already figured that
out. Also the fact that if they brought their own pilot along
they could choose their moment to drop him into the
ocean. Okay, but they'd need a little Windex to get his
brains off the windshield—he wasn't going easy.

XVI

A scuzzy young dope pilot, who claimed his true name was "Rodger Dodger" and seemed amused by that presumption even if no one else was, flew the plane. Over Casey's objections, of course, which had gotten the same hearing as his other objections. Roger had a Rasputin beard and long, presumably blondish-but-too-dirty-to-tell hair bound in a loose pony tail, a personality loose to the point where you had to assume he doubled as a product-tester of the material he transported.

Casey sat beside him, Vigiletti and Joe Peck behind them, two of the rented killers filled the remaining seats and the third sat cross-legged on the floor in the cargo area in the rear of the plane smoking ganja. The Italians had automatic pistols on their persons, the posse members carried a spread composed of an Uzi, a Skorpian and a Kalashnikov assault rifle, all of which they kept in first rate condition, oiling, polishing and checking even as they went to war.

They scarcely spoke to the Italians who were supposed to be their bosses in this, and what they said to each other although putatively English was unintelligible to Casey. Looking very much alike, absent any discernible personality, they most resembled what they were, killing machines in a human form. He doubted they had mothers or names.

As they left the coast of Andros and headed out to sea, Casey felt a totally unfamiliar, ineluctable spurt of something like joy. When what he should have been feeling was fear, anger and despondency at his prospects. But he was in

the air, in the wind, the element where he felt most complete, where he knew that at least a part of him was spirit.
He glanced down and thought that the Caribbean had never
looked so lovely. Was this how you felt when you knew to a
certainty that you were going to die?

Had it been like this for Max, who must have gone
through something similar, forced to fly with a gun to his
head? He suddenly felt this kinship with Max, an extraordinary man, the brother he had never really known and now
had lost.

To avoid going into the tank over poor Max he decided
to be nasty to the pilot. "I guess you see a lot of Colombia
from the air in your job."

The pilot looked at him and said, "Fuck you, man."
That becoming the entire warp and woof of their conversation.

Vigiletti leaned forward to say, "What makes you think
they're out here somewheres?"

Casey leaned back to speak in a loud voice over his
shoulder. "I did a search yesterday and I found this little island. I didn't actually spot any aircraft but there was a place
on the ground that looked kinda like maybe somethin' had
landed there once."

"Yeah," Joe Peck said, "a flyin' saucer."

Vigiletti was in no mood. "Lemme tell you somethin'
that's gonna be news, bigmouth. We don't get it back, the
money, somebody gets bent over. I been told. Who you
figure that's gonna be?"

Fear broke into Joe Peck's cool; even with the free flow
of air through the cabin there was a detectable rancid odor.
"We gotta talk about this, Marty." He looked around as if
thinking of stepping outside for a moment.

"Get the money back, we won't have nothin' to talk

about. We don't, we won't be talkin'. Now you know. Serious business out here today."

"That what we're talking about, babe?" the pilot asked Casey, indicating a green dot on the horizon only a couple of miles off their course on the left.

Casey took up binoculars, pretty sure it was "his island." He had made a mental note of the particular shape of the surrounding coral reef that was discernible through the lucent green water. Even Casey, who was hardly given to philosophical speculation, thought it strange that anywhere so pristine might conceivably hide evil.

On the island itself, Tony, Doc and Jack were standing on the verandah, arguing about how many bags of money they should have. It had all been loaded on the aircraft but Doc said he had counted and they were taking out two fewer than they had brought in. Of course he was drinking long swigs out of a bottle of vodka as he spoke.

It led to a lot of paranoia and loud quarreling about whether one of them had hidden some of it. Either in their possessions or intending to come back for it. Charges and counter charges followed, becoming increasingly noisy and violent.

They could hear it down where Max was cleaning up around the Cessna, collecting tools and stowing them in a container. Lalo was bringing cans of fuel from where it had been buried in the sand on the beach, as he had been for the last hour, and even Diana carried a few loads out of boredom and nervousness.

Max was the first to become aware of the sound of the aircraft. He tried to look up with his eyes only and find it without drawing attention. There it was, coming up from the southwest, no doubt from Andros and straight for them.

The deliberateness of its course confirmed it.

As Lalo came up he heard it too and, alarmed, looked around for some direction. Max was wondering what kind of signal he might get away with when Tony's shout came down from the house.

"Plane! Everybody outta sight, quick. Lalo, watch those two, you hear me?"

Lalo answered with a shout and pulled a .38 revolver, the one he had shown when he was sleeping in the Cessna, urging them under the canopy of branches and fronds. Still, everyone, including the prisoners, strained to peek out from under whatever cover they were utilizing as the plane came closer, descending.

On the verandah there was panic. Clearly whoever was up there was looking for them. Why else would a private plane seek out and fly low over an uninhabited little piece of coral bearing only a ramshackle, disused house? Everyone instinctively had their hand on a weapon.

No one watched with more interest than Max and Diana. She reached out and took his hand. His lips formed the word "Beechcraft" but she was looking up at the plane.

As they circled everyone in it strained to see below except the Jamaicans, who showed no more interest in the landscape that was to be their killing ground than would a falcon or hunting dog. When the prey was sighted they would look.

"I don't see no plane," Vigiletti said.

"Looks like somebody's been hangin' there recently," the pilot said. "But I don't see anywhere you could put a plane down. Don't see a boat, either."

A subdued Joe Peck tried to cover it by asking Casey sarcastically, "You got any more bright ideas?"

Casey said he didn't. "It looks different today somehow."

The pilot said, "So it's not the right island. There's a million of 'em out here. Let's go out farther and make a sweep."

Casey knew it was the island he had been talking about but insisting on it didn't seem like the healthiest choice right now. The pilot banked and started away.

"We better find somethin'," Vigiletti said, without intending it as conversation.

On the verandah they began to relax, but only a little.

"They could come back in boats," Doc said. "Like the one we usta have." He looked at Tony who refused to rise to it.

"They was lookin' for us," Jack said. "Ain't no doubt."

"We're goin'." Tony went back into the house to get the last of his belongings. The other two followed, moving swiftly.

"It's leaving," Diana whispered, digging her nails into Max's hand.

Lalo was still watching the plane go away but his body had gone off point. Max remembered something and knelt beside the tool box. He lifted a tray containing assorted parts and beneath it was a flare gun. He withdrew that and the spanner with it, whispering to Diana, "You run well?"

She had no idea what he was intending but the mere sound of it brought a resurgence of hope. "Many times."

Max stood, everything smooth, measured, and took one silent giant step to within reach of Lalo, then slammed him along the side of his head with the wrench. The Cuban made a horrendous sound but was only staggered. He turned slowly, blood streaming, to grimace at his assailant.

"Jesus," Max said, unbelieving, and hit him again. At

least he had slowed the man's reactions to the extent that he simply took the second blow without defending against it. This time he went down to one knee, but unfortunately the spanner went flying out of Max's hand. Lalo lunged along the ground, reached out and caught his attacker by the legs. Max began to suspect that he had misjudged.

Struggling to remain upright with this boa constrictor winding about his extremities, squeezing them together and preventing him from moving off the spot, he lateraled the flare gun to Diana with his other hand, shouting, "Shoot!"

Grabbing it with both hands, she pointed it skyward and pulled the trigger simply because she didn't know what else to do. The flare rose to an admirable height and blossomed with a bang and a hiss just like fireworks, and that followed immediately by shrieks of rage from up at the house.

Seizing their weapons, the three poured out onto the verandah, leaped off of it and went pelting down the path, Tony screaming that this time he would kill Max. This time, no contradiction.

Lalo finally succumbed to at least the accumulation of blows, his grip slipping away but slowly. Max tried to kick his legs free like a broken-field runner caught in a tackle, yelling all the while for Diana to go. She refused to leave him, instead picked up a heavy branch and began hitting Lalo's arms. Finally Max broke loose with only seconds to spare.

Grabbing her hand he pulled her from the path and into the bush just as a burst from Tony's MAC-11 shredded wood and leaves, sending shards flying all around their heads. Much too close to have been meant as a shot over the bow; a blood lust running now that was indifferent to consequences.

"Take it back!" Casey said with authority that, if nothing else, grabbed attention. He had been the only one looking behind them because he was the only one who was certain that was the right island.

"Whatsa matter with you?" Vigiletti rasped. Fear had grown with a clearer view of his own destiny forming out there in the glare of an empty horizon, grown to where it blinded him to any overtures, even hopeful ones.

The pilot looked where Casey had indicated. "What's that?" He was already banking to come around when he asked.

"That's Max."

"What kinda bullshit is this?" Vigiletti demanded.

"That's what he'd do. That's Max."

The plane headed back and went down again, everyone except the Jamaicans craning forward.

"I think you're fulla shit," Vigiletti said, "an' lemme tell you, we go back without the money, you don't go with us."

Casey felt compelled to say, "I got a wife and two little kids."

"I'm cryin'. I got five."

"Vig, lookit," Joe Peck said, pointing down.

As they approached the house there were running figures on the ground, first two, dodging in and out of the bush, appearing and disappearing, and then three more at some distance behind, but all seemingly oblivious of the plane overhead. They were running, that was enough.

"Take us down there," Vigiletti ordered.

The tone of his voice made the pilot try very hard to find somewhere that was, if not suitable, at least possible. His practiced eye swept the whole island. "Mr. Vigiletti, in my line of work you land in a whole lotta funny places . . . but there isn't anywhere."

"Find somewhere."

"I'm telling you, that's a body-bagger if I try to put it in down there." Desperation had made him bold.

"We don't get the money back, whaddaya think's gonna happen to all a us anyway?"

"I'm just a pilot, Mr. Vigiletti, I'm not a part of it. Please . . ."

"I know where," Casey said. "Gimme the controls." He looked back at Vigiletti. "That all right with you?"

"Somebody better." He had the automatic out now, his badge of authority.

Jack said prison had made him forget how to run, he was huffing and coughing. Tony told him to go back and see what could be done for Lalo; they could use another beater out here.

Doc pointed. "They seen the goddamn flare. They're comin' back."

Tony, watching the plane, wondered out loud, "Who the fuck? Okay, gotta get these two. Then I'm gonna put the muzzle a this"—he brandished the MAC-11—"up her cunt and leave it till we get to Mexico. He'll do what he's told. That way." He swept the air with his hand. "Divide up. Nail 'em against the beach."

Max and Diana were still on their run, but the sandy, scrubby terrain made for hard going, full of little dips and rises and vines that were usually not seen until you were tangled in them. There was not the density of trees that would constitute good cover in many places so they had to stay low and keep dodging.

At a point as far as you could get from the house in one direction on this small island, they had to decide which way to go while sticking to the shoreline. Diana, breathing hard, flopped down to rest. Reluctantly, Max joined her.

"What's the good, Max? Are we going to just keep

running around this island in a circle?"

"If we have to. That was Casey's plane up there."

"So what? It went away."

"No, I can hear it. He's coming back."

"But there's nowhere to land. And if he goes for help he'll never get back before—"

She broke off at the sound of Doc's voice, distant though not distant enough.

"I think I see 'em," he cried out to someone.

"Oh, God," Diana groaned, as Max hauled her up roughly and started them running again. Once she got going, she was, true to her promise, a swift runner.

Thirty seconds later Doc and Tony, in tandem again, stumbled into the same area, fatigued, carrying heavy metal, of course, but mainly betraying their urban origins. It had been a long time since either of them had run anywhere. Tony was driven by rage that, as much as anything, had turned his skin a kind of dark purple, a color threatening an implosion, and Doc by greed which had sucked his lungs dry and turned him pale, but neither motivation made them any faster.

Casey knew exactly what he wanted to do, the only choice. A cold euphoria swept over him, a literal sense of the body cooling, eyes becoming keener, narrower in focus, nerves singing a song of restoration, severely tight yet beautifully controlled. The same way it had worked for Max, for a thousand pilots.

Max, maybe a mixed blessing but still a part of the firm, an employee, trapped down there on that tiny piece of real estate with no other hope save his reaching him somehow.

"What're you doin'?" someone demanded, and someone else asked, "Why's he smilin'?" Casey didn't have time to worry about who was unhappy. They would have to take the risk with him whether they liked it or not.

"Hey, hey, hey . . . ?" Vigiletti said. The pilot joined the chorus, a tenor reaching for soprano, "You can't land on that, man!" Even the Jamaicans were making noises.

A beach was rushing up at them at seemingly incredible speed, like the dramatic charge of some exotic long white animal intent upon eating them. Casey threw the switch to lower the landing gear and the sound of it going down escalated the panic.

"You know what you're doin'?!" Vigiletti asked in a kind of interrogatory shriek.

"You better hope so." Vigiletti's terror exhilarated him. "It's just a big aircraft carrier." He cackled, raising hair on hoodlum necks, and added, "With sand."

The formidable surf reared up hugely in the windshield to where it seemed they might reach out and touch it just before they went straight and deep into its viscera.

But they didn't, Casey put it exactly where he wanted it, at the waterline, where the sand was packed hard and the shallow water would provide a slight drag without causing them to somersault. He had got the nose up at just the last second and barely grazed the surface of the water while reaching for the sand.

It sounded like a pancake landing, a mighty "whomp!" causing a violent spume of water and sand to cascade all around and over the plane. After that, it was thrown back by the propeller and wheels while he tried to fight the plane to a standstill. A spectacular watery rooster tail with a rainbow soared behind.

Sand whacked at the windows as if thrown by a catapult. Even the pilot covered his eyes. The hoodlums managed to suppress their terror once it was upon them, merely squeaking and grunting a little and keeping the volume low. Slowly the plane shuddered to a crawl. Finally it stopped and the prop was idled.

They climbed out cautiously. Everyone except Casey and the pilot had a weapon in their hand when they alighted. There was a moment where they froze, silent, while they listened and took stock. No sounds of alarm anywhere.

This was a new kind of warfare for all of them, even the Jamaicans to an extent. Vigiletti showed some instincts in sending one of them up into the growth that lined the beach in order to guard against surprise. They checked out their weapons, Joe Peck bringing a sawed-off shotgun to the party, everyone taking a large supply of ammo in pouches and pockets. Clearly they were expecting a war.

"You stay here," Vig told the pilot, "with him," indicating Casey. He turned to Joe Peck. "Give him your .32. Anyone comes," he said, turning back to the pilot, "kill 'em. Anyone, you understand that?"

"Hey, listen, man, I'm just a pilot, not a—"

Vigiletti hit him in the mouth, bloodying it and sending a five-hundred-dollar cap flying through the air. It was a good shot for an aging overweight father of five but it didn't justify the result—the pilot staggered backwards and then fell, sprawling with outstretched arms. The fall had been deliberate; like Diana, he knew he was safer supine, baring his throat to the alpha wolf.

No one else was surprised. Vigiletti stepped over him, saying, "I told you what to do, do it," and went on up the beach, the others in the raiding party following.

Casey, remaining with the plane, remembered the shotgun hidden under the seat, but it was not to be. At the tree line Vigiletti stopped and called back to him, "You know, it's better you come with us."

233

Casey reluctantly fell into line. The trek inland would have had the appearance of a guerrilla column save for Vigiletti's brown and yellow check sport jacket.

Diana and Max had heard the plane coming down at the opposite end of the island but had no idea as to whether it had landed safely or what it might mean for them if it had. Having no way of knowing the pursuit was off, they kept right on running, stumbling to nowhere with aching lungs and limbs that threatened to go south any instant.

Jack and a patched-up Lalo, having scouted closer to the beach where the aircraft had landed, failed to hear anything that sounded like a crash. More alarming were several voices, none sounding *in extremis*. It was enough to send them scurrying off in search of the others, calling out their names until they found them.

Tony immediately called off the chase. With enemies already on the island, there was no hope of capturing Max in time to get away. He asked himself what Caesar or Hannibal, backs to the wall, would do, and decided to go on the offensive.

He addressed his troops in the clearing in front of the house. "Hey, we don't know who they are, but who the fuck cares? How many can they get in that little airplane, huh? That's the big thing here. 'Cause there's four a us, right? We can handle it. We take down this crew and we're outta here. Outta here and rich!"

Jack nodded, Doc blew his continually dripping nose but no one said anything. Lalo was ordered back to determine who were the invaders and how were they armed. The rest were to spread out and ambush them when they came, as they were bound to, in the direction of the house.

Tony kept the need of his heart to himself, one fixed

234

idea, to lead the invaders away from the airplane and the millions already loaded. Over the past weeks he had succumbed to the grip of a powerful obsession, a criminal apotheosis that pinned his whole life on this one score as if it were something for history, the discovery of the General Theory of Relativity, a cure for cancer, conquering Rome. If not, better they should all die.

Antonio Ciufini, third son of Angelo and Carmela Ciufini of Brooklyn, New York, had stumbled upon and embraced the most dangerous sentiment of all—glory!

Max tripped, banging previously damaged ribs against a coconut log and Diana had to help him up in order to get them going again in a hurry. With him staggering, they zigzagged through scrub to reach a copse of pine, and then Diana fell. This time they both stayed down, laboring for breath as quietly as they could.

Max yanked off his shirt, suggesting that they might both tie them around their heads to keep the sun off. He crafted his version of the "Bedouin Look" and leaned back against a tree to rest.

Diana's turban carried more chic but left her in her brassiere. Modeling, she said, prepared you for running around in your underwear.

She flopped onto her back, indifferent to the sand that stuck in her hair, on her skin and in her clothes, and regarded Max's turban with desperate amusement. Pointing, she had to stifle a giggle and soon had Max threatening to do the same. Pure hysteria.

"We better go," he said, shaking it off but unable to rise, holding his ribs.

"Where?"

"I don't know."

"I can't run any more, Max."

"You can always run more. I'm living proof of that."

He raised his head and listened to distant yelling, shots. Instantly energized and grabbing up her hand, he started them moving. "Back to the house. Find some weapons, or maybe I can jump one of them."

She struggled along painfully, gasping, "*We'll* jump them, Max," while flailing the free hand at her hair, trying to shake out the sand.

They left the water's edge and turned inland, seizing on a narrow, overgrown footpath. A few minutes along and Diana grabbed Max's arm to hiss, "Lookout!"

At a distance but directly in front of them loomed the figure of a man, silhouetted by light that streamed through some palms behind him but with the face in shadow. They froze momentarily, before Max tumbled them both into a small depression having the dimensions of a shallow foxhole, pressing down hard to prevent their bodies from showing above the lip.

"Who?" she whispered in his ear.

He shook his head. "Coming this way."

"Oh, God."

Max pushed her head down and edged his upwards, straining to see without being seen. He was just starting to get a fix on the man when pistol shots came from behind them. Max ducked and tried to throw his body over Diana's in that cramped space.

Someone came thumping close by on their left. When they looked again, it was Lalo advancing at a kind of trot that shook the ground in the direction where the silhouetted man had been. He passed within a few yards and, had he looked down, would have seen them easily. Both swallowed their breath and held it down; Diana closed her eyes.

Lalo paused and fired a shot from his Smith & Wesson, a weapon absurdly unsuited for combat on open ground. There were answering shots and Lalo, past them now, fired again, twice. He would have to reload after six, yet he continued to move forward. Max and Diana heard someone cry out in pain, then a roar of anger from a third presence.

Without knowing about the Jamaicans, Max detected some sort of accent. There was an answering burst from something heavy and when next he looked it was to see one of the Rastamen limping away in pain and another firing a Kalashnikov.

There was another shout or very loud grunt and Lalo fell from behind a small tree where he had sought cover by turning himself sideways. The AK-47 rounds had passed through the tree. He fired two or three more shots out of reflex as he went down. No sooner had he struck the earth than he struggled back up to one knee and fumbled with his buck knife. Either he had used whatever ammunition he had or he was too hurt to reload.

The Rastaman shot him again, then rushed over and did a little dance while firing into him as he lay prone, bouncing the body up and down and raising dust around it. When that paled, he kicked his victim several times, shouting insults. Max thought he caught the word "Motherfucker"—why not? the universal pejorative—pronounced with something like a working class British accent and, having spotted the dreadlocks, understood now.

He wished he knew why they had arrived in Casey's plane; he couldn't think of any way that was good. A horrified Diana covered her face and made sounds of revulsion; he put them both back into their hole and squeezed her tightly, hand over her mouth.

More shots in the distance, some automatic, some

single. Max thought he had heard the MAC-11 and a shotgun, and possibly that played-with carbine of Jack's but he was no expert on weaponry and the sounds overlapped. Was it coming their way?

No sign of the two Jamaicans. "Stay here." He scrambled out onto level ground and ran, bent over, to where Lalo lay, still breathing but on the way to death. The gun was empty and, as he had feared, there was no more ammunition in the pockets. While he was struggling through them Lalo made a hideous gurgling sound and half-rolled over, popping his eyes open for an instant. It made even Max, who had an intimate relationship with violent death, wince.

He tried to wipe off the blood he had accrued from touching him and, taking the knife, ran back to Diana.

"No bullets."

"Who were those men?"

"Nothing good."

"That's who's come to save us?"

"C'mon, let's keep going for the house."

He gripped her firmly to overcome what he saw as an ominous passivity, but she went without hesitation.

Casey had found himself being prodded along through the center of the island by Vigiletti and Joe Peck, the latter two stumbling, lurching, swearing, actively hating the primitive environment. The Jamaicans were dispatched to make a sweep.

The Vigiletti party managed to move more or less steadily in the direction of the house. Not having spotted the Cessna, it was the only objective they could think of. The boss carried a Ruger pistol and Joe Peck his sawed-off shotgun. Listening to distant gunfire in this heated atmosphere made them jittery enough to blow up anything that moved.

One thing they were not was quiet, tramping on dried palm leaves and kicking vegetation out of the way, complaining out loud. Casey knew better but wasn't going to say anything that might save their lives, even at the risk of his own. They started across a small clearing.

Suddenly, there he was, Tony, seeming to loom hugely as he stepped out of the trees opposite. The only thing that saved them was that Tony proved to be more mobster than Che Guevara. Having all three dead in front of his MAC-11 with a full clip, he chose to stop and shout insults so they would know who killed them. "Hey, Vig! Fuck you, you loser!"

By the time he got off a burst all of his targets were halfway to the ground. Even on urban streets you knew enough to hit the concrete when facing a gun. It was a long burst, using up a lot of ammo, and savaged the shrubbery all around where their heads and torsos had been. Some of it rained slowly down on their prone figures. The rest of the clip was spit at them in fragments, sending up little geysers of sand but failing to hit anyone.

When Casey raised his sand-covered face to see over Vigiletti's bulky figure, he caught a glimpse, a fragment of purple shirt, across the clearing. His impression was that it was moving away from them. Running. Probably trying to reload as he went.

Vigiletti agreed. "Get the cocksucker," he shouted to Peccarino, who fired off a round with the shotgun and then went clumping after. Grunting and puffing, Vigiletti pulled himself up and lumbered behind; he wasn't hugely fat but it still suggested a hippo running. Casey stood and looked around. He was alone.

XVII

Max and Diana reached the clearing that surrounded the house just in time to see Doc come stumbling and lurching from a different direction. He was being pursued by the Jamaican with the Uzi who loped so easily across country while firing short, controlled bursts from the hip that you had to wonder if he wasn't playing with his victim. Especially as Doc was clumsily returning the fire with his Magnum, a powerful gun at close range but another bad choice for combat.

More than halfway across the clearing, with the house tantalizingly close, Doc tripped on a tree root. The Jamaican closed rapidly to within easy range for his weapon. Doc tried to aim and fire at him but the chamber clicked on empty. Prone and propped on one elbow he fumbled in his pockets for some more bullets.

He never would have gotten it loaded in time and would have died right there, but Jack Biggers came running from the house in a Kamikaze charge, a true berserker. "You want my money, nigger? Come and get it!"

Looking out from behind a fallen tree facing the side of the house, Max and Diana watched. Even from here they thought they could see amphetamine at work. Nothing either of them had witnessed previously would explain all that crazed speed and energy on the way to self-destruction.

Jack kept firing as he ran and the Jamaican, surprised, frozen in place for a moment, finally managed to fire a burst. Jack was hit full in the chest, so that it was impossible

240

to imagine his frail body continuing to function, but it did. He staggered, fired again, looking straight ahead, seeking his opponent's eyes even at a considerable distance. After firing several rounds he at last stumbled to a stop and, weaving, stood there a moment before flopping to the ground like a wind-blown scarecrow.

Max couldn't understand why he had been allowed to remain on his feet so long, why the Jamaican hadn't simply blown him away. But when they looked, he was sitting on the ground just out from the tree line, holding his belly, looking down at it with his mouth a perfect "O" expressing amazement at the prospect of his own death. When finally he fell over and lay there in the hot sun, his chest heaving, insects instantly swarmed on the blood.

Max actually got them up for the rush to the house, but caught sight of Doc disappearing inside. Now Vigiletti and Joe Peck appeared amongst the palms and shrubs fronting it. Unknowns to Max and Diana, they were nevertheless a flagrant threat.

The third Jamaican arrived now at the edge of the clearing to one side, then moved along behind the cover of scrub to join his employers in the center, all the while supporting or dragging the one wounded by Lalo. Diana whispered that she thought she saw blood on both of them. Max thought not.

The sound of breaking glass at the house indicated that Doc had spotted them, too. Pretty soon he was keeping up a steady rate of fire. Obviously he had found some other weapons.

It was difficult to tell whether it was one or two men firing from inside. Maybe Tony was there; someone was shouting out threats and insults, but the voice, too, was difficult to make out. Could be that Doc was trying to make it appear there were more.

Max said maybe now that the house was lost to them, they could slip away and run for the plane.

Someone was coming up behind them, running, cutting them off so that they had to go to ground again. Having no idea as to how many gunmen had come to the island, they clawed their bodies as deeply as possible into the sandy soil under the log.

The runner seemed to be zigzagging, a good idea for anyone, but his course brought him relentlessly towards where they crouched. The steps would draw nearer, then go off on a tangent, raising hopes, only to come towards them again. Now they could hear the man's snorting and huffing, the engine of an oncoming train when you can't get off the tracks. Diana covered her ears with her hands, her eyes already deep in the sand. Max pulled a large palm frond over their hiding place and prepared his muscles to bring himself up fast.

Like all confluences that portend collision and seem inevitable, this one was. The man ran right into their nest, tumbling onto their prostrate forms when the foot that was intended to propel him over the log instead sunk into their soft flesh. He let out a panicky yell as he crumpled. Max managed to half-turn his body despite the weight and put his hands out for the man's throat before the news could reach his central nervous system that this was Casey.

"Muldoon, you dumb bastard!" Casey said, gargling his indignation.

Max, relieved, could only smile and murmur, "Jesus Christ."

"Oh, my God," Diana said, "it's you. You brought all these killers?!"

Casey demanded of Max, "What's she doin' with you??"

Max told them both to shut up while he reared his head

to look for any sign that they had been spotted.

The firing had become desultory on both sides for the moment, an occasional round coming from the house but almost none from the vegetation along the edge of the clearing.

Casey wanted explanations on the spot but Max cut him off. "We don't go for it now we won't have a prayer."

"Where's my goddamn airplane?"

"Way the other side of the house. There's a camouflaged strip—"

Casey raised his voice again: "You brought it in here??"

"Yeah," Max said, "twice. And it's ready to go up again. Where's yours?"

"Mine's—they're both mine, dammit—on the beach on the south side. But it's guarded and I don't know—" He was staring at Diana. "She's okay?" he demanded.

"Yeah," Max said absently, "she's okay," starting to get up.

Diana grabbed his shoulder to pull him down as a loud, extended clatter of gunfire from more than one weapon sounded within the house. Front windows were blown out and smoke and dust erupted from them. Someone began howling. A series of crashes and bangs, then curses. The climax came when the one healthy Jamaican strutted from the main entrance grinning and brandishing his weapon above his head to signal a victory.

"Shit," Max said. No one knew exactly who was accounted for and who wasn't, but there was no time to worry about it now. With one mind they took off back into the bush, Diana between the two men, and started their run for the plane.

If they had remained, they would have seen Vigiletti and Joe Peck come out of the brush, their city clothes and even their faces torn and dirtied, with only their zealous hate to give them any dignity at all.

The Jamaican went back into the house and dragged out his trophy, the still twitching but very shot-up body of Doc, trailing a dark red smear across the floor of the verandah. Though the Italians bellowed for him to desist, he booted his victim several times and then spat on him before crowing his triumph to the setting sun. Doc was the only one who didn't care either way.

On their long trek circumventing the house to the landing strip, Max, Diana, and Casey had to fight exhaustion, but what oppressed them most was the silence. No more gunshots. Fighting over, the thoughts of these men, who had come to kill everyone on the island, would naturally turn to those who were unaccounted for. And the money, which was packed in the plane. The gunmen could already be on their way.

When they got to the landing strip, it took ten minutes for the three of them to clear the major pieces of camouflage off the plane and remove any obstacles from its path. Max climbed in first and Diana followed. Casey stood for a moment looking at the so-called runway, disbelieving. He wet his finger and put it in the air.

When he got into the cockpit, he found Max in the pilot's seat and ordered him out. Max argued reasonably that he was better equipped because he had already landed and taken off from here. Casey said that he was the better pilot, and besides it was his plane and he didn't believe for a minute that Max had ever landed it here. Diana blew and began screaming that someone had better get them off the fucking ground or she would take over the controls herself.

"Okay," Max said with a shrug.

Amazingly Doc was still alive. Vigiletti shoved the Jamaican aside roughly when the latter seemed prepared to pump more rounds into his victim.

Kneeling, Vig whispered in a voice like crunched gravel, "Where's the money you stole from us?"

Doc looked up at him blankly.

"The money, asshole?" When he didn't get an answer he pulled out his Ruger and put it to one of Doc's staring eyes. "You wanna die?"

Something like a grotesque laugh bubbled up through the bloody spume. "Whaddaya call this?" Doc said, barely audible, and made the sound again.

Joe Peck, having quickly surveyed the rest of the house, was standing over them, looking down. He kicked Doc a couple of times. "You can feel pain, can't you?"

"Feel . . . nothin' . . ."

Vigiletti leaned close and gripped Doc by the collar of his sport shirt. "The money." An ominous rattling began in Doc's throat. Vigiletti, not knowing what to do, fell back on old forms. "Listen, I'll find your family. You got kids? I'll find 'em. I'll kill your dog. I'll bury you head-down in pig shit." Finally he yelled in frustration. "Where's the fuckin' money??"

"Got . . . any . . . blow?"

Though it was barely intelligible, it was enough to provoke Vigiletti to stand and shoot him several times. Then he leaned over and asked the question again. The answer came in a faint whistle of escaping air and gasses that signaled Doc had gone to the Great Coca.

"Nothin' inside," Joe Peck said. He looked at the fury and bewilderment on his boss's face, enjoyed the moment and then added, "But . . ." He let it hang there for a couple of seconds, until it was dangerous not to go on, ". . . There's stuff packed, baggage like, so they musta been just ready to leave. I dunno how."

"There's gotta be a plane."

The Jamaican had seen it.

"Strap in," Casey, always a stickler for the forms, insisted.

"Just get the goddamned thing in the air," Max said, as he twisted in his co-pilot seat to help Diana behind him do hers. Looking at her he laughed; he couldn't help himself; she had finally managed to look like someone who had been pulled through a swamp by their feet. Casey, oblivious to everything except the aircraft now that he was in his role, started the engines.

The propellers began to whine and turn slowly. Casey never spoke unnecessary words at a time like this; it was unprofessional. He did, surprisingly, speak to Max, "It feels heavy."

"How can you tell? We haven't moved." Max slapped his head like a Levantine. "Aw, shit! The money! The bank money's on here. Thirty-five million in bills."

For the second time that day Casey was stunned by the reciting of a sum. He stuttered badly when he tried to say "thirty-five million dollars," never quite getting it out.

"We had the same problem after the bank," Max said. "The dumb bastards wouldn't throw out a nickel and it nearly got us killed." He started undoing his seatbelt. "I'll get rid of it."

Casey got one word out all right: "No!"

Max stopped. "What?" he shouted over the accelerating engines.

Diana pleaded with Casey, pointing out what should have been obvious, their lives were more important than pieces of green paper no matter what their worth.

"If either of you touch that money I'll shoot you." It didn't seem to occur to anyone, including him, that he didn't have a gun. "Get in your damn seat, Muldoon." Max sat back. "I'll get us outta here. If you did, anyone can."

Finally he just clamped his jaw down hard and started to taxi. Through flying, he could disassociate himself from the wholly unsettling fantasy of unimaginable wealth a mere few feet away.

Adjusting slightly to improve the angle for takeoff, he raced the engines and shouted a suggestion to the others that they pray. Having meant it literally, he began one himself.

All Max heard was something about being in a little boat on a big sea but it did sound like Casey was doing enough for all of them. Just to be safe, he said a "Hail Mary" himself under his breath.

Casey's religious fervor scared Diana, who whispered, "Jesus, he thinks we're gonna crash."

Max was trying to reassure her that Casey, being very pious, did this with every takeoff when the first bullet hit the cabin. The shot had been muffled by the engine sound. Max darted a look out the window and saw Vigiletti firing with his pistol. Joe Peck was just bringing up his short-ranged sawed-off and behind them, still at some distance back in the bush, the Jamaican hurrying forward while jamming a clip into the submachine gun.

"Go!" Max shouted into Casey's ear. Throttle wide open, they tore down the "runway," bouncing on the uneven ground and occasional small obstacles but Casey with a master's grip on the reins.

Like Max at the bank, he had made a calculated decision not to hold back anything; no last minute change of mind would be possible, get up on the first try or die.

Just as the plane reached the end of the runway, it began to lift, dragging some vines with it. They were slow falling away, then it brushed the top branches of trees and, finally, when it dipped dangerously low, the ocean spray. But in the end the aerodynamics were right, the props clawed at the air and pulled the plane skyward.

Everyone was too limp to cheer. Collectively they settled back in silence, breathing again, deeply, enjoying each breath. It didn't seem important to look around and ascertain the situation on the ground; that was irrelevant now. It was enough to be free in a clean cerulean sky, turning gracefully to follow the lingering sun westward, trailed by shadows on a sea of lavender, pink and twilight gray.

Behind them even the Jamaican, Jimmy Postlewaite, whose code when he was working on loan-out from his posse was to ask nothing and see nothing but the objective, was consumed now by rage and despair. Vigiletti recovered quickly and ordered that they reclaim their "own" airplane, the Beechcraft, and pursue. Joe Peck reminded him that the pilot had said they would never get it up off that beach.

Vigiletti said the pilot was a pussy and they were going anyway. As soon as he caught his breath. He was clutching his ample ribcage, gasping, color alternately filling and draining from his face in mortal tides.

For the first time the Jamaican had begun to suspect how much he or his comrades were worth to these Italians. Now he demanded to know what they intended to do about his wounded friend, left near the house when they set off for here.

When Vigiletti said, without pretending that he cared, the man would die anyway and to leave him behind, Jimmy's response was to point his automatic weapon at

Vigiletti's genitals. He had heard that Italians had a special affection, greater even than most men, for this organ, and it was indicated by the fact that they were often seen on the streets grabbing it to make some sort of statement.

The other two sputtered but they caved quickly; it was conceded that Joe Peck would go with him to help carry the wounded man to the beach and, not so incidentally, to act as a hostage. A wider knowledge of the world would have spared Jimmy his next mistake; he assumed that the issue had been decided, therefore they were once again working together.

All for one and one . . . He had never heard of Machiavelli.

Vigiletti went ahead to secure the plane and its flaky pilot, literally grinding his teeth as he tramped through the tropical brush, curses rumbling up from his belly like gas at the thought of himself taking orders from a colored. Consoled only by a silent promise to kill him the first time he turned his back.

It might be that Joe Peck, who had witnessed all this and was an insolent prick anyway, would have to be put down, too. It was a matter of being able to hold up one's head on the streets of Bayonne.

Vigiletti need not have worried. As the other two dragged up the path to the house, Joe was feeling unbearably hot, fatigued and disgraced. Their chances of getting the money back were obviously attenuating. It was all the boss's fault; Vig had screwed up royally and placed them both in deep shit. A man who always liked to have a lot of options, Joe had suddenly found himself with very few. Hope of forgiveness on the part of the Messinas was not one of them.

Run was one choice. Die another. Or, if he ratted to the feds he could probably get in the Program okay, but you ended up packing lettuce in Omaha and jumping on forest fires the rest of your life. If that wasn't enough, here he was playing ambulance attendant for a couple of smokes. It was degrading.

Thinking, as it always did, was getting him highly agitated. Like Jack Biggers, he knew what he needed—what action would clear his head and cleanse a gangster soul—to kill somebody. He wanted to feel good again.

At the house he thought he could already smell the dead bodies cooking in the sun. Joe was hardly squeamish but he did feel that there was something unnatural about death out in nature; the place was beginning to get to him. They found the wounded Jamaican by following his moans, as he had instinctively crawled into some shrubbery to hide, and lifted him not gently for the long haul to the beach.

Jimmy naturally wanted the Italian walking in front of him where he could see him—he was not that incautious—so hefted his friend under the arms, leaving the feet for Joe. That suited Peccarino just fine. Since the Jamaican had taken on the heaviest burden it was necessary for him to attach the gun to his belt. Joe Peck, on the other hand, was able to cradle his lupo under one arm. They began trudging back along the route they had come with a long way to go, all the while with the wounded man groaning and spitting up blood.

In addition to the other discomforts, and Peccarino was not accustomed to physical labor beyond carrying a case of something in or out of the back of a restaurant, he found it impossible to keep the insects off his face as they staggered along. He hated bugs!

But he knew what he had to do and wearing the other man down was part of it. His purpose, and here he was experienced, lay in shaving seconds or even fragments of them from the Jamaican's reflexes, from his acuity.

Forget honor for the moment, and taking orders from a dinge, if it was going to be difficult to get up off that beach like the pilot had complained, two more people wouldn't make it any easier. Besides, this stud was bound to demand that they take his buddy to a hospital or some craziness like that.

Postlewaite's labored breathing could be heard over that of his wounded comrade's, and when the former stumbled a bit that was the Italian's cue. He jerked forward, pulling Jimmy's arms away from his body, and then dropped the wounded man, who screamed in pain when his friend, struggling to keep up, lost him too.

That time the other spent trying to compensate and prevent the helpless Jamaican from striking the ground was all Peccarino needed. He spun, the sawed-off immediately slipping down into his hands, and fired one shot. It wasn't necessary to aim at six feet.

All he saw in front of him before the blast ripped Jimmy apart were two wildly expanding eyes and hands flung up in entreaty. There had never been a hope of his getting at the Skorpian. Dreadlocks springing loose as if hit with fifty thousand volts, Postlewaite's body was lifted up and jerked backwards, spraying blood and small pieces of him on the trees, ground and even Joe Peck.

The latter jumped away, instinctively concerned about his clothes even though they were already badly used. The shot echoed like an explosion all through the island and left a desolate silence in its wake. Even Peccarino was paralyzed for a moment.

He was brought back to the world by a cry from the man they had been carrying, still sprawled where dropped, looking up at him and pleading with his eyes, his mouth working spasmodically. Peccarino realized that he had never reloaded the shotgun after he fired at Tony in that clearing. He dug into his pockets and withdrew two more shells, inserted them into the chamber.

What the hell did the man expect, that he should be left there perhaps to recover? And they were supposed to be so "baaad." Joe Peck would have known better.

The air and sky were soft, Casey cruised at ten thousand feet, uncharacteristically in no particular hurry, humming snatches of *Oklahoma* under his breath in tune with the smoothly running engines. That was a pleasant surprise; he had assumed all along that anything under Max's aegis for several days would have to be in a state of advanced deterioration.

Distracted by the euphoria of their escape and chatting eagerly with Diana behind him, it took a few minutes for Max to realize that Casey was heading back to the airport on Andros, and to challenge him on it.

"We gotta go to Andros," Casey said. "There's one of these bastards there holdin' Billy at gunpoint."

"Casey, you're worrying about somebody else? As amazed and touched as I am, I got to point out a couple of things. The Bahamians'll hold us for a year while they sort this mess out. That means they hold the money for investigation, too, and that'll take about a hundred years, at which time it'll only be a memory anyway."

Casey went "Hmmm," and then found that he could at last say the words, "Th-th-thirty-five million dollars," without trauma. He began testing them in different rhythms, tonalities, and colors, trying them on this way and that. Billy's name seemed to have been forgotten.

Max suggested they simply make an anonymous radio

call to Nassau to report that there was a terrorist holding the airport manager on Andros prisoner. Casey liked that and put it through. Afterwards, he set a course direct to Key West.

Max had another idea. "I better get busy dumping the money."

"Dump . . . the . . . money?!" In a voice that erupted in shrillness with each word, Casey asked him if he was joking or insane? "You just said we'd lose it if we went to Andros!"

"The idea's nobody should ever know we had it."

Max's tone was so reasonable and full of assumed understanding that it threatened to drive Casey mad. He began to screech and yell and wave his arms, an unnerving sight in a man who's flying an airplane and one that greatly alarmed Diana. She yelled at him to calm down, before turning on Max and demanding to know if he *was* insane?

"It's mob money, for Christ's sake. If we keep it, they'll hunt us down wherever we go and as long as it takes. They got very long memories, those guys. Somebody's gonna have to die when it's this kind of money. Ask yourself, how could any of us spend it without drawing attention?"

Casey started to argue again, but Max nailed him with the clincher, "The rest of your life, you'll be afraid to have little Jane and Bucky ride in the same car with you. Or some day Mary Beth'll be in a hurry to get the kids to school, she'll forget and take your car. You want that?"

It worked, the deliberate infusion of the kids' names had turned the key. Casey moaned and cursed but he was beaten.

"Boy, you guys give up easy," Diana said, "we could run, we could hide." But she knew better and sighed, "I never had anything anyway."

The only person to disagree with the decision was Tony C.

XVIII

When Vigiletti, limping, puffed onto the beach where the Beechcraft rested, another disaster awaited him.

"Heeeeey, bro . . . The big man! The bossman." Roger threw his head back like a coyote. "The boss of bosses *di tutti di* bosses." That made him giggle. "Biiiiiig bosses—you dudes eat too much pasta, man. Always eatin' . . ." He dropped his head between his knees.

"What the fuck's the matter with you?" Vig demanded, squinting at him as he approached. "Get in the plane."

"Whoooaah! I don't need no fuckin' plane. I'm already airborne, man . . ." He cackled while Vigiletti stood over him, unbelieving, his face on fire.

Rodger Dodger was squatting on a coconut log resembling nothing so much as a stoned grasshopper, arms and legs pointing at four angles, head bobbing, wearing only his jockey shorts and a silly smile. Having felt himself under a certain strain, he had exhausted his small supply of coke, popped some ludes, had a ganja doobie dangling between his bruised lips and several butts in the sand under his wiggling bare feet. His toes jumped up and down like the keys of a player piano, a sight that revolted Vigiletti.

When Rodger kept grinning and licked at the blood from his last encounter with this boss, the Italian determined that the solution was to give him some more to work on; he picked him up by the hair and slapped him with an open hand, this over and over again while screaming every obscenity he could think of in two languages.

254

At first, the pilot, anesthetized, reacted only slightly to the pain and refused to sober up even when he was covered with new blood. Unlike his underboss, Vig didn't care if he got it on his clothes; his wife always said, "Cold water."

After the tenth blow, when Vig's hand was starting to swell though he wasn't half appeased, the pilot complained, "You shouldn't of hit me back there"—never mind that his face was at this very moment being converted to *papier-mâché*— "I got my pride, man. I'm a professional . . ."

"I'm gonna kill you. I'm gonna kill you!" Vigiletti kept yelling over him, spit flying.

"Let that other asshole . . . flyer . . . take you . . . I'm stayin'. I like it . . . here . . ." He drifted into song, "Sweet Lelani."

In his frustration, Vig resorted to his fists until he had knocked out two teeth and the man was an unconscious pile at his feet. He tried kicking him awake and probably would have killed him if Joe Peck hadn't appeared, running onto the beach, shouting for him to stop.

Joe went so far as to push his boss away from the scene. Snorting, Vigiletti looked for a moment as if he might kill him instead, but sanity clicked in and he began working to calm himself, stomping around in tight circles, his chest heaving dramatically.

When Joe Peck was satisfied that it was safe to turn his back, he picked up Roger, dragged him down to the water's edge and threw him head-first into the surf. Then waded in and sat on him. When the pilot's head came up to vomit salt water Joe would let him finish, but then shove him under again.

It both mollified Vigiletti's anger and served to bring the pilot at least part of the way back. Finally he was pulled out, an amphetamine that Peccarino customarily kept in his wallet for emergencies was jammed down a gaping throat, then yanked to his feet and half-walked, half-dragged up the beach where he was stood up before Vigiletti like some sort of present.

Vig sat on the same coconut log, in his case looking not at all like a grasshopper but huge, violent and poisonous. His shirt was torn open, face scratched, sweating rivulets through the dirt, oiled thinning hair sticking out in an unintentional punk haircut. He appeared to be glowering at both men as they made their appearance before the frog king.

The pilot drooped but he managed with help to stay upright, and fortunately he had lost the inane grin that provoked. Perpendicular but more like the corpse of Rodger Dodger.

"What are we gonna do, Vig? This asshole can't fly."

"You put your hands on me."

"Hey, I know, boss, but I had to. I'm sorry, man, but Jesus, you'd a killed him we'd never've got off. Stuck, just us an' all them fuckin' dead bodies out there. Wouldn't a helped nothin'." He shrugged big and Sicilian in a bid for tribal solidarity. "Whadda we gonna do?"

"Fly."

"When?"

"Now."

Joe Peck actually raised his voice. "He's wasted! He'd get us all killed. Look at 'im!"

Vig stood and brushed himself off as carefully as if he were going to a meeting. "I got one word for you, Joey— 'Messinas.' Put him in the fuckin' plane. You wanna go, get in with him. You got no belly for it, makes it easier for us, him and me."

"I wouldn't fly me," the pilot said, grinning again and shaking his head.

Joe Peck shoved him to the ground, to preempt Vigiletti doing something worse, and told him to get his clothes on, he couldn't fly like that.

The pilot said, "Why not?" but put them on anyway.

"Where we goin'?" Joe Peck wanted to know. "I mean, we could wait. Where we're goin' right now's worth dyin' for?"

"Where the money is. Where them come from that stole it. Key West."

He never asked what had happened to the two Jamaicans.

Tony crawled forward from the cargo area of the cabin, where he had hidden ever since his failed encounter with Vigiletti, behind hung webbing and curled up in the bags and stacks of money. He had remained there only because of a total lack of options, without a plan, simply praying as he hadn't since he had drunk all of the altar wine back at St. Genisius across from Aqueduct that this would somehow work out for him. Maybe it had.

He slid along in his own blood, oozing from minor wounds where some of Joe Peck's shotgun pellets had reached him, dragging the MAC-11 with him as he came. With deliberation, he placed the muzzle of the gun against Diana's head and in a hoarse voice shouted a single word: "Mexico!"

Startled, she cried out and foolishly tried to bob her head out of the way, the gun following while Tony screamed into her ears to sit still. Finally, he grabbed her hair, pulling her back and forcing her to remain stiff and upright in one position.

The men swore in tandem even as they turned their heads. Tony's absence from the final equation had nagged at Max's subconscious since the bloodbath at the house, but in their desperate flight there had just never been time to act upon it. And once off the ground elation drowned every instinct.

"Not enough gas," Casey said, recovering quickly.

"Bullshit," Tony said, indicating Max, who had turned all the way around and was staring at him while placing a reassuring hand on Diana's. She scarcely seemed aware of it, sitting as straight as a mannequin with that icy mouth pressing her neck. "He figured it out before you come," Tony insisted. "We got enough to reach the 'Yukkatan.' "

"He doesn't know. I'm the pilot. They're my planes."

Max was concerned for Diana, who looked about to crack, drained of color and life. "Take the gun away, huh," Max suggested. "We're not armed."

Tony who had crouched behind her, edged up onto the seat in the last row and gradually lowered the weapon, although he kept it pointed forward.

"Lemme explain somethin' here." He addressed Max, " 'Member, you told how you had nothin' to lose if your honor was taken or some shit like that? Now that's me. They hang you in the Bahamas, burn you in Florida, and I'm gonna have every wiseguy in the country on my ass. So you wanna crash in the ocean, go on, I don't give a shit. Why should I?"

"That's what's gonna happen," Casey told him.

"You go for it anyway. Only chance I got's to get to Mexico and start spreadin' that money around."

"We gonna make it?" Max asked quietly in an aside to Casey.

Casey shook his head. "Weather ahead, weight of the money." It was intended to be overheard.

Tony forbade any more whispering or he would kill one of them. Only needed one to fly the plane. After that, he muttered on to his own audience, "I never had no luck, man. Messinas treated me like shit. Wasn't nothin' I didn't do for those pricks, an' they acted like I was a punk for it."

Taking no chances, Max spoke in a loud, clear voice easily comprehensible above the hum of the engines, "Casey, with bad weather ahead, shouldn't we . . . ?"

Casey looked ahead into the benign, pacific sky stretching almost to Key West. "What?"

"Shouldn't we strap in?"

Casey glanced over and around. "You are strapped in."

"Hey, hey, whaddaya tryin' to do, Muldoon?" Tony demanded. "We goin' towards Mexico now or not? 'Cause I figure we're not, I kill her first."

Looking at Casey, Max said, "Better get in a safety belt, Tony."

"What's this shit?" He craned his neck to look out of the windows. "I don't see no bad weather."

"Casey, you ever see one of these tough guys in a safety belt? Even in a car? Against their nature."

"You wanna get me tied down or somethin'. Well, fuck you, I'm—"

"Aaaah!" Casey interrupted, when at last he caught on.

Without thinking, sensing that he couldn't afford to, he jammed the yoke over violently as far as it would go, rolling the plane onto its back and creating chaos. Risking a dangerous stall because the engines didn't work when inverted, risking everything, he held the plane there for an instant to defeat centrifugal force.

Diana, hanging upside down, screamed, but it was the scream of the roller coaster passenger. Tony's was something else, exactly what Max wanted to hear but still hideous, the mortal scream of an animal caught in another's jaws.

It was hardly a large drop to the cabin roof but he hit it

without getting his hands up, head first and then with all of his big body at a devastating angle. Through all the shrill cries a cruel snapping sound was heard. Adding to the confusion, bags of money and everything else that wasn't tied down went with him to smash open, spraying bills. Casey, holding his breath, tried to continue the roll, but he had hesitated too long.

With the airspeed dropping rapidly, the controls failed to respond; it remained frozen in a half roll with the aircraft balanced precariously on one wingtip like a circus act, with Tony bouncing around, squeaking and groaning pathetically, and millions of dollars creating a blizzard through the cabin. After an agonizing moment perched like this, it began to fall away with the engines hacking.

Plummeting earthward on its side, Casey tried a desperate maneuver, daring to let go for a moment, like giving a horse its head, accepting the slide. Then, when it began to flatten a little in the manner of a falling leaf, he pushed the nose over to increase airspeed. The plane shuddered; it hadn't been built for this kind of punishment.

As they hurled themselves towards the black water of twilight, throttle open but the engines remaining inconstant, almost staccato, it was impossible to imagine them ever pulling out. But Casey held his nerve and the dive; the engines caught suddenly and roared but he wanted them stronger yet and kept putting off the moment, knowing that when it came it would have to be acted upon in a fragment of a second.

Tony was jammed against the last row of seats, plastered with money, locked there with or without his MAC-11 by the same G-forces that prevented Max from getting out of his seat to deal with him.

At a thousand feet Casey knew in his scrotum every bit

as much as in his mind that it was instantly now or die, and pulled back on the yoke with all he had left. The engine noise rose in volume until it sounded as though they must explode, the plane creaked and moaned in all its vulnerable parts but finally, a few dozen feet above the whitecaps it leveled off.

Sweat poured off of Casey's face in such profusion it sprinkled the shoulders of his shirt as if he had just come in out of the rain. Only an effort of will pried his hands off of the yoke and then he couldn't bring the fingers to close again without repeated flexing, holding it instead with his vibrating knees. He knew that until someone else spoke up he was incapable of saying a word. After a deep breath he began to take the plane back up to a safer altitude.

It was going to be up to Max to subdue Tony and he wanted at him. Even before they had entirely leveled off he let out a yell, scrambled over his seat and the one in the row behind that, causing Diana to duck down out of the way. The unrestrained fury of his attack frightened her almost as much as the prospect of his failing.

She had had only a glimpse of this capacity for sudden, lethal violence back on the island, but failed to grasp what it said about him. One of the assumptions on which she had based her life was that she understood men, all kinds. No one ever seemed to understand Max.

In an instant he was all over Tony, assuming he had his weapon beneath where he huddled. In that cramped space without a weapon of his own there were few options. He hung on to the nearest seat with his left hand in order to punch with his right while the plane bucked and bounced, then switched hands. He was looking for the one sensitive place that would open his target like an oyster.

All of a sudden Max stopped the assault. "Oh, man . . ."

He grabbed Tony, lifted him up only to discover him breathing coarsely, making small spongy sounds and unresisting. He shouted past Diana, who had ventured to turn and lean over the back of her seat now, "Casey, I think he's bought it. The fall or me or he had some bullets already in."

Casey's first instinct was to say, "Thank God!" over Diana's heartfelt, "Oh, my God."

"He's still breathing." Max felt around on the darkened floor. "I got the gun."

"Aw, sweet Jesus in the mornin'!" Casey said, abruptly, very upset. "Now his friends are gonna come to kill us. And then the damn cops'll make us prove we acted in self-defense and we gotta hire lawyers and meanwhile they impound my . . . aw shit!"

"Casey," Max called forward with a new, ruthless authority in his voice, "there's no question here. He goes out. Take us down and cut the airspeed."

Diana jumped out of her seat and tried to see into the shadows behind her. "What are you saying?!"

Max wasn't saying much, except to repeat what he had said to Casey, who was hunching into himself the way people do when they want to separate from a course of action.

Tony was already being dragged the few feet to the cabin door and propped up beside it. The plane slowed and descended, at the same time turning away from its island destination.

"What are you doing, Max? Answer me!" Diana demanded, grabbing his shirt.

He pulled her hand loose without looking at her. "He's going out of here." To Casey, he shouted, "Slower—I don't want to go with him."

Casey called back, "I'm down to a hundred—we can't risk a stall at this altitude. Key West's on the horizon. If you're gonna do it, do it."

Diana continued to plead, "Max, don't. He's still alive. You can't just murder him."

Max's voice was cold and metallic, all at the same impersonal level, one she had never heard before. "He'll have family, friends, and he ties us to the money. Get back in your seat."

"Please, Max."

"I said get back in your seat and strap in. I'm going to open the door."

She couldn't seem to move so he grabbed her firmly, put her in a seat and strapped her in, cinching the belt tightly to make a point. Diana put her head down in her hands and cried.

Having made jumps, Max knew something about being in the open door of a plane at a hundred knots. He had to slam the handle several times but at last, with great effort, got the Dutch doors open. He braced himself, reached down to drag Tony almost to his feet, then with a tremendous effort, using his shoulder, stuffed his limp figure through the opening.

And, caught by the wind, almost went with him.

Thrusting backwards in a panic, he hit the opposite cabin wall, bounced to the open door again only to find Tony caught on the steps that constituted the lower half.

He could hear Casey's frantic cries of, "Get him off! Get him off!" as the plane reacted to the drag, tilted, yawed a little and threatened to fall away again.

Max gripped the doorway on each side with whitening fingers and, murmuring childhood prayers, again subjected his body to the punishing wind. He thrust his pelvis out over space to reach one foot out and down, kicking at Tony's clothes at the place where they had caught on the steps. Several kicks, he would never know how many, the wind blowing his leg this way and that, whipping his shirt and pants, threatening to yank him out.

There were no books or courses on how to do this. He had to close his eyes to squeeze the water out of them. Suddenly there was a ripping sound and a sensation of emptiness, of loss, of himself being suspended weightless in air. He forced himself to see. Tony was gone.

Frightened as he was, he remained clinging there to see the body plunge towards the ocean, pursued by a small storm of blowing, twisting hundred- and thousand-dollar bills. That seemed appropriate.

He got the doors shut and leaned back a moment to recover his strength. Breathing hard, he bent his head and crossed himself. No one saw him and he wouldn't have explained if they had.

Casey, relieved, was straining to look in every possible direction from where he sat. "I don't spot any ships or other aircraft," he called back. "Nobody saw it, but I'm goin' out in the Gulf and come in the other side just in case."

Max nodded his head wearily and said, "Wait until I get the rest of the money out." He reached out to touch Diana, but she pulled away without looking at him; her disillusionment too deeply felt for small gestures.

Silently, he set to work dumping the money. When he glanced forward he saw Casey, alternating hands on the controls, clumsily stuffing some of the dollar bills that had blown forward into his shirt and down into his pants. He let it go; there was no protecting people from their own folly.

Working in the terror of the open doors, he heard Diana's faraway voice, accusatory, "He was a human being. It's a horrible way to die."

"Not so bad," Max said, no regrets and weary of defending

the indefensible. He knew that he loved her, but also knew that he was helpless to explain it to her. A rare sense of despair swept in. It was just what happened when you started caring.

"Max, back when you told . . . him you'd crash the plane and kill us all if he raped me, you meant it, didn't you?"

"I told you before, you have to mean it when you say it."

She looked at him finally. If he had changed in the last few minutes, so had she. "I don't know you."

She waited for him to say something.

What? Max had said it all.

XIX

When they landed, it was getting dark. Casey taxied to the most remote possible parking space. Diana said she wanted to go into the canteen for some coffee and aspirin. They got some cleaning supplies out of a shack and Max went to work eliminating signs of Tony's presence there.

Casey said he had to go to his car for a minute and Max understood that he just wanted to get the money out of his shorts and hidden somewhere more comfortable. When they returned, they spent over an hour scraping and scrubbing, using caustic on blood spots and burning any shreds or shards of money or clothing that might yield forensics. Max was too focused to wonder why Diana hadn't come back.

When they finished he went over to the canteen to look, but she wasn't there and no one could tell him where or exactly when she had left, although the waitress thought it had been some time ago. He tried to accept it, unwilling to admit that he was stricken, even to himself. He went back to Casey and reported that she was tired and upset and had gone home. It struck him even as he said it that he had no idea what might constitute "home" for her.

They went past the office to pick up a couple of pistols and then spent a tense evening together at dinner, a bar, a motel, waiting for some sign of Vigiletti. The next day, still nothing. Casey, unduly encouraged, went to report to the authorities that his Beechcraft had been stolen and was relieved to have them treat it routinely.

Max spent his time trying to locate Diana without success. How could she not know that he was capable of that, of what he had done, and why couldn't she forgive it? He wondered if anyone ever really understood another.

When finally he admitted that she had walked out, Casey with his usual sensitivity reassured him that there were plenty of great-looking bimbos out there for a stud like him.

Casey had his own heart's secret hope and the beauty of it was all in tax-free cash, the kind of money you could see, feel, sniff, and even chew on, it appeared to glow in his hands. His fervid hope was that Mary Beth would take him back, renew her marriage vows and jump on his bones at the mere sight of it, loving money as she did.

Things didn't quite turn out that way. When he arrived at the house she said she had serious things to say to him but still wouldn't let him in to say them, instead addressing from that damned upper story window. Who wanted a "serious" Mary Beth, anyway?—an oxymoron.

"Casey Moon, while you been runnin' all over the Caribbean chasin' colored girls with that bunch a bums you hang out with, I have discovered the Lord through the grace of Reverend Andrea of the Celestial Light."

This was not promising. Casey, defenseless against untrue charges, chose to defend himself by the most direct method in his arsenal of social graces; he began pulling bills handful by handful out of his money belt, exhibiting them like a magician and then letting them flutter to the lawn.

Amazingly, Mary Beth covered her eyes as if he was exposing her to a giant spider and shrilled, "I don't want to see it. Take all that unholy stuff away, it gives me the chills."

Casey was stunned and totally disarmed under a falling sky. He pleaded with her in turn to drop her hands and look. She refused, saying she couldn't be bought any more with mere money, her "personhood" was not for sale, her body either, for that matter—something miraculous had happened and she was more "spiritual" now.

"Whatever in hell you talkin' about, woman?"

"I heard a sermon while you were away that give me a whole new way to think. I finally understand you, Casey Moon. And it's not a pretty picture. In fact, you're scum, you and your whole sex. I'm sorry to have to say that."

"Who in hell's this Andrea and what right she's got takin' my family away from me?"

"She's a woman spiritual person from Malibu, California, who wears the most wonderful designer suits and's preached to all the Hollywood stars, everyone famous. She said if a married woman's doin' bad things, it's her husband makin' her do it. That's what I got out of it."

"Goddammit! Mary Beth, those Hollywood stars are morons."

"You don't need to swear. It's just more immorality around here. Now go away, I'm not doin' that dirty stuff with anyone any more."

Casey got down on his knees, fully aware that half of the neighborhood was probably looking on and laughing. It was intended as a plea, but also facilitated his picking up the money before it blew away. He'd look down at the money, then up at her, pitiably, and try to win her over with the tale of all he had gone through. For her!

Mary Beth said, "You can just begone, vile son of Adam," and slammed the window.

He stood slowly. The idea that a woman with breasts like that would become religious. Would God never stop playing mean tricks on the world?

Out on the lawn he turned and shouted back at the

house at the top of his voice, "Mary Beth, I love you!" The elderly gay couple sitting on their lawn across the street applauded. He tipped his cap.

Three months later a yachting party found Casey's plane not far off of the beach where he had originally landed it. Evidently it had cartwheeled into the surf and ended upside down. The three men inside had been knocked unconscious and drowned. None were wearing seatbelts.

Vigiletti's family were not particularly surprised by his death, only by the geography, as they had always assumed it would occur in a parking lot in Las Vegas.

Max visited Earl in the hospital once but never returned to the office. Casey began to search for him in turn, seeking everywhere without success. A couple of people claimed to have seen him in passing but commented that Max appeared distracted, not his usual social self. One day it became general knowledge that Max was not anywhere. He had simply disappeared without notice to anyone. Had he gone seeking Diana? Were the lovers together somewhere?—those were the romantics (by now there were several versions of the story abroad), particularly the writers. The fishermen thought they knew better.

For a long time Casey simply refused to accept Max's disappearance as fact, proving that he was also among the legion who had never known him at all.

Three months later Earl received a thousand-dollar bill in an envelope postmarked Costa Rica, but with no other indication as to the sender. Casey told him that thousand-dollar bills were illegal and he would be arrested if he tried to cash it. Earl hid it in his son's mattress along with the dirty magazines, where it remains.

It was Maude Sheldon who provided Max's epitaph. As the exotic nature of the story escaped the confines of the Keys and traveled through the marginal world on the Eastern Seaboard, the curious came avidly seeking. Often they were steered to Maude, the unofficial font for everything.

True to the local code, she told a lot and nothing. When two old bull detectives from Miami bellied up to the bar at the Rendezvous and asked oh-so-casually if Max Muldoon was around, she pretended that she hardly knew the man.

"That Irish aviator? He's in the wind."

About the Author

JAMES DAVID BUCHANAN was raised in Michigan and attended a variety of colleges. He has worked in a brokerage office, as a jazz musician, stage hand, radio announcer, tour guide, television director, school teacher. Latterly, a long time Hollywood screen writer/occasional producer. *Moon & Muldoon* is his eighth novel. One, *The Prince of Malta*, became the film *Curacao*. He lives near Los Angeles and spends time in Dublin, Ireland.